Operation Neurosurgeon

Operation Neurosurgeon

by

Barbara Ebel MD

ISBN 1441481370

For all the patients I've put to sleep

as well as the professionals

on both sides of the blood-brain barrier.

Chapter 1

- 2009 -

Through the desolate winter woods, she could see a run down single story house. She firmly pressed the accelerator to climb the hilly, rutted road as pebbles kicked up from the gravel, pinging underneath her sedan. All around her, tall spindly trees stood without a quiver, the area still, quiet and remote. On this damp, cold February afternoon, she had come to conclude a deal with a man named Ray.

The road narrowed past the house, fading over the hill, but she veered slowly to the left, a barren area in front of the peeling house, where a dusty red pickup truck stood idle and a black plumaged vulture busily scavenged. Deliberately she left her belongings, clicked the lock on her car and walked to the front door. She threw the long end of her rust scarf behind her shoulder. The raptor grunted through his hooked beak as he flew off to the backwoods. The door opened before she knocked.

"Nobody visits a feller like me," the man said, smiling at her while adjusting his baseball cap, "unless we're buying and selling. You must be the lady with the book."

The tidily shaven man wore a salt and pepper colored beard and mustache and an open plaid cotton shirt with a tee shirt underneath. The boots peeking out from under his blue jeans had seen muddy days.

The woman smiled pleasantly at him and went in the front door empty handed. If the man had any furniture, she wasn't aware of it. Car parts lay strewn everywhere, which made her wonder if he slept in a bed.

Ray followed her glance. "You nearly can't find one of them no mores," he said, pointing to a charcoal colored, elongated piece of vinyl plastic on the floor. She looked quizzically at him and shoved the woolen hat she'd been wearing into her pocket.

"It's an original 1984 Mercedes dashboard. See, the holes are for vents and the radio. Got a bite on that one from a teenager restoring his first car." She didn't seem interested though. She eyed the dust, in some spots thick as bread.

"Are you sure you have twelve-thousand dollars to pay for this?" she asked, unbuttoning her jacket.

"You come out thirty miles from Knoxville? That baby in your belly may need something," he said, pointing to her pregnancy. "You want a soda or something?"

"No thank you," she said, grimacing at him.

"Oh, yeah. I got the money," he said. "All I got now to my name is seventy-five thousand dollars. I got ruint in Memphis. Was a part owner in a used car dealership. Went away for a little while, and the other guy cleaned me out. Can't afford nothing like a lawyer to chase 'im down."

She tapped her foot.

"Anyhow, I won't bother yer with all that. I got a thing going good on eBay. I got a reputation, it ain't soiled. You can trust me, I give people what I tell them, whether I'm buying or selling."

A beagle-looking mutt crawled out from behind a car door. "Molly, you're milk containers are dragging on the floor. Better get out to your pups," the man said, prodding her out the partially closed door.

"You like dogs?" he asked.

"I suppose so."

"I got no use for people who don't care for dogs. Something not right about people like that."

The woman turned and followed the clumsy dog outside, grabbed a bag from the front seat, and came back in. She took out a book, opened the back cover, and handed him a folded piece of paper. *Certificate of Authenticity*, the man read, from a company in New Orleans, verifying the signature on the front page to be Albert Einstein's. He inverted his hand and wiggled his fingers, gesturing to her if he could hold the aged book.

"Where'd you say you got it?" He observed her carefully.

"It's been in the family for years. I took my precious belongings with me when I left New Orleans because of Hurricane Katrina. Since I lost my house there, I decided to stay in Tennessee. Now I'm selling my expensive things. I have to make ends meet, especially with a baby coming."

"Good thing you got this certificate with it, then. Twelve-thousand dollars, we've got a deal."

He walked away to the back of the house while she held on to the physicist's 1920 publication. He came through the doorway with a stack of money and a brown paper bag. She nodded once when she finished counting the bills, so he handed her the empty bag.

"I still got your email address and phone number," he said. "I keep track of what goes and comes."

"You won't need them," she said and left abruptly.

He watched her back out, stood there until the car disappeared out of sight down the gray road.

Chapter 2

- 1989 –

"You dawdling over there?"

"No. Peeing, Dad." Danny zipped his fly and wheeled around, his boots sinking in soft leafy earth. His father, Greg, stood on polished creek stone at the river's edge beside Danny's wife. "And on rounds, the proper term is urinating." Danny slipped from the woods and approached them.

Greg threw a few red salmon eggs into the Caney Fork River and handed Danny his spinning rod. "I better catch up to the better half of you newlyweds."

Sara propped her pole on the cooler, held up a rainbow trout in front of Danny, and exclaimed "Tah-dah."

"We're just here to have fun." Danny grinned at both of them. "It's not as if our lives depend on it." But Danny knew the Tennessee Wildlife Resources Agency had recently stocked the river. The three of them had been bottom fishing since before the morning fog lifted like a friendly ghost drifting away to expose the slow but noticeable current.

"You're right, Danny. You know what I say."

Sara plucked algae off her four-pound test line and looked questioningly at her father-in-law. She waited to wade into the water, figuring one of Greg's metaphorical sayings or idioms were forthcoming. She'd dated Danny throughout his four years of medical school at Vanderbilt and had spent so much time at his Dad's house, where Danny had lived, that sometimes more lipsticks and tampons had been in Danny's bathroom than her own.

"You may want to fish for dinner," Greg said, "but if you must fish to catch dinner, you've screwed up."

Sara pushed dew-misted hair behind her ear. "Danny's one of only two residents they've accepted into the neurosurgery program, Dad. That doesn't qualify as, umm, messing up."

Danny beamed at his wife. During med school, almost two dozen students were already married or headed that way, but some couples split with the strain of exams and deadlines, hours in labs, physician's offices and clinical rotations with overnight calls. Sara kept busy teaching high school biology and running, and always helped Danny focus. When he needed long-term perspective, objectivity, or softening after his brain was slammed shut for hours between pages of Principles of Pharmacology, she could turn him around. She would run her hand through his hair, or massage between his shoulder blades, or whisper to him under the sheets after they made love.

When they took their vows a month ago, Danny secretly promised to nourish the effect they had on each other.

Greg had forgotten to bring wading boots, so he stayed on shore while Sara and Danny carefully picked their steps. Occasional diehards just sucked it up and waded in. The water was as warm as it would get, a cold summer temperature, unforgiving for anyone without proper gear.

Quiet spread across their sanctuary except for a small surface splash or a fish tail grazing the surface. A young man in a small canoe paddled by and without any fanfare hoisted his baby boat onto a jeep rack and left.

Danny and Sara finally came to shore, each with a brown trout. "Both about the same size," Sara said. Danny agreed, leaned over and pecked his wife on the cheek as they crouched, holding their fish like new baby birds. The trout squirmed in their hands, then darted away. Sara smiled, pleased with their release.

"Time to go Dad. They'll be generating soon." Danny nodded at the Center Hill Dam, the nearby Goliath. Sara picked up their poles and Danny and Greg grabbed the unused salmon eggs, cooler, and tackle boxes; they walked slowly up the road to the parking lot as they heard the generating dam gushing Center Hill Lake water into the Caney Fork.

"This is the last load, Dad," Danny said.

Greg waved his hand as Danny walked by him with a flat cardboard box and suitcase and entered his bedroom. Inside, ebony blue curtains framed windows to a view that appeared as if by magic despite his Mother's illness. She had died three years ago from ovarian cancer.

Danny looked out over south facing slopes of grown hickories, southern red oaks and maples, white and Virginia pines. Donna had assisted the native habitat by producing a real show for early spring. She'd worked with Mexican migrants from a wholesale nursery to plant rows of redbuds and terraced beds of mountain laurel, rhododendrons and wildflowers. Specks of white, hints of pink and tinges of purple had helped her to divert thoughts of a possible short life expectancy to reminiscing about her family and their accomplishments. She would leave behind a wonderful marriage, two fantastic children, and a beautiful estate.

Danny turned his head to find Greg at his doorway. "I miss her, Dad. There's not a day …"

"Me, too," Greg said, gazing at his shoes, his thick dark eyebrows practically covering his eyes. "I still can't believe I'm without her at fifty-two years old."

Greg walked in and sat on Danny's bed, his shoulders slumping over. Greg had gotten married in 1960, after only dating Donna for six months. They never missed Sunday devotion together until Donna had been bedridden. Greg's gaze averted to the outside hallway where one of his wedding pictures hung, the loving couple fixed in an embrace.

"You know what I told her?"

Danny shook his head no.

"A girlfriend who prays with me is worth keeping."

Danny did know that, as well as the adoration his father had shown his mother for as long as he could remember. He patted his father's knee once and got up. Danny unfolded the cardboard box, and then dumped it in front of his dresser.

"Dad, Sara and I can't thank you enough for the wedding present. The house is home already. Sara's summer vacation and my break before residency made it all work out." Danny looked around. "Will you turn my room into a guest bedroom?"

"Yes. And I'll keep it the same. For visiting grandkids?"

Danny laughed. "Are you prying, Dad?"

"If there are plans for me to be a grandfather, I want to be the third one to know."

"Done deal," Danny said, checking his top drawers to make sure he'd emptied them on a previous trip. He opened the last drawer and threw his winter stash of sweaters into the box. A large baggie still sat at the bottom, which Danny picked up, then sat next to Greg on the cream-colored bedspread. The mattress indented with their weight and their knees lined up together, their six foot two frames carbon copied from similar blueprints.

Danny's eyes gleamed. Greg reached to touch the plastic storage bag, an uncanny method to preserve the emotionally stirring and valuable treasure. Danny opened the bag and took out the brown hard-covered book as gently as he had held a hummingbird the previous week after he had found it stunned from hitting Sara and Danny's glass front door. He placed the small item on his lap and opened the faded cover to the yellowish tinge of aged paper.

"Your sister will wear your mom's jewelry," Greg said, "but you? Someday you can bequeath what your mother gave you to your children or a museum. Or sell it."

Danny whistled, knowing it's price tag would have plenty of zeroes, with more added as time went on.

"I still remember when your mother purchased it. She drove a hard bargain and requested that the store manager in New Orleans have the book and the signature verified by an authenticator of such things."

They both looked at the front page: Einstein's 1920 *Relativity: The Special and the General Theory*. Many copies existed, but this was one of the few remaining from the early 1900's. Two-thirds down on the page was the author's signature: *Albert Einstein*. Which wasn't the usual way the historical genius had autographed his books. Almost always, he had signed *A. Einstein.*

"It's the real McCoy," Greg said. "And with Einstein's full signature, you've inherited a diamond in a trowel of white sand." Danny slid it back in the bag. "Perhaps you should put it in a safe deposit box."

"Perhaps. But occasionally I look at it, Dad. I think of Mom." Danny paused, looking again to the summer's day, tree shadows beginning their leftward crawl. "It's inspiration for entering a field where I'll surgically be in the very matter which spawns incredible ideas and discoveries like his."

When Greg left, Danny packed the last shirts and shoes left in his closet, a few medical texts in the nightstand and a bottle of Sara's shampoo from his bathroom. He opened it and smiled. Orange ginger. Sara's hair.

Danny glumly endured his first postgraduate year, then six months of general surgery, a few months of neurology and one month of neuro ICU. He knew how important these rotations were for establishing his clinical knowledge and skills; but he couldn't wait to focus on physical brains, the control panel of it all. As he tolerated these months, he tried to listen to Greg, who kept telling him, "It's not the end result, but the journey that matters."

Finally, late in his second year of residency, Danny was smack in the middle of his first true month of neurosurgery. He pushed through hospital health care providers in scrubs, police officers, and uniformed ambulance personnel in the ER hallway, to see three stretchers in the trauma room. Someone yanked at his arm.

"Dr. Tilson, the one in between. The anesthesiologist is intubating the difficult airway over there, the driver. The ER physician will probably declare that patient on the right, another driver who went off the road to avoid them." The navy blue uniformed man, the same age as Danny, spoke quickly and sped Danny to the head of the middle stretcher.

Danny had already begun assessing the patient while gesturing for the young man to continue. "This patient. Right front seat, wasn't wearing a seatbelt. A ten-pointer buck ran from the ditch, driver slammed the brakes, trophy rack came through the front window. Brown body and appendages followed. She was talking when I arrived, but became somnolent en route. To be on the safe side, I intubated her."

Danny glanced at the monitors. Vital signs okay, but not great. Dirty, dark blood covered the sheet and neck brace behind the motionless woman's head. He slipped on gloves and felt around the endotracheal tube protruding from the patient's mouth, palpating facial bones for stability and orbital area for swelling. Danny checked her pupil size and reaction to light. A general surgeon had arrived and simultaneously examined her abdomen and chest. They assessed quietly despite the chaos around them.

Danny finished, stepped back to a tray covered with the patient's ER paperwork and grabbed physician order and progress sheets. "I'm going to need a non-contrast CT scan of the brain," he said to the general surgeon and nearby nurse.

The surgeon nodded. "Looks negative down here." A gloved nurse waited for Danny's other orders.

"Nice job, driver," Danny said to the man who had given him report. He pressed ahead with his writing without looking at him.

"I'm not just an ambulance driver," the man said sarcastically, "but a highly trained EMT. A paramedic. And unlike you, I'm launched in my career. You'll be pussyfooting around for the next five years before getting yourself established."

The female nurse didn't move.

"Shut up, Casey," Danny said with a small grin.

The nurse exhaled. "Phew. I thought you two were for real." She untwisted a pretty ivory earring.

"We're throw backs to grade school. It's just that he never grew up." Danny glanced sideways at Casey. "And I still think you should've been a quarterback. Thick neck, muscular build and all."

Before Casey could open his mouth, Danny continued, "I'm not touching a book tonight, so pop over. Sara and I could use some deck time."

"Okay. For Sara. But don't let that baby fall asleep until I see her awake. What do you two do, tranquilize her?"

"That's what babies do, Casey, they sleep."

Casey weaved out of the trauma room through the diminishing gawkers. As the patient's stretcher rolled past, Danny paged his chief resident to give her a report.

"When the CT is finished, meet me in radiology," Dr. Welch said.

Chief residents, in their final sixth year of neurological surgery, were in charge of lower residents and had an attending physician available for counsel. Danny had an appreciation for Dr. Welch, a thick waisted, fast talking female whose gender in her specialty made her rarer than lobster ice cream.

Karen Welch stood in the CT scanning office when Danny arrived. She had evaluated the patient before they had transported her to the ICU. She glanced up and down the CT images on the viewer, hands on her hips.

"Dr. Tilson, glad you could join me. So your college bound, buck startled patient has a high-density area on CT," she said, pointing.

Danny carefully looked through the images, careful not to let Karen bait him into hurrying the probable diagnosis, or missing something else evident.

"A cerebral contusion from a sudden deceleration of the head."

"Is there more to that story?"

Danny took a step off the imaging room's platform to establish better eye contact. "The brain impacted on bony prominences. A coup injury occurred where the skull struck the brain. A contrecoup injury is an injury directly opposite the impact site."

Karen Welch turned to her resident. "Surgical treatment is not indicated at this time. When will surgical decompression be warranted?"

"With threatening herniation. If she becomes refractory to medical management. With increased ICP."

"Ah, yes. The magic three letters for increased intracranial pressure. You know what to do." She winked at the radiologist sitting in front of his equipment.

She handed Danny the patient's chart from the table and began walking out. "I'll talk to the general surgery resident. Most of the patient's scalp wounds are only a few inches. They can clean and suture them without bringing the patient to the OR."

That evening, Danny left Vanderbilt University Hospital and traveled southeast to the wedding present Greg had given them almost two years ago. Greg had hired the builder, but Danny and Sara had approved the plans and construction, giving the builder lots of latitude with his work. Since they chose a lot in a newborn subdivision, their split-level ranch at the end of a cul-de-sac faced woods in the back. Danny and Sara liked the outdoor, natural environment and had a wooden deck built on the front and back of the single story side of the house.

Danny hit the remote and pulled his four-year old Toyota into the garage. "Hi girls," he said, entering the door. Melissa sat in her high chair, her right hand swinging a red rattle, the other hand holding a small white stuffed dog with a ribbon collar. She shook with glee when she planted her eyes on

Danny. Sara graded the sprawling papers in front of her but got up to meet Danny halfway.

Danny put his right arm around Sara, pressing his head into her blonde peppered hair. Her bob cut accentuated the contour of her cheeks and her silky hair made him linger and revel in its fragrance. He pulled back. Sometimes her hair stayed behind her ears, but sometimes she'd purposefully leave it up front and kink it softly around her face. Danny liked it either way.

"Good day, night and day?" Sara asked.

"Actually, yes. I got an entire eight hours of sleep," Danny said. "Did you have a nice day?" He planted a kiss on Melissa's forehead.

"Every day is fine with Melissa in it." Sara sat back down, crossing her trim legs, exposed from a burgundy corduroy skirt. "I finished meiosis and mitosis at school today, so tomorrow I start high school biology's version of human anatomy. Although for fourteen and fifteen year old boys, that may only mean this …" She waved an outline of a shapely female in the air.

Danny laughed. Sometimes he accentuated his laugh, and added some on at the end for effect. Sara liked it. Along with his wide, white smile, and his jovial manner, he entertained her.

"You eat yet?" Danny asked.

"Homemade soup. And the salad's over there," she said, pointing with her whole arm.

Danny went to the counter and came back to sit with her carrying a bowl. "Casey's coming over later. He wants to see Melissa awake."

"Did you tell him babies don't keep single guy's hours?"

Danny wolfed down two servings while Sara finished putting A to D on test papers. He grinned. "Come on," he said.

Danny opened the back glass door while holding Melissa. Sara followed with Fluffy the dog and a light cotton baby blanket. Outside sat two oak porch rockers and one double, which Danny and Sara eased into. Melissa cooed and clutched Danny's fingers as she sat on his lap, facing forward. The early evening hinted of summer. Tree buds were making their debut and a few sparrows flew limb to limb, singing to each other.

Empty hooks like horizontal question marks hung from the porch beams. "Time to put out the feeders," Sara said, following her husband's gaze. "The hummingbirds are depending on us." She buttoned her camel sweater as Casey jauntily came around the side of the house.

"Not even a front door greeting," Casey boomed, standing in front of the railing. "A bunch of rocking chair slackers." He walked up the steps and handed Sara an elongated brown bag. "Home grown," he said.

Sara pulled out a bottle of wine, the label from Stonehaus, a Tennessee winery. "Sweet Muscadine. Thanks, Casey. Have a seat after you go inside." She swept her arm forward, pointing directly with her index finger. "Glasses upper right."

Casey squatted in front of Melissa. "Wow. You're beautiful, for a baby," he said, bouncing his head for her amusement. Melissa sputtered gibberish, her diaper bound bottom squirming in Danny's lap.

Casey brought three thick wine glasses. "So how's Jane Doe?" he asked Danny. Danny eyed him wondering if he had meant to be facetious by using the name Doe, but Casey was being straight.

"Who's Jane Doe?" Sara asked.

"Deer accident this morning on a side road off 40. College girl with a cerebral contusion," Danny said. Sara crossed her legs the other way and Danny resumed slowly rocking. "I checked on her before I left and she's showing progress. She opened her eyes, responded to commands. Cerebral edema is getting better, but I've ordered another CT in the morning."

"That's good," Casey said, turning his head towards Sara "Her boyfriend driver got intubated and went for surgery, but another driver averting the accident got killed." Danny clasped Melissa closer and Sara shook her head.

"Sara, Casey and I'll put Melissa to bed tonight, if you'd like. I'll change her diaper, put her pajamas on, skip a bath. That okay?"

"Sure. I'd appreciate that."

Sara dripped a few more ounces of Muscadine into her glass then Danny resumed rocking. A hummingbird scout whizzed by, taking a momentary pause near the roof gutter to view them, determining if they had yet placed a plastic bulb with red nectar. Danny broke the silence, and poked Casey. "Anybody new?"

"Got a date with an x-ray tech on Saturday. We're going to see John Mellencamp at the Ryman Auditorium."

"Bet she's a knockout," Sara said. "You date the most beautiful and intelligent women. I don't know where you find them."

"He doesn't find them," Danny said. "They find him."

"She's a nice lady," Casey shrugged. "I've taken her out a few times."

"Come on, then," Danny said. "Help me out. Get lessons for what comes after the wedding rings." Danny got up, swung Melissa once in the air, the glee of the ride spreading across her face like sunshine on the horizon.

"Daddy's little girl," Sara said. "You three have fun." She chuckled as they left, Casey's gym bulk noticeable in blue jeans and a cotton shirt, and Danny's tall height. Two grown men, all their attention centered on a little baby girl.

Upstairs, they went to the bedroom directly across from Sara and Danny's. Casey took a back seat to the bedtime routine, but gave Melissa a kiss after his friend laid her down in her crib. Danny nestled a lightly frayed blanket around his daughter as her movements slowed and her eyes closed.

Chapter 3

"That crazy bitch. She nailed me."

Danny listened to a patient on an ER stretcher, intrigued by two inches of nail jutting out of the man's head. Maybe a five-inch nail including the part imbedded in his brain. The hem of the man's blue jeans were caked with mud and his olive Henley shirt had missing buttons. He wore a two-day five o'clock shadow and his offensive odor masked background smells of open wounds and vomiting.

"What did you do to her?" Danny asked, urging him to talk. Danny wanted to assess the man's reasoning and appropriateness, look for mental deficits due to his injury. On second, thought, however, Danny figured his baseline might be someone else's deficit.

"Are you stupider than my wife?" the man asked, wiggling his body all over the sheet. "What the fuck difference does that make?"

"Whether or not you walk around the rest of your life as a coat rack depends on me. Maybe you'll talk to me nicely."

The man's eyes opened wider and he grinned in disgust.

"You need to tell me what happened and if you passed out," Danny said, putting on gloves to examine the injured man's scalp.

"I was drinkin last night. But I fished yesteday. Drinkin then, too. All I know's is she was mad when I got home. I must'ta passed out in the garage, where I got a little workbench and tools there. I dunno."

"So you were in a drunken stupor before you got nailed in the head?"

"Yeah. I reckon."

Danny assessed his patient's pupils, which were equal and reactive to his penlight and obtained a negative previous medical history from him. Danny went to the desk to sit down and write orders, but first stopped to tell the secretary to call radiology for a CT scan.

Danny was in his fourth year of residency, a PGY4. He'd been thrown into the trauma month because a resident was out on medical leave, and Vanderbilt needed the coverage. Otherwise, he would have finished his sixth month at the VA. The beginning of the year, he had done six months of pediatric neurosurgery, but found it depressing. It made him more appreciative of Melissa, now two and a half, and his second daughter, Annabel, six months old, who were both the picture of health. His little girls could undo the pediatric neurosurgery blues any day.

Danny slid into a rolling chair and scooted around Casey, who half sat on the desk, legs extended and crossed at the bottom.

"I'm working a graveyard this week," Casey said. "He was my last run. His wife called it in. When we got there, she waved an automatic nail gun and asked me if I wanted the weapon. I told her I wasn't the police." Casey leaned backwards and selected a glazed Krispy Kreme from the donut maker's box of twelve on the counter top. "You going to do the surgery?"

"Probably. I'm hoping Mr. Rhine's blood alcohol level is low enough that anesthesia clears him. I'm the highest-ranking resident on this service right now besides the chief, so I think he'll let me do it if he supervises."

Casey took a napkin to hold the uneaten end of donut and nodded. "How's Sara and the girls?" A nurse stalled while grabbing a chart behind him. She opened a tab and glanced alternately between the page and Casey.

"They're fine. You're welcome to meet us all at Downtown Italy tonight," Danny said, referring to his parents' original Italian restaurant on Broadway.

"I'm going to the gym. Then I have to get back here for another tour of duty. I'll take a rain check." Casey got up, smiled at the nurse and left after pitching the wadded napkin into the trash.

Danny called his chief resident, Dr. Vince Aaron, and shortly later met the group rounding on patients in the CT room. After the other residents saw Mr. Rhine, the gaping mouths of junior residents closed and they congregated around his CT results.

"Clean penetrating injury," Vince said, waving his pen at the scan and addressing the PGY2. "Do you see the bleed inside the skull?"

"No, sir, I don't see any evidence of that."

"Very nice. Correct. So we suspect the nail avoided major blood vessels. Now, Dr. Tilson and I must be careful not to cause bleeding while surgically removing it." Dr. Aaron spun around, sat on the desk, and continued. "What about the nail's location?"

"Lucky guy," the PGY3 said. "The right frontal lobe. Probably forgiving."

"What if it had been his temporal lobe?"

"The dominant hemisphere of the temporal lobe houses Wernicke's speech area. But no telling if a penetrating injury there to this Tennizzee hunter would have enhanced or deteriorated his speech."

"Fisherman," Danny corrected him.

"Whose name is probably Bucky," the PGY3 said.

Laughter erupted from the residents in the back.

"Okay, very funny, Mr. New Englander," Vince said. "Now, everybody get down to business. Danny, I'll meet you in the OR after the case is booked, you've got consent and labs, and the anesthesiologist gets the ball rolling." Vince pocketed his pen. "In the interim, I'll be the photographer."

Danny scrubbed while watching the attending anesthesiologist and resident say goodnight to and intubate his patient. The anesthesiologist probably didn't bother to ask him to count backwards. When Danny walked through the double doors, the OR table had been turned ninety degrees from the ventilator, the anesthesia circuit carefully secured; one arm of the patient was wrapped on an accessible arm board for IV access and the other arm tucked alongside his body. A blue warming blanket covered the patient and draped over the sides of the table.

A nurse unfolded Danny's surgical gown allowing Danny to slide into it. The circulating nurse tied it from the back as he stepped to the patient's head. The area around the nail had been prepped and shaved. Danny affixed a bolt-like contraption to hold the head and put a sterile drape with a hole to expose the surgical site.

The scrub nurse stood closest to him, her instruments laid out neatly on moveable tray tables. Danny incised a wide circular margin, cutting down to skull. "Drill. Suction," he said. The nurse handed him both, and he started to drill, applying pressure to bone. Danny knew his chief resident had scrubbed and readied after him, and he now looked closely over Danny's right shoulder.

Vince dripped saline over Danny's drill bit and surgical area. Danny continued drilling firmly, then eased up when he felt no resistance, which meant he was inside the skull and near the brain.

"Dr. Tilson, you scattering bone dust around here?" the anesthesiologist quipped.

"I'll be sure to glue it all back together before we leave," Danny said, smiling under his mask.

Danny suctioned. He slowly pulled out the incised skull bone. Perfect. The major venous sinuses weren't anywhere close and the nail wasn't too far in. Vince kept quiet; Danny had the situation under control. The small defect in the pulsating brain wasn't bleeding, so Danny and Vince turned their attention to pushing the nail out of the bone from where it had entered.

"Fine job," Vince said. He stepped back and took off his gown. The scrub nurse took the suction tip from Danny. He appreciated her methodical style and her respectful treatment of residents, who often weren't assisted with the same professionalism as senior staff.

Minus the nail, Danny inserted Mr. Rhine's skull piece back into the hole like a single cardboard piece into a puzzle, and stapled the scalp flap back onto the adjoining skin. He was grateful that the case had been straightforward and that a good senior resident had done the anesthesia. He'd get out at a reasonable time to spend the evening with Sara, Greg and the girls.

Greg's chef, Gianni, eyed his pesto sauce for color and texture. He sampled it and nodded his approval. He slid chopped onion and garlic to Greg from a butcher block, for

Greg's customary part in preparing the appetizer while Sara and Danny were on their way. Greg sautéed them, added browned eggplant, and stirred in tomatoes. He mixed capers, anchovy paste and olives in the pan drippings, spooned it over the eggplant and covered it. "Sara's favorite," Greg said.

Greg and Donna had foreseen Nashville's potential for a fine, pricey Northern Italian restaurant. While entrepreneurs concentrated on pulled pork and ribs, Greg and Donna figured the country superstars and entertainment folks had a ton of cash, and there was only so much barbecue people could eat. So when downtown Nashville was in its infancy, springing more and more café's, buffalo wing restaurants and sports bars, Greg and Donna had bought a large, old bookstore and renovated it. Sending for Gianni from Italy sealed the deal. Later, when they opened a second and third restaurant, they sent for two more chefs, but remained attached to their original Downtown Italy.

Greg went to the dining area as Danny and Sara arrived. Melissa ran to him with outstretched arms, plowing into his legs and hugging tightly. Two fancy rubber bands held her fine hair in short ponytails off the side of her head, and long eyelashes swept almost to her eyebrows.

"Pop-Pop, guess what I did today?"

"What did you do today, sunshine?" Greg said, crouching down to her.

"I gave Annabel a carriage ride up and down Mrs. Emily's driveway!"

"You are something else," Greg said.

Greg greeted his son and daughter-in-law, then went to the kitchen and brought out his eggplant and toasted focaccia. "Chow down," he said, placing the appetizers on the table. A waiter stepped over, bringing them ice water and a bottle of Pinot Grigio while Melissa handed Annabel a piece of Italian bread. Her baby sister sputtered with delight, legs wiggling from the highchair.

Sara took the vase with a sprig of flowers and placed it on the floor against the wall behind them, then put a napkin on Annabel's tee shirt. She dipped into the herbed vegetable in the middle of the table. "Thanks, Dad," she said.

"Come on, Dad, join us," Danny said. Greg poured wine and sat. Danny and Sara ordered shrimp scampi since Gianni made fresh pasta from scratch every day. "And ravioli with fresh mozzarella on top for the girls," Danny said to Angelo, the waiter.

"Angelo, my usual," Greg said.

"Yes, sir," Angelo said. He winked at Melissa and left.

"Danny," Greg said, "that internist put me on a diuretic today and gave me my lab results. My good cholesterol's high and my triglycerides aren't elevated. Since I'm not diabetic and don't have cardiac risk factors, we can't figure out why my blood pressure is high."

Sara leaned in closer to her father-in-law. "Dad, you certainly aren't obese either," she said, waving focaccia in her hand before taking a bite.

"No one in the family had premature heart disease from bad genes, did they?" Danny asked.

"Not that I'm aware of. Your grandfather died young, but as you know, he died swerving off the road in an automobile accident."

Danny pondered that a moment while two small speakers piped in Pavarotti. His parents had a flare for atmosphere and interior decorating; a mural of a Mediterranean piazza and vineyards plastered one wall.

"Dad, maybe granddad had a heart attack."

Angelo slid Greg's pasta in front of him. Greg acknowledged it with a nod of approval and looked at Danny. "That would explain it," Greg said, frowning.

"Dad, did you talk to that man interested in your restaurants again?" Sara leaned back as Angelo placed their scampi plates. She cut ravioli for Annabel while her hair fell forward, then she swiped it behind her ear.

"He's offered me a mint for the two other restaurants. He asks only that I give him the first opportunity to buy Downtown Italy when I'm ready to sell." Greg twirled some angel hair after dipping it into extra parmesan at the rim of his plate. "Managing all three has gotten to be too much, especially without your mom."

Melissa squirmed out of her chair headed for her baby sister. She spooned a small piece of pasta and airplaned it towards Annabel's mouth. Annabel banged her arm but quickly reached for her sister's ponytail. Melissa jumped back and giggled. Greg and Danny laughed, too, and Sara leaned in smiling, putting her hand on Danny's shoulder to give it a squeeze.

"Well, I think your slowing down is a good idea, Dad," Danny said. "Although managing Downtown Italy is hardly slowing down."

"Okay, I'll make the deal. Let's all toast to it."

Sara raised her glass, pretending to clink it towards Melissa and Annabel.

"And let's toast to only three more years of residency," Danny said. "And to a great teacher and magnificent wife."

Angelo placed a cream linen napkin over his arm and smiled at them.

"More wine?" he asked.

"No," Sara said, waving her hand. "But we'll take Gianni's prized sacripantini."

"You know, Miss Sara," Angelo said, tilting his head, "sponge cake made with rum is a Luciano Pavarotti favorite. But, of course, Gianni's is the best."

"Yes, we know," Danny said. "And please, Angelo, a shot of espresso with a shot of liquor. Brandy will do. I can be festive today."

"Something you're going to tell us?" Sara asked, kneading his shoulder.

"Before and after surgery pictures of my patient today made it into the department's photographic archive. Projectors will be showing those slides in lectures all over the country."

Sara beamed and they both kissed. When their lips pressed, they lingered.

Sara held Annabel snuggly in her arms for a few minutes before leaving the porch and going inside. Annabel had fallen asleep on the drive across Murfreesboro Road and the winding gravel roads into the subdivision. Two motionless deer stood on the outskirts of the woods. They had lost their white spots, but weren't fully grown either. The deer stared at Sara and Danny and realized they weren't a threat, so started eating at the brush. A nearby whip-poor-will called loudly, listened, then emphatically spoke again after a distant response from a fellow bird.

Danny and Sara headed inside. Sara carefully changed Annabel and tenderly placed her in her crib. She kissed her baby girl on the cheek and pressed her small fingers into her own. While Sara peeled away to take a shower, Danny helped Melissa wash and change. Melissa wrapped her arms around Danny's neck as she stood on her pink bedspread.

"Tonight you can dream about those graceful deer visiting you in your backyard," Danny said, returning the hug. "Their eyes are as bright as yours."

Danny turned off Melissa's light. He went into the master bedroom, closed the fauxwood blinds facing the woods, then sat on the bed and took off his shoes. Sara's gray tee and loose cotton briefs she wore to sleep lay crumpled in the middle of the bed, and the chocolate colored quilt with a popcorn texture looked like they had just crawled out from it in the morning. Danny liked Sara's taste in decorating, a cross between country style and modern. He moved brown throws and gold shams toward the headboard, thought about lying down, but heard the shower water and imagined his wife sponging her curves.

Danny unbuttoned his shirt and slid it off as he walked into the steamy bathroom to slick tiles and a hazy mirror. "Would two be a crowd in there?" He opened the shower door and narrowed his eyes, taking in the view from top to bottom.

"No. It needs to be steamier," Sara replied.

"I can fix that." Danny took off his navy trousers and briefs and stepped in. He inhaled the aroma of the shower stall, saturated with orange ginger. Already the sight of water hastening down her silky hair and smooth skin aroused him.

Sara leaned into Danny, who was a good six inches taller. She pressed her hands into Danny's back muscles. Her breasts sunk into his chest as she felt him embrace her with firm arms. She explored his lower back, gliding her hand around. She squeezed while their lips and tongues explored, all wet and moist from each other and the pounding shower head.

Danny inched his hand behind Sara and between her thighs. He pressed closer while Sara raised her leg onto the soap dish ledge.

Chapter 4

The salon was wedged between two posh women boutiques. The chatter inside diminished as personnel snapped down bulky dryers and stashed away rinse colors in plastic bottles. The last hairdresser with a client combed and snipped the parched hair of a customer in her chair, the wife of a prestigious partner of a major law firm in Elvis's hometown.

"You have the longest legs, my drape isn't doing your cream silk pants any justice," the hairdresser said. "Here." She placed another cloth over the woman's knees.

"Thank you darlin. I'll be shedding them soon enough. I'm donning my most recent holiday splurge for tonight. And if my husband asks me about the gown's price, I'll just tell him it's one of his Christmas presents to me." She laughed over her shoulder. "That works for everything this time of year."

The younger woman combed her client's hair forward around her face, scrutinizing for any unevenly cut areas. "Mrs. Rose, in retrospect, what would you do differently? Regarding men, that is?"

"First off, you've used the correct term. Never stop with one."

The hairdresser squirted a creamy product in her palms and massaged it into the woman's hair, creating a silky sheen.

The older married woman didn't offer any more advice. "Are you still taking that course you told me about?" She spied the study guide on the hairdresser's busy counter.

"I am. I take it online. It's so easy and it's only for twelve months. I sit for the certified surgical technician test in a few months."

"Wow. There's good money in medicine."

"Not as a tech."

"You're not after lawyers, then, are you?"

The young woman smiled.

"Smart girl. You strap on one of those masks they wear and you'll knock them male surgeons dead with those eyes."

"Thank you for the kind words, Mrs. Rose. And enjoy your holidays."

Mrs. Rose squeezed a twenty-dollar tip into the woman's hand, paid the bill at the front register and left. The beautician swept her space. The salon was quiet and almost empty.

The co-owner left the cash drawer open and pulled the window blinds. The pretty twenty-four year old picked up her study guide and gathered her purse from the bottom drawer of the front desk. With her eyes fixed on the inattentive co-owner, her hand smoothly slid a fifty-dollar bill from the register into her blouse pocket.

Casey tugged at Danny's sleeve, a canvas jacket that Sara had bought him last year. "Good thing you're not this slow in surgery," Casey said. He depended on the crisp early December air to enliven his friend after his grueling day. They walked west of Vanderbilt so Casey could share his refined bachelor taste with Danny, to pick out Christmas gifts for Sara and the girls. Like Sara, Casey had observed and encouraged Danny in his senior resident year.

Danny had more responsibility than ever before, running the spine service for six months, coordinating the residents below him, and trying to figure out where he'd work in another six months. In addition, Danny had his hands full at the house. Sara and Danny had another baby girl, the "last one," Danny had said.

"Casey, we could have gone to the Mall near Opryland, where we could've bought something from the Bass Pro Shop. Sara likes things in there as much as I."

"You can do that, too," Casey said.

"Not before this Christmas," Danny said, "unless someone donates me more shopping time."

Casey stopped short and pointed across the street to a pretty boutique with a red cobblestone sidewalk out front. They sauntered across, passing a black lamppost and wooden bench out front. When they walked into Grace's, a hanging doorbell rung and they smelled mulling spices. Fine stationery, leather items, frames and gifts lay on shelves and tables, and baby trees stood with festively decorated splendor. Casey walked to an oak table and thumbed through an album of font choices for personalized stationery.

"Danny, I'm ordering my girlfriend note paper with matching lined envelopes, her name embossed on both. That might also be a good idea for you, too, for Sara."

"No jewelry for your girl?"

"No. Too early for that."

"Maybe for you," Danny replied.

"We'll probably fizzle out. She says she likes my clean, military haircut, but it's really my biceps she wants." Casey laughed while pointing to the rose lined envelope. "I'll order this and buy her some CD's and poinsettias."

"I'll get Sara the pale blue paper with the fine script font for her name." Danny felt the paper, almost like linen, which gave him another idea. He spotted small satin pillows and walked over to the hardwood shelf. Neatly stacked beside them was an assortment of baby-blue linen cases.

A saleslady walked over, noticing Danny's interest. "Besides personalizing the stationery, you can get a lovely monogrammed pillowcase for the pillow as well."

Casey joined Danny. "Nice idea," he said.

Danny decided on personalized pillows for each of the girls and Sara. He continued looking and picked up a soft, burgundy case, the length and width of letter paper. He looked questioningly at the woman, who took two steps to answer his forthcoming question.

"Can you monogram this?"

"Yes. And it can be ready for Christmas."

Sara opened the oven door to peek at the sixteen-pound turkey, the thick aroma and heat escaping onto her face. Its skin crackled as it browned and its juices ran into the black roasting pan. Danny snapped in the kitchen table leaf, then spread a gold vinyl tablecloth and put four Santa Claus candlesticks with green holly on top.

"Daddy, is this okay?" Melissa stood in front of him with the windows to the backyard behind her, light catching the silver ribbons Sara had put on her hair. She wore a red satin dress with pale leotards.

Danny couldn't count how many times he hugged and kissed Melissa since they'd opened Christmas presents that morning. He took the milk bottle, shook a few drops onto his wrist. "That's wonderful," he said, "just like you."

With twinkling eyes, Melissa smiled widely, willing to please. She lifted her baby sister, Nancy, from the playpen, sat on her painted rocking chair and Danny handed her the bottle.

Annabel skipped over, holding a stuffed reindeer with large floppy ears and flew it around her sisters.

Sara lowered the stove heat while Danny started setting the table. "I'm almost ready but some surgeon needs to do the carving," she said, pointing to Danny.

Greg walked through the kitchen entrance bundled in a thick coat and a Russian warm hat, the wool almost meeting his eyebrows. "Merry Christmas everyone! It smells like turkey in here." He placed a large aluminum pan on the counter. "Keep it warm," he said, giving Sara an embrace. He bent over and squeezed Annabel, who turned around, displaying her velvet green pants and top. "Come on, you help me," he said, dashing to the car for another tray and a shopping bag of presents.

A red hat with a white pompom jingled as Casey and his date walked up the back porch steps and entered the family room. Casey handed Danny a heavy bag with eggnog and apple cider. "This is Carolyn," he said. "Carolyn's a physical therapist at the hospital."

"Glad you could make it" Danny said, while she handed him a bottle of wine. She rubbed her hands and asked them how she could help with last minute preparations.

Casey put two small packages under the tree for Annabel and Nancy and walked to Melissa as she placed Nancy back in the playpen. "This is for a very pretty angel I know," Casey said, waving for Melissa to follow him to the family room fireplace. He sat on the stone hearth, the crackling fire behind him, while Melissa put her hand on his cotton trousers, eyeing the gift box wrapped in gold foil.

"For me?" she said in a whisper.

"Yes," Casey whispered back.

Melissa ripped the paper and opened a white box.

"It's your modern birthstone," he said. "These are called opals and I'll give your Mommy some links, so it can expand. When you get bigger."

Melissa's small fingers felt along the oval opal bracelet then Casey clasped it around her wrist. She wrapped her arms around his neck. "Thank you," she said. "I love it, Uncle Casey."

Danny sliced breast meat while Sara tossed hot biscuits into the breadbasket. Greg placed a second platter from Downtown Italy on the table.

"Time to eat. Food for thought," Greg said, as everyone swarmed around the festive feast.

"Oh yuck," Melissa said, covering her plate with her hand as Sara tried to add spinach.

Greg pretended to scowl. "Children should be seen and not … "

"Spanked," Melissa blurted.

Greg laughed. "You four year old smart aleck."

Greg questioningly looked at Carolyn sitting next to him. "May I?" he asked.

Carolyn nodded while she placed her plate closer to the serving spoon. "Thank you all for inviting me," she said. She wore a knit teal dress, like a ski sweater, hugging her figure like black skin on a seal. She owned a good sense of humor and spoke enthusiastically about her job coaching patients in physical therapy.

Sara's left hand pushed her hair behind her ear. She had meant to put on a wide barrette with teeth to hold back her hair, but she had changed Nancy after applying moisturizer, put on silver earrings and slid on a skirt. She'd pulled the snow pearl sweater overhead that Danny had given her last year for Christmas, and had forgotten all about it.

"Dad, has Danny told you that it may be my last year of teaching?" Sara asked. She lightly poured gravy on her dinner. "At least until the girls get older."

"He mentioned it. It'll make things easier at the house. But you love your teaching."

"Danny's income is going to soar, so we won't be dependent on my salary. Miss Emily doesn't want to sit for us anymore, and yes, Dad, I will miss it. But the girls need me more right now, and I can resume teaching in a few years."

"Sara can give the girls early biology lessons," Danny said.

Greg reached around the candlesticks for the wine. He poured another glass. "Maybe this will help my blood pressure. It's high again Danny. The doc increased the beta-blocker."

"The best cure for that is to go fishing, as soon as it warms up."

Casey and Carolyn helped Sara clear the table when they finished and Melissa stood on a standing stool scooping apple cobbler into bowls.

Greg took the opportunity to take Danny aside to the family room, where they sat in the recliners next to the porch windows. Except for a few cedars, there was a clear view in the woods of hilly terrain saturated with fallen leaves. Just once, Danny thought, a white Christmas would be fun for the girls, but that would be too rare for the Music City.

"So, any concrete prospects?" Greg asked.

"Dr. Bruce Garner."

The thick brows on Greg's forehead rose. He put down the wine and leaned forward, looking at the girls unwrapped presents from the morning. "He lives in the estates, nearby. Even I know about him. Fantastic reputation."

"He hired someone two years ago, whose emphasis is backs. Bruce does fifty-fifty spines and craniotomies. He'd like me to join, round out the group with my emphasis on intracranial surgery."

"Is he going to slow down?"

"No. But he's territorial of his practice. It may be awhile before he makes the other doc a partner."

"Well, I'd be territorial, too. He's responsible for the success of his practice, so he better know who he's handing the plate to."

Danny nodded, leaned over and stirred the fire with a wrought iron poker.

"It's not a well kept secret that he makes over a million a year. He said he'd start me at one fifty the first year, but raise me to two fifty the second year if things work out."

The two men let this thought settle. "Which brings me to what I wanted to discuss with you," Greg said. "You know I received a few million selling the two restaurants. I'm having my estate plans changed. You and Sara are going to be fine, financially, with you going into practice."

"I agree, Dad, no worries there."

"I want you two to enjoy yourselves, not worry about the girl's later or their college education. You two live on and plan your future based on your neurosurgery income. I'm having a trust drawn up with everything going to the girls, payable to them equally, in installments, when they turn eighteen."

Danny pondered this. "Dad, that would be fine. Wonderful, I mean. It's generous of you. Sara and I won't need the inheritance. You already gave us this house."

"Another thing. Instead of bothering you or your sister with the trust paperwork, I'm appointing the bank as the executor. Is that okay with you?"

"That's fine," Danny said. "Can I ask you about Mary, though?"

"I'll leave your sister my house. She can come back from Sitka to live here in Nashville if she wants. Or sell it. Someday maybe she'll get tired of selling winter artwork and giving fishing boat tours in the summer."

"I don't know about that, Dad." Danny laughed. "She's the environmentalist."

Greg took a sip of wine. "But this is all premature anyway, because I'm going to see my grandchildren become young ladies. They're going to fish with me when I'm ninety."

"You'll teach those girls to come home with full stringers," Sara said, walking in. She gave Danny a kiss, picked up her pillow present and hugged it to her chest. After dessert, Greg, Casey and Carolyn said good-night and Melissa poked through her new treasures under the tree.

In the confusion of gifts, Danny picked up a bag and walked upstairs to the master bedroom. He pulled out the unwrapped leather burgundy case he had bought himself, monogrammed with his initials DT. Sara had also liked it. On the edge of their bed, he felt the soft leather. Precisely the right size. He leaned forward, opened his bottom drawer and rummaged in the back, pulling out the plastic bag. So much for a safe deposit box. It was more fun having Einstein at the house.

Danny thought back to the day his mother told him about the historical hoopla. He'd been sixteen when Donna had shown him the *Time* magazine in 1979 with Einstein's picture splashed on the cover, the hundred-year anniversary of his birth. Although Einstein had been dead twenty-four years, his image and accomplishments kept getting larger, an icon growing like the importance of his formulas.

Danny fished into the plastic baggie, pulled out the book, and stared at the great genius' signature. After some moments of reflection, he lightly inserted the publication into the leather case, slid the cover under the leather strap and stuck it back under his clothes. The old treasure holder, the plastic bag, spun as Danny dropped it into the bathroom garbage can.

Chapter 5

Dr. Bruce Garner concurred with Danny. They stood in front of angiography studies, MRI and CT results. Bruce pointed to the angiography, tracing the external carotid artery feeders to the meningioma. Nice to get a second opinion, Danny thought. Danny turned to Karen, one of their office nurses, and asked her to send Susan Kempler to his office, where he could inform her of her diagnosis, treatment and probable outcome.

Danny had assimilated well with The Neurosurgery Group for Middle Tennessee. With only one other junior colleague, Dr. Harold Jackowitz, Bruce maintained control of a successful, reputable practice and worked as hard as his younger employees. Danny thought of him as a presidential figure. He had Danny's build, but he dominated their specialty with his authoritative manner, intelligence and refined manual skills. His thick graying hair and twinkling, narrow slotted eyes made him stand out in a crowd.

"I'm going over to the hospital to flip-flop lumbar discectomies with Harold for the afternoon," Bruce said. "Just see my two remaining office patients after you talk to Mrs. Kempler." Bruce took off his long white coat and folded it over his arm. He tilted his head to adjust for his lower bifocal. "Try and get a spot on the schedule for Mrs. Kempler next Tuesday.

Then you and I can share backs after your craniotomy and Harold can mind the office."

"All right," Danny said. "I'll ask if Tuesday works for her."

Danny walked into his office, acknowledging the waiting couple. Mrs. Kempler's husband placed his hand on her blouse, her forearm resting on the mahogany armrest. At forty-six years old, Susan Kempler had been healthy, a workout fanatic, so couldn't understand why she had developed seizures. While waiting for the referral to see Danny, the neurologist had prescribed antiepileptic drugs, but the medications had been unsatisfactory in controlling the frequency or severity of her episodes.

Danny hated telling people grim diagnoses, but this one, compared to many, gave Mrs. Kempler a promising recourse. However, Danny sometimes noticed that patients did not grasp what the diagnosis of their particular tumor, aneurysm or metastasis meant. They focused too much on the fact that they needed surgery inside their head, and sometimes, that could be the easy part. If they had a severely malignant tumor or a mass growing in a precarious region of the brain, it could affect their eyesight, their balance, or their cognition. Their intracranial pressure could go too high. Those were the things to really worry about.

"Mrs. Kempler," Danny began, "all your studies are back and I can safely assure you we've found the culprit responsible for your recent symptoms."

Danny paused as they became more attentive. Mr. Kempler focused on his wife as she moved her forearms to her lap and wrung her hands.

"You have a meningioma. Most times, they are slow growing and benign." Danny spoke softly as Mrs. Kempler's facial muscles slightly relaxed.

"What exactly is that?"

"First, I'll tell you what it isn't. It's not a metastasis. Something that could have spread from somewhere else in your body." Mr. and Mrs. Kempler nodded their head. "It is the most common primary intracranial tumor. In your case, it's between the brain and the skull."

Mr. Kempler leaned forward. "So it's not in Susan's brain tissue?"

"Of the three membranes of the brain, there is an intimate layer on the surface, dipping in and out of its grooves, or fissures. Its two components are the pia and arachnoid. Sometimes there's a large space between them which contains CSF, a protective cushion. Susan's tumor originates from arachnoid cells."

"What are my treatment options?" Susan asked.

"Dr. Garner and I agree that surgical removal is the treatment of choice. Radiation therapy is considered ineffective and we would not suggest letting this go."

"If it's benign, like you think, then why not?" Mr. Kempler asked.

"If it keeps growing, Susan's seizures won't be the only symptoms. More will follow. But of more importance, at present, is that we detect some cerebral edema on the CT. Susan should have the surgery."

"Cerebral edema?"

"In simple terms, Mr. Kempler, consider the brain inside a closed, inelastic skull. There are three things in there. Blood, CSF and brain. Each takes up a certain volume. If there is an increase in volume of one of these, in this case, a growing brain tumor, it must be offset by a decrease in another. If not, the pressure inside the skull will rise. We treat high intracranial pressure; even have methods to monitor it. High and uncontrolled intracranial pressure can be fatal."

"If I have surgery," Susan asked, "what is my prognosis?" She stopped fidgeting with her hands and held her husband's hand.

"Outcome is good. Five-year survival for meningiomas is ninety percent.
Preventing a recurrence mostly depends on how successful we are in removing the entire tumor."

"What would you do?" she asked.

Sunlight filtered through the blinds in Danny's office. A glare reflected off the glass-framed print above the couch.

"Have the surgery," Danny said without hesitation.

Mrs. Kempler glanced at her husband whose empathy showed in his moist eyes. He remained silent. It was his wife's decision.

"Okay, as soon as you can fit me in."

Danny nodded. When they left, he stopped to contemplate his Norman Rockwell *Grandpa and Boy Fishing* print.

Dr. Simon, the anesthesiologist, busily adjusted Susan Kempler's IV access and the radial arterial line he had inserted for continuous blood pressure monitoring. Now he could easily take blood samples out of the radial line, to send for evaluation of the patient's blood gases, to adequately hyperventilate the patient to a pCO2 between 30-35 mm Hg. Blowing off CO2 would cause vasoconstriction, decreasing cerebral blood flow, which would decrease intracranial pressure or ICP. Danny glanced his way, knowing anesthesiologists dealt specifically with neuroanesthesia. Dr. Simon also hung mannitol and piggybacked it into the patient's IV. A diuretic, it would draw fluid out of the brain, also a measure to decrease ICP.

Danny fixed Mrs. Kempler's head position. He penetrated the scalp and outer table of the skull with pins and grimaced under his mask with the effort. He planned on macro work for the meningioma, which meant he'd be standing for the case, and hoped its removal would be complete and wouldn't take all morning. He had not gotten a full night's sleep because Melissa had a cold. Sara and Danny had awoken with her coughing intermittently throughout the night.

Eileen, the scrub nurse, wheeled the instrument table closer. She had everything aligned precisely the way she wanted it. "How are your girls, Dr. Tilson?" she asked.

"Melissa has a cough, but she'll be fine." He pinched the drape around the suction tip, then clipped it together with a hemostat. "The second one is a tomboy. Annabel sulks every time she looks in the mirror at her crooked tooth."

"She may not be a frilly little girl," Eileen said, "but she must already understand that a girl's smile is one of her assets."

"Must be," Danny said. "And my wife says that our three year old, Nancy, is growing like suburban Nashville, but she doesn't like her ears. She thinks they're too big."

Dr. Simon looked over from writing on the anesthesia record. "Braces for the crooked tooth and a hairstyle to cover the ears will fix that."

"Then it'll be something else," Eileen said. "Boys are easier."

"I wouldn't trade them, though," Danny said while Eileen passed him the drill. Eileen was a full RN. Danny had found out that one of the scrub nurses wasn't a nurse but an unlicensed technician, or surgical scrub tech. Due to an increasing nursing shortage and high health care costs, hospitals could have an RN supervise several ORs, but have unlicensed techs fill the scrub and circulator roles. Danny preferred, and had requested, only registered nurses to assist him.

OR banter diminished as Danny's work became more involved. The morning disappeared as Danny removed the brain tumor and excised some dural attachment and abnormal bone. Luckily, there was no involvement of a sinus and Danny believed his removal of the meningioma was complete. Danny started his closure when another nurse gave Eileen a short break, then Eileen came back to resume her duties.

In sterile fashion, the relief nurse helped Eileen gown and glove on her return. “Dr. Tilson,” Eileen said, “Casey, the paramedic from the ER is waiting for you in the doctor’s lounge. He told me to tell you that your wife brought your daughter in to the ER because of her cough but she’s better now.”

Danny’s heart thumped. Sara wouldn’t have just brought Melissa to the ER if it weren’t serious. “The ER? What else did Casey say?”

“That’s all. He said he would wait for you.”

The circulator refrained from turning on a CD at the end of the case. Danny remained quiet, focusing on closing, but thinking about Melissa, who was so thoughtful of others, like a miniature of his wife. And yet, perhaps he’d missed something. Melissa always seemed paler and more out of breath than Annabel and Nancy when they ran in the yard.

Danny removed the drapes and left the OR. He walked into the doctor’s lounge where Bruce Garner and Casey hovered around the hospital’s complimentary lunch spread.

“Melissa’s been seen,” Casey said, as Danny approached him. “They’re just waiting on paperwork and a prescription in the ER.”

“What happened?” Danny asked, tugging his dangling OR mask off.

“Sara said Melissa’s cough kept getting worse. Then she had difficulty breathing.”

"I'll get the backs started," Bruce said. "Link up with me when you get back from the ER. Is Mrs. Kempler off the table yet?"

"No," Danny said.

"You can tell me about your resection later. I'll check with anesthesia before I start the back. Go see about your daughter."

"Thanks, Bruce." Danny removed his shoe covers and grabbed his white coat from the locker room. He and Casey ran down the staircase to the ER.

The ER had the usual semi-emergent day crowd without any hectic trauma cases or acute heart patients. As soon as Danny and Casey stopped at the desk, the ER doctor came around and escorted them into Sara's room. "Danny, your daughter came in with bronchial asthma. A respiratory tract infection probably triggered it." Danny hung on the physician's every word. "She responded to a bronchodilator."

"No shot of epi?" Danny asked.

"No," he said. "And she was thrilled about that."

Sara sat stroking Nancy's hair as her daughter leaned across her lap. Melissa smiled at them as they walked in, opening her arms from her perch on the exam table. A deer stared at Danny from Melissa's favorite short sleeve slate top. Danny felt his daughter's opal bracelet at the back of his neck while he squeezed her. Sara came over and rubbed Danny's upper arm.

"Are you okay, sweetheart?" Danny asked, and kissed the top of Melissa's head. "I bet you scared your mom. We'll get you better."

"I'm okay, Daddy. Did you fix somebody this morning?"

"Yes, I did, sweetheart. But right now I'm worried about you."

Melissa lightly shoved her father to look at him. "It's okay, Daddy. It was just a little cough."

"She can go home," the ER doctor said. "We'll give you an inhaler. But, Sara, make an appointment with the pediatrician. Your daughter will need to take maintenance medications."

"I will," she said, "and thank you."

"Daddy," Annabel asked. "Mommy said she'll buy us an ice cream going home. Can you come with us?"

Danny crouched to her eye level. "No. But why don't we all go fishing this weekend?"

At that, Annabel wrapped her fingers around Nancy's hands and shook them up and down. "Yes-s," she exclaimed, then felt her crooked tooth with her tongue. Danny spied the white rounded front end of her sneakers, which wore a mud-stained smile, and the Life is Good baseball cap she wore. He couldn't help grinning at her as he straightened up.

Sara pondered over the 2003 calendar on the kitchen counter. Although it was the beginning of October, she already had scribbled things to do in the little squares for November and December. School functions, a 5K charity run, piano lessons for Melissa, soccer practice for Annabel and Nancy, doctor's appointments. The pediatrician had just prescribed a preventative daily pill for Melissa's asthma, and he had also announced the disappearance of Annabel's lingering summer bout with poison ivy.

"Come on girls, everyone will be waiting on us," Sara yelled up the stairs, swaying her arm although no one could see her. It took her by surprise when all three girls sprang down the steps, in reverse chronologic age. Perhaps there wouldn't be any eight, ten and twelve year old sibling rivalry today. She picked up a camel corduroy jacket that matched her skirt and draped it on her arm. She tightened her sandals; until her toes got cold, she refused to put real shoes on. Until then, the only shoes that deserved tying were her running sneakers.

"Is daddy going to be there yet?" Annabel asked. She plucked a light hooded jacket from the closet for her bare arms just in case she needed it, but skipped a cap, knowing Danny and her grandfather frowned on wearing hats inside restaurants.

"He's on the last back of the morning," Sara said. Every other weekend Bruce, Harold and Danny ran a Saturday morning elective surgery schedule for cases that couldn't be fit in during the week and had piled up. "We'll see him there. Casey is meeting us, too."

Sara relished the occasional Saturday or Sunday lunch gatherings at Downtown Italy, especially since she wouldn't cook the rest of the day. As the three girls and Sara opened the restaurant door, Angelo put the finishing touch to their table, a vase of carnations and a pitcher of cold water. "Ciao bella," he said to Nancy, pulling out the chair for her. "Buongiorno," he said to Melissa and Annabel. "Your Grandpapa is not here yet."

A few customers came in, and Casey followed. He hastened his step, a full smile crossing his face. "I'm having lunch with the prettiest women I've eaten with all week. Is this the right table?"

"Here," Nancy responded, and pointed to the chair next to her. She giggled, wishing she was older than eight, and felt her hair to make sure it wasn't behind her ears.

"Danny's on his way. Let's order," Sara said. She let the girl's select their lunch and asked Angelo for a small salad and lasagna.

"Any dates this weekend?" Sara asked Casey.

"Last night, an attorney from Bowling Green. And I've got the whole weekend off." Casey extended his arms and rolled up his blue shirtsleeves. "I'm playing poker tonight with the guys."

He buttered bread and handed it to Nancy, who took it and looked away. Sara could swear she blushed.

"Daddy's here," Melissa said.

Danny nodded hello to Angelo and sat. "If Gianni made Zuppa Di Minestrone today, I'll have a cup," Danny said, "and thanks."

Danny unfolded his napkin. "Where's Dad?" he asked Sara. "Is he in the kitchen?"

"No. He must have slept late."

Danny smiled. "He deserves it. We'll call him in a little while."

Sara rose from her chair and swerved around Melissa. She tugged her husband's shirt collar towards her and pecked him on the cheek.

"Sorry, Sara," he said, and returned a kiss on her mouth. "Cases went well this morning and I'm off the hook for the rest of the weekend. Harold is officially on call."

"How's it going with Harold and Bruce?" Casey asked.

"I think fine. No complaints."

Danny and Harold had become partners in The Neurosurgery Group of Middle Tennessee. They had almost as much input into the business and schedule as Bruce, but Bruce still controlled the finances. Danny felt grateful to have fallen in with Bruce to begin with but now thought he deserved a higher salary.

Sara finished lunch first. "Time's up for Dad," she said, reaching for Danny's cell phone. "I'll call." She let the phone ring and ring. "There's no answer at the house," she said. "Maybe he's on his way."

"Call his cell," Danny said.

Sara dialed and waited, then left a short message.

"I'll go by the house when we're finished if he's not here by then," Danny said, "and you can take the girls home."

"But I'm going with you," Casey added. "Both of us can give him grief if he's been dragging his heels."

Danny drove into the circular drive and both men got out of the car to a bright white sunshine almost like a hot summer day. They walked to the house where Danny tried the front door knob. Casey pressed the bell while Danny reached for his keys when his Dad didn't appear.

Danny and Casey walked through the two-story foyer looking in rooms to both sides. The back opened up to an expansive kitchen. Danny sighed, "Not here either," he said to Casey. But they heard a low sound, like a whimper.

Around the island, Greg sat on the floor in his pajamas, his index finger poking at the tile, as if he were squashing bugs. Danny squatted in front of him. Greg stared at his finger then at Danny. "I don't know what I'm doing here." His eyes were moist, he started crying.

It was late at night when Danny headed through the lobby. He took his cell phone out of his pocket as the automatic doors opened, and dialed Casey. After a few hours at the hospital, Danny had insisted that
Casey go home.

"Stroke, for sure," Danny said. "They'll do some more tests tomorrow."

"You worried about his residual? You think he'll be able to go home?" Casey asked. He took a poker break and took a beer from the fridge.

"He needs a nursing home, at least to start, with physical therapy. If he makes progress maybe he can go home, and if he can’t manage on his own, we’ll hire him some assistance during the day.”

Danny got his car keys out. “I’ll be back here in the morning.”

“Danny, you told me that you and Sara were taking the girls hiking in the morning.”

“We can’t do that now.”

“Yes you can. Hiking won’t take that long with the girls. I’ll go to the hospital in the morning to stay with Greg. If anything important comes up, I’ll call you. I’ll see you when you finish.”

“Casey, you sure? Don’t you have something else you need to do?”

“I’m positive. Look, I worked out earlier this evening. Now I’m playing poker. I’m free as a bird.” Casey heard grumbles from inside. “Two pair, big deal,” one of the players said.

“Okay, thanks. I’m going to call my sister in Alaska again. It’s earlier there. She’s thinking of coming home for awhile if Dad needs help.”

“Talk to you tomorrow,” Casey said, and went back inside for another hand.

Chapter 6

Sara grinned at her sister-in-law's trademark gait, a toeing in of her right foot, and wondered if her right leg was shorter than the left. Sara and Mary were just a year apart, Sara thirty-eight, and Mary thirty-seven, but Mary had remained single. Since Mary had her own businesses, the cost and time necessary to visit her family in Tennessee made her visits rare. But when she did, she slid into their lives like a bursting silk cocoon near a butterfly bush. She also loved her far-away lifestyle in Sitka, Alaska, where during the five warm months she chartered salmon fishing trips in her gas guzzling boat and painted all winter. Local galleries luring cruise ship tourists would turn her art work over twice a season.

Mary hoisted her backpack onto her shoulders and wheeled her luggage away from the carousel. She and Sara hurried out the door to the short term parking garage across the street.

"Flights okay?" Sara asked as they zigzagged between yellow cones placed to help the flow of traffic.

"No problems and no delays," Mary replied, dragging her black suitcase.

"Kids are in school," Sara said, "they'll be so happy to see you. And I hope Danny is now visiting Dad. He's been seeing him at least once a day." Sara raised her arm to shoulder level, pointing to their aisle. "Did you board up at home?"

"Not exactly," Mary said. "A friend is staying there for minimum rent. She'll pay the utility bills and look after the place. It's a deal for both of us."

Sara rummaged in her bag for her car keys. They placed the luggage on the back seat and left Nashville International Airport.

"Let's stop at Dad's to leave your things," Sara said.

Danny nodded to the therapist coaching Greg to slowly walk along a wooden plank. Greg inched his hands along the rails and wore a frown as Danny stood close.

Greg scowled at his left ankle, which wouldn't cooperate. He willed it to straighten and step down like it used to. Under his breath, he cursed the clunky black footwear the nursing home made him wear.

"Dad, I'm so glad to see you," Mary said, entering the sterile room of machines. Sara trailed her as Danny reached for his sister.

"Your look gorgeous, despite the drag of traveling," Danny said, giving her a hug. Mary's long dark red hair hung loosely tied behind her back. She embraced her brother around his white coat and gave Greg a light hug.

"You look fine, Dad," she said. "You'll be sampling pasta downtown and fishing before you know it."

"My girl, from glacier country," he said. "See, I haven't lost it."

"Dad, you'll never lose anything," she said. She gingerly patted his hand on the railing as moisture accumulated in the corner of her dark blue eyes.

Greg glimpsed down. “It’s too cold,” he said, referring to the silver handrail. His forehead wrinkled and he started sobbing. “What’s wrong with it? Do I have to hold onto this?” he said to the therapist on his left side. He began to cry without restraint.

“It’ll be fine Dad,” Danny said.

After work, Danny went straight to his father’s house. Annabel and Nancy sat at the kitchen table doing homework while Sara made chili, concocted from ingredients in Greg’s pantry and ground beef that she had brought from home.

Mary changed into a sweatshirt, gray sweatpants and pink slippers and brought out a stack of photographs. She pointed to fish and birds, naming them as she went along, showing Melissa, who leaned over the armrest. Mary’s Kodaks made a pile between her legs, which were crossed and pulled up into the cushiony chair.

“Melissa, I see students on field trips all the time. The University of Alaska has a campus site at Sitka, where you could study for a BS in Biology. Can you imagine leaving your classroom and walking to an ice field?”

Melissa shook her head. Her eyes got glassy imagining the experience, crunching along the tundra in spiked boots, or cramming for a marine biology test while rocking in a boat at sea.

Melissa’s rescue inhaler sat on the end table, a constant reminder that she hadn’t outgrown her asthma. Despite daily meds, she struggled with occasional flare-ups, particularly in the fall and spring, even prompting another visit to the ER for a shot of epinephrine. The injection had magically bronchodilated her breathing passages, causing more oxygen to be absorbed into her bloodstream, providing fuel to her tissues. Even though Danny was a doctor, he had felt useless to help her and only relaxed when her gray color turned neutral again.

Danny glanced out the back window, where leaves tossed around on a breeze, and those caught by the back of the house piled outside the glass door. His mother's evergreens held onto their forest and teal shades and he frowned at a withering flower bush in a stone patio planter. His father's patio furniture stayed outside all year, he only brought in vinyl chair cushions and bird feeders that needed emptying and scrubbing. Danny sat on the couch facing his sister and daughter as Mary handed all the pictures to Melissa. Sara slid a lid on the chili pot and perched herself next to Danny.

"What's the doctor's update? Is Dad going to improve?" Mary asked.

"The neurologist said Dad has a condition called emotional incontinence." Danny took Sara's hand and turned it over, as if looking for Greg's perfect outcome. "I hate to see him this way, with labile behavior."

"I don't understand," Mary said.

"Dad may seem depressed and he's going to get frustrated. The stroke damaged an area of the brain controlling the normal expression of emotion. He's going to cry readily and have outbursts that don't fit the situation."

Sara nodded to her sister-in-law. "Danny's got a good neurologist taking care of Dad and his partner, Bruce, is pitching in, especially if he's going to need any surgery."

"You know I can stay through the winter," Mary said. "I can help take care of him after they discharge him from the nursing home and PT program."

"Then let's plan on that, to keep him home as long as we can," Danny said. "Just ask us when you need some extra assistance with him; we'll get more help if needed."

"What will you do with the restaurant?" Sara asked them.

"Mary's in charge of Dad's finances, if needed. And Mary, you know you get the house if anything happens. But I think right now, he'll want to sell the restaurant. You'll have to talk to him about it. The owner of his other two restaurants will buy, if Dad is ready."

Mary leaned forward. "Is he capable of making sound decisions with me or us?" She brushed her fingers through her hair.

"I think so. If you patiently discuss things with him."

They heard Annabel as she took off her new fly-fishing cap and thumped it on the table. "Annabel, what's wrong?" Melissa asked.

"Stupid math."

Melissa walked over and kneeled on the floor, peering at her sister's arithmetic problems. "I finished my homework. Want some help?"

Annabel gave her sister a pencil and scratch paper. "I've messed up," she said, pointing. When I multiply my division answer with the denominator, it doesn't give me the numerator."

Melissa worked the problem as they huddled together. "I see what you did wrong."

Nancy stopped reading. She smirked while pulling at the collar of her orange turtleneck. "Melissa, you always help her," she said. "Can you read for me?"

"Nancy, that's not true. Just ask me. Besides, you're so smart. When did you last get something wrong?"

A small smile formed around Nancy's mouth. "Well …"

Melissa slid her hand along Nancy's swatch of hair in front of her left ear. "See? You made a mistake, what, a year ago?"

"Come on girls," Sara said. "Let's clear some space and set the table."

The front doorbell rang and Danny sprang up. “It’s open,” he said loudly. Casey sauntered through the hallway and handed Danny a long brown bag. He slid off a gray parka.

“It’s the baguette delivery,” Casey said. He elbow locked Annabel by the head while his other hand patted Melissa’s hair. Mary rose awkwardly.

“Mary,” Casey sang, giving her a hug. The curves under her sweatshirt felt warm and unrestricted by any undergarment as they pressed against his chest.

“Casey, how are you?”

“Fine. It’s your dad we’re worried about.”

“Dad’s in great hands, even though his son is a doctor.”

“I’m not touching that one,” he said.

Danny sliced bread while Sara ladled her spicy mixture into soup bowls. “Grab the bag of cheese in the fridge,” Sara told Melissa. Danny looked through Greg’s wine rack and selected a Tennessee blackberry, popped the cork and poured four stemmed glasses half way. Danny extended his glass.

“To the best family and friend.”

When Danny and Sara got home and their bedroom turned dark as sleep, they whispered in bed like school kids as Sara lightly massaged Danny’s shoulders.

“Chow it …,”

Greg stopped. He dropped his head, turning it sideways to look at the Italian wall mural for the correct words. He thumped several fingers on the top of the tablecloth. “The sea is over there, not here,” he said, stalling. Small sobs like a child’s unexpected hiccups emanated from his sad spirit. Danny and Sara waited; Melissa coughed, crouching next to her grandfather. Greg looked into her eyes, smiled through his weeping. He then fumbled for a warm focaccia that Angelo had placed on the table in front of him. "Chow down," he finally said.

"Angelo, thank you for working with Dad all these years," Danny announced as he glanced at Gianni standing across the table, a white chef's hat perched on his graying hair. "You, too, Gianni. We'll still see you and patronize the restaurant. And we wish you luck with the new owners."

Greg, Sara, Mary, and the girls lifted wine and soft drinks with Danny and toasted Downtown Italy's staff. The next day, the legal paperwork would sign over ownership to the buyer of the other restaurants. Almost a year had elapsed, with Greg suffering yet another stroke, minor, but with cumulative effect.

Mary had weathered the heartache of seeing her father's deterioration and steadfastly cared for him while shifting artistic subjects, giving creative license to the state's lakes, wildlife and barns. Even simple Black Angus cattle didn't look drab when Mary painted them.

Danny and Mary had stalled the inevitable, but Greg now required full time care and monitoring. Besides his emotional lability, his long and short-term memory failed him frequently, and urinary incontinence forced most excursions to an abrupt halt. He walked laboriously, trudging along caged in the three sides of a walker. Often, Mary pushed him in a wheelchair, his body wearily resigning to her destination up and down the driveway, like a baby in a carriage.

Everyone's order arrived. "Angelo, tell Gianni everything is marvelous," Danny said. He lowered his voice to Mary, sitting next to him. "The nursing home said Dad's room will be ready at the beginning of the week. It's the only solo large care room available. You've been doing more than your share lately, so Sara and the girls can bring over pictures of him and mom, the girls and us, and his most cherished items. Dress up the room beforehand."

"Sorry, Danny, but I'm going, too. And Sara," she whispered, "we'll make sure we adorn it with pictures of Dad fishing at the Caney Fork, and that opening day at Downtown Italy picture with Mom."

Nancy listened in. "Mom, let's put a picture of Grandma's garden on the wall, too, and put bird feeders outside his window."

"Excellent idea, Nancy," Sara said. Her daughter's eyes shone back.

Danny leaned forward to catch Greg's attention across the table as he analyzed fork prongs. "Dad, we're talking about decorating your new room before you go there." Greg stared blankly at Danny. "Your new home next week, at Wellington's Life Care," Danny added. "Dad, you'll see one of us every day, just like now."

"Hmm," Greg answered. He picked up a small plastic cup of Italian dressing and tilted it to drink its contents, in lieu of his iced tea. His lips quivered with dissatisfaction at the taste of the strange liquid. Melissa patted his arm.

When they finished, Angelo cleared the plates. He came back and flanked Danny's right side for dessert orders. "How about cannoli to share?" Danny asked everyone. Sara looked at the girls and nodded, Melissa barked a cough.

"Angelo," Sara added, "please put it in the center of the table and bring us some small plates."

"Excellente," Angelo said, flipping his notepad closed.

Melissa cupped her hand over her mouth, coughing, then drew in air like yanking at a tug of war. She twisted her hands and looked at her father with widening eyes. Wheezing replaced audible breathing, her chest muscles retracted through a teal Danskin pullover, and her respirations increased.

Annabel sat next to her. Hastily she shoved away from the table and disappeared towards the floor, rummaging through Melissa's woven tote. "Do you have it?" she asked while Sara and Danny also rushed to Melissa's side. Melissa could only nod. Annabel dumped the contents of the bag onto the table, spotted the blue plastic inhaler, and shoved it into her sister's hand.

Danny arrived at the Rehab Institute late in the afternoon after finishing his last surgery and post-op orders at three p.m. He never advertised it, but along with a neurologist, he volunteered occasional services to Fort Campbell's, Kentucky soldiers, to evaluate them after they returned from Iraq and Afghanistan. Danny figured since he had never served in the military, it was the least he could do. These soldiers were surviving brain injuries better than men in previous conflicts because of improved body protection. Blasts from mines, grenades and other explosives had become survivable but caused common war disabilities when the women and men arrived back in the United States.

Danny first called Casey, knowing Casey had worked a graveyard shift and would be awake by then, chugging his black java, watching CNN headlines or catching the bold headlines of the daily paper.

"They called me to see a soldier who returned from Rustamiyah. Eastern Baghdad," Danny said. "He's got memory loss and a host of other symptoms. A traumatic brain injury."

"I bet the poor kid is half our age," Casey replied.

"He is. I'm not sure if there's anything surgical I can do for him. A rocket sailed through the building roof where his unit was." Two occupational therapists passed Danny at the front desk of the therapy room, acknowledging him as they left for the day. "Casey, if you're free, can you help Sara and Mary pack a car load at Dad's before work?"

"Sure. I'm meeting Susan in a little while for dinner. I can get over there between dinner and work."

"You still dating her?"

"A little bit. It's not serious. Besides, she's moving to Oregon for a new job."

"Undoubtedly moving because you broke her heart."

"Not a chance."

Across the room, a soldier in a camouflaged combat uniform stood with a therapist near a corkboard plugged with red and blue pegs. "Say hi to the girls," Danny said, as the young man picked a peg from a hole and placed it in a different row for a coordination test.

Casey left his jacket in his Jeep and rapped on Greg's front door. He never owned a house key of theirs, like he carried for Danny and Sara's place, so he restrained himself from trying the door. Especially since Mary lived there now.

The heavy front door opened. Mary's face lit up as she tossed a handful of hair onto her back. Casey's tongue tripped and the words tumbled, as if he couldn't control them if he wanted. "You look great," he said. "Despite the smeared orange and rust paint on the side of your face."

"Painting myself comes natural." She laughed, blushing, and then turned around. Casey followed her, infatuated by her easy but unconventional gait, and tried to pinpoint her aroma. Glorious geraniums.

Sara opened the cardboard box on the counter. "Plenty of pizza left," she said.

"No thanks. I just ate with Susan. Plus, I'm working tonight, so I'm at your service for a limited time."

"We'd like to bring over Dad's rocking chair," Mary said. "My mom had picked out the striped fabric to reupholster it when she was ill. It's a family heirloom."

Casey pushed up his off-white shirtsleeves. "It'll fit in my car. No problem."

Melissa and Nancy came bounding down the stairs, each with a storage container of pictures to sort through at Wellington's.

"My favorite screenagers," Casey said.

"Thanks for coming to help," Melissa said.

Greg sat inside on the couch. Annabel took his plate and the pizza crust he'd been flicking on his leg, and brought them to the kitchen. "Don't take my radio," he told her.

Casey leaned over, in front of him, to brush crumbs off his pants.

"Who are you?" Greg asked.

"I'm a friend," Casey said.

The girls stayed with Greg while Casey, Sara and Mary shuttled memorabilia and small furniture to Wellington's. They walked to the left side of the two-story building; residents on the opposite end lived in assisted living. Casey paused in the front lobby to smirk at the plastic flowers in a ceramic vase. Mary followed his gaze. "They'll last longer if they're artificial," she said, then grinned.

Greg's ground floor room at the end of a nurse's station hallway had a large bathroom with handicap accommodations. Mary and Sara began hanging hooks and pictures in the extra large single room. Sara put Greg and Donna's wedding picture in the center of the empty wall - the metal swirled frame, mat, and their pose dating it later than the mid 1900's. Both women stood side-by-side.

"Dad always said 'If your girlfriend prays with you, she's worth keeping,'" Mary said.

Sara peeled her gaze off the photo and touched Mary. "He's still with us, but I miss him already."

Mary nodded. "Me too."

Sara commenced rummaging inside a box for the new birdfeeders they had bought. She slipped a suet bar into the wooden one, and stepped through the end hallway door to hang it outside Greg's soon-to-be window. When she walked back in, she quietly marveled at Casey and Mary. They were making Greg's bed, spreading a soft white bedspread, laying his favorite patchwork quilt at the bottom, fluffing sham pillows near the headboard. Sara had never seen Casey engaged in a family chore like this one.

Chapter 7

Danny's thirty-eight year old patient furrowed his forehead while being examined. "I've never had a headache before," Mr. Donaldson said. "Now I'm walking around for two months with one. I can't stand it."

Dr. Singh, the neurologist, had started the man's work up, but Dr. Singh would be away for two weeks and believed his patient had signs of increased intracranial pressure, so he had referred him to Danny.

Mr. Donaldson put on his navy blue shirt and began buttoning it. He worked as an architect-engineer, sometimes at building sites in Tennessee, sometimes at a project outside Mexico City. He rubbed his stubbly beard and leaned back on the examining table. "Lately I've been getting nauseous. But the other day? I didn't go to an important meeting because I thought I'd vomit."

"We'll try to get to the bottom of your symptoms, Mr. Donaldson," Danny said. "Radiology sent me the CT and MRI that Dr. Singh ordered. I've looked at them. We can discuss the results as soon as I have more information." Danny checked boxes on his lab order sheet. "I'd like you to stop in our lab down the hallway to have your blood drawn."

Mr. Donaldson left, then Danny flipped his brain imaging results on the viewing box, perplexed by the solitary space-occupying lesion he saw. He'd confer with Bruce as soon as he returned from a cruise with his wife, and when all results were back.

Melissa's goal to pursue biology hadn't budged. She seemed ahead of her high school senior classmates filling out college applications because she had narrowed her interest - all she had to do was look at schools with good biology departments and availability of marine classes. Danny and Sara told her not to worry about a school's tuition or financial aid forms. They encouraged her to continue getting high grades and promised to foot the entire four-year bill – whether she attended a college nearby or went away.

During the late winter, Melissa had spent a few weekends barricaded in her bedroom submitting on-line applications and further investigating school possibilities on web sites. She conscientiously filled out forms, got letters of reference from previous teachers, wrote essays about jobs she'd had, and wrote the reasons why she wanted to attend a particular school. Despite sending out seven applications, she only had two serious choices – University of Alaska and Wake Forest in North Carolina.

Melissa and Sara had toured Wake Forest. North Carolina was as gorgeous as their native Tennessee, and the campus was as spectacular as an overgrown southern plantation with nice student housing. When they got home, Melissa told Danny how much fun she'd have taking a tropical marine ecology class off-site one summer in Jamaica. But Melissa still hadn't gone to see the campus sites in Alaska.

"No prob," she said. "If Mary says it's impressive, it is. And there I'd get a ton of marine ecology, mammalogy and rainforest studies." Now she waited tentatively for mail with return addresses from her college choices, worried if their contents contained a rejection.

Melissa doubled her steps up the back deck into the house, dropped her backpack, and slit open The University of Alaska Southeast's envelope with the bold UAS letters. The day before Wake Forest had accepted her. Sara put down the grocery list she had started and slid onto the stool next to Melissa.

"Yesss," Melissa exclaimed. Melissa held onto the letter as if it were a treasury note. Sara got up and mother and daughter hugged.

"Mom, this is so exciting. My top choices. I'm in! I can't wait to tell everybody." But just as quickly, she aborted the enthusiastic gesturing and slid onto Sara's stool.

"Oh," she said.

"What?" Sara asked. Her daughter put the letter on the granite countertop.

"It never sunk in before, Mom. I wouldn't get home as often if I went to Alaska, wouldn't see Pop in the nursing home like I do now."

Sara put her hand on her daughter's high school sweatshirt and patted her shoulder. "Sweetheart, that's what happens when young people leave for college. It's time for your most important educational years; it's the beginning of your new life."

"But Mom, Pop isn't going to be around forever. If I go to school in North Carolina, I can see him at Wellington's every time I have a long weekend or a break."

"You think about this carefully. Your father and I won't meddle."

Sara embraced Melissa again and whispered into her ear. "You need to make your own decision." She let go of her daughter and smiled. "I'm making a grocery list for your graduation party. I'm going to make marinated meatballs as hors d'oeuvres and freeze them."

"Thanks Mom. And it's a good idea to have it before graduation, like you said. All my friends will still be here, before they go away or start working summer jobs."

Sara smiled. "You're welcome. You're going to have a super party."

Melissa started to walk away, but drew in a breath and stopped. "Mom? My mind is made up. I'm going to accept Wake Forest. And we're bringing Pop here the day of my graduation party."

Melissa's words froze Sara to the spot. Her daughter's thoughtful choice stemmed from startling maturity. Even if she wanted to, Sara realized she couldn't argue with her. Melissa now held her own reins. With a glow in her eyes, not to her complexion, Melissa turned on her heels and left, her decision solidly rooted in its place.

Danny stood in his office on Monday morning listening to Bruce bubbling over with details of his trip. With a few minutes to spare before seeing patients, Danny donned his white coat, told Bruce about Mr. Donaldson's medical and social history, and waved him towards their imaging room.

"His lab results show a high sed rate and a seventeen thousand white count," Danny said, as he put the patient's imaging results on the screen.

Bruce shot Danny a glance. "CSF has a similar density to this lesion. Did you get a differential on that high white count? Are his eosinophils high?"

Danny nodded his head. “Yes. He has eosinophilia.”

Bruce’s towering frame swung around to Danny. “I think you better get an infectious disease physician in on the case and schedule surgery.”

Danny felt Bruce’s excitement. Although every case was different, most of the time they were dealing with recurrent diagnoses. “Are you implying this is exotic?”

“You ever hear of echinococcosis?”

Danny had heard of it. “Oh my God. Hydatid disease? He has a highly lethal and an aggressive parasite? In his brain?”

Bruce nodded and when Danny shrugged his shoulders to acknowledge he couldn’t remember more facts off hand, Bruce continued. He pointed to the round lesion. “This hydatid cyst is probably caused by the more common species of Echinococcus granulosas. From the dog tapeworm.”

Danny squirmed. He remembered spitting this out on an exam. “Dogs are the definitive host of the adult worm,” Bruce said. “The intermediate host of the larval stage is a human, sheep or species that your soon-to-be infectious disease physician will enlighten you about.”

“This thing has probably been growing for years, hasn’t it?” Danny asked.

“Precisely. And your job?” Bruce dabbed the cystic image. “This thing contains hundreds of thousands of parasitic particles. You have to surgically remove this cyst intact. If you rupture it, scoleces will contaminate your patient’s brain or cause a severe allergic reaction.”

By the end of the week, Danny conferred with an infectious disease specialist who further tested Mr. Donaldson and confirmed the diagnosis. “Humans are infected by tapeworm-infected dogs,” said the balding physician. He and Danny poured coffee in the doctor’s lounge. Danny grimaced, but Dr.

Ngo continued. "Mr. Donaldson was infected either by direct contact or by eating food with viable parasitic eggs. The eggs hatch in human intestine, their embryos slither through the mucosa, traveling to other target organs in the blood." Dr. Ngo told Danny he would start Mr. Donaldson on the medical drug of choice, albendazole, but concurred that the definitive treatment lay in the hands of a skilled neurosurgeon.

Danny and his office nurse made the necessary arrangements with the operating room for his patient's craniotomy. He booked it as the first morning case, allowing ample time even though he had to-follow surgeries. He did not want to feel rushed because spillage of the cyst's contents would be disastrous. Danny wasn't sure if the case could be done as all macro work. He'd also set it up microscopically, in an electrically operated moving chair, to be safe.

As professional courtesy, Danny alerted the pathologist who would be working that day and stopped by the anesthesia office the day before to inquire, "Who's doing my morning case tomorrow?"

The CRNA closest to the drug rep food spread pulled the next day's schedule from her scrub pocket. "Dr. Ebel," she said.

"Good. I'll catch her before I leave and tell her the pertinents." He tailed his words with his trademark chuckle. Barbara will love this one he thought.

That evening, conversation centered on Melissa's college choice; her enthusiasm still bubbled over. Danny had also given her full latitude with her selection. Both parents marveled at her for forsaking her first choice because of her attachment to her grandfather. They couldn't be more proud of her.

Danny told his family about his craniotomy for the next day. As he explained the lifecycle of Echinococcus granulosas,

Annabel twirled the enamel trout earrings dangling from her ear lobes, which had been pierced when she turned fifteen. “Dad,” Annabel said, flippantly, “like that’s more information than we need.”

“Okay, but I may have to tell you how this ends tomorrow night,” Danny said.

Annabel stopped fidgeting and finished her chicken before Melissa and Nancy, who still sat there dismayed that a worm thingamajig could end up in someone’s brain.

Danny spoke with Mr. Donaldson before Dr. Ebel slid in a radial arterial catheter for continuous blood pressure monitoring. As Danny parted the preop curtain, the Versed she had just injected into Mr. Donaldson’s IV caused his lids to slide down to half-mast. Thirty minutes later, after a bagel and his second cup of French roast, Danny stood in the operating room while his patient was put to sleep and intubated. They turned the table away from the anesthesia machine, the flurry of activity continued, and then Danny scrubbed outside the room. Bruce stopped by, promising to break later from floor rounds to peek at Danny’s ongoing case.

Danny reentered the room. When the scrub nurse shook the sterile blue gown to unfold it, he slipped into it; and when she opened and parted the sterile latex gloves, he pushed his hands into them. Then he noticed her … her aqua eyes fixed on him. Wide eyed, undistracted except for Danny, as if she were a hypnotist, mesmerizing her subject. For a second, Danny forgot his case, the moment robbed by the salacious stare from above the pale blue mask and below the white OR bonnet.

“Danny, good positioning?” asked Debbie, the OR circulator. She pointed to the video system, and he focused again on his work.

Danny nodded okay, so Debbie stepped behind him to tie his gown. He glanced at the IV pole for the bottle of mannitol, the osmotic diuretic, and saw Katherine adjusting the patient's foley bag near her side of the table. Danny sat. Everyone was ready to start and he made his incision.

Little chitchat had enveloped the room, but now fewer words were spoken after the hum of the drill. Danny rested his elbows on the armrest, his wrists on the patient's head. The scrub nurse transferred instruments efficiently by following his procedure. Most of the noise in the room originated from the comforting beeps of the EKG. The pulse oximeter remained quiet.

Moist gray matter under the skull plate looked healthy. Danny gingerly explored to the left of his exposed site. Once he glanced over to the MRI and CT just to assure himself. There. Right there. Like a virus alert on a desktop screen, the top of the round cyst stared at him. Its fibrous capsule gave him courage. It looked substantial enough to withstand removal without splitting open. Perhaps underneath this capsule, the laminated membrane and germinal membranes also gave it further toughness.

Bruce entered, stood to Danny's side, then took a step back. The scrub nurse had forceps poised at the edge of her instrument table. Danny followed the hydatid cyst's edges … around, around, slithering it away from the gray and white, blood vessels, neurons and memory itself. He held his breath. He took the large ball from the man's head and placed it into a plastic cup. Life in its host ended. It was now destined for pathology.

Phew. Danny's bottled-up tension drained from both arms. Dr. Ebel sat on her stool to chart the last five minutes and Bruce nodded and left.

"Nice job."

Startled, Danny looked to the velvet voice he just heard. The eyes again.

"Are you a new scrub tech?"

"I'm not new to being a scrub nurse, but I'm new here."

"Oh, sorry. The hospital knows my position about covering my room. I want scrub nurses, not scrub techs," he said.

"My name is Rachel." She tugged the suction tubing gently, checking for slack as Danny placed the tip into the surgical site.

"Dr. Tilson, is it adequate?" she asked, rolling the words slowly off her tongue. "The amount of sucking?" She said it softly, leaning slightly forward for Danny to hear.

Danny's pulse quickened. He lifted his head too fast, but stopped when their gaze locked. Those eyes. He gulped under his mask.

"Anybody mind if I turn on the CD's?" Debbie asked. She counted surgical laps by the wall. "I'll keep it low if you'd like. Pick your favorites Dr. Tilson, Dr. Ebel."

"Sure. How about John Mayer's Continuum? That okay with you, Barbara?"

"Sure, that'll work."

"How's the patient doing?"

"No problems here," Barbara said.

When Danny got home, he perused *The Tennessean* in his easy chair, waiting for the girls and Sara to arrive. They burst through the back door after purchasing science project supplies, and scattered to set the table. Danny helped while Sara put white rice in the microwave. When it finished, they spooned garlic braised beef from the crockpot and sat down.

"We stopped by to see Pop," Melissa said. "He smiled the whole time, Dad. We thought he knew us when we got there, but then he told Mom not to feed the customers until the food was ready." Melissa looked down. "But I gave him a huge hug, Dad, and I swear he understood we all love him."

Sara sat next to Danny, her shapely legs crossing at the knees and the ankles. "Well," she said, leaning towards him. "We can't wait to hear."

"Yeah, Dad. We can't believe you haven't said a word yet."

"What did it look like?" Nancy asked. She twisted her fingers and pulled them off the table to her lap.

"I took it out successfully."

"And that's all?" Melissa asked.

Danny smiled and shrugged his shoulders.

"Kind of anticlimactic?" Sara asked.

Danny didn't say anything.

Chapter 8

Danny snapped the power button on the desktop computer, clicked, scrolled and found what he wanted. Hematocrit, potassium, creatinine, and further down the page, he evaluated Mr. Donaldson's other postop labs drawn at dawn. Everything looked fine; next, he had to make hospital rounds, and then start seeing patients in the office at nine.

He put his white lab coat on the back of a chair and walked to the coffee pot. He poured two-thirds of a cup, split a bagel and slipped the halves into the toaster. Two younger physicians sat on chairs in front of the television, the volume low. Several came and went from the dressing room. The bagel popped up and he spread thick pats of butter on each. He took a napkin and bused the bagel on a plate and remaining coffee to a round table.

There were three large windows facing the hallway. On the other side of the hallway were identical windows to the nurse's lounge. It looked a lot busier in there, Danny noted, as he slid his chair out. The doctor's lounge door opened and a woman with an untucked pink and white checkered blouse walked hurriedly towards the counter.

"Oh, Dr. Tilson, good morning."

Without scrubs, mask and OR bonnet, Danny knew who it was because of the voice, then the eyes. “Good morning, Rachel.”

“Perhaps the Doctor’s lounge is better supplied. I just need some type of rag or wash cloth to rub this off.” She stood next to Danny and pointed to dried dirt on the leg of her blue jeans. “Good old Tennessee clay,” she said. A smile crept across her lips.

She was a blonde, more like a dirty blonde. Her hair loosely curled to her shoulders, and pearl skin gleamed over sculptured cheekbones. She brushed the spot on her jeans with her right hand and some of the clay disappeared.

“There may be a cloth in a drawer beside the sink,” Danny said. “How did you do it?”

“Do what?” She tilted her head, grabbed a little lower lip between her teeth. “Oh, that,” she said. “My dog got more mischievous than usual this morning.”

“Your dog?”

“Mm hmm. He’s a Chesapeake Bay Retriever. Normally I unleash him for a little while every day. This morning he ran down the hill to the pond behind my townhouse, and when he came back, he couldn’t resist jumping on me.”

“Come to think of it, it does resemble a paw print.” Danny laughed. “Sounds like you’ve got your hands full.”

“Actually, he’s fantastic.” She stopped her animation and sunk her stare straight through him. He has a canine good citizen certificate, but also, he’s a therapy dog.”

“Really?” The melted butter had sunk into the doughy bread so Danny took a bite.

He wiped his mouth on a napkin, and as Danny put the napkin back on the table, Rachel’s hand approached it. Her fingers touched his, gently running over them. She eased the paper napkin out of his light grasp, put it to her mouth and moistened it. Danny stared as she rubbed the soiled spot with the paper.

"There. That made it so much better."

Danny sat spellbound, then his pulse quickened. He sipped the last remnants of his coffee and got up. He nodded towards the door and started to walk as Rachel stayed at his side.

"What exactly does your dog's job entail?"

"Like your rounds," she said. "Sometimes I bring him to see patients. Especially old people who don't have their pets any more. I used to bring him to a psychiatric facility when I lived in Cincinnati. Now I bring him to nursing homes. Like Wellington's," she added.

"You visit Wellington's Life Care with him?" Danny opened the door, held it for her.

"Oh yes. Patients love my visits, with him, I mean."

Danny took a step out the door behind her. She definitely had curves. She wasn't the skinny model type; she probably wore a size eight. He knew those numbers because of Sara and the girls.

Rachel turned. "Nice talking to you, Dr. Tilson. Your skills yesterday were extraordinary."

"Thank you. I try. Actually, I'm going to see Mr. Donaldson right now."

"He's a lucky man to have you give him a new lease on life, freeing him of that virulent parasitic ball." She scrunched her face. She still looked pretty.

"Thanks. Later, Miss Rachel." Danny slipped on his white coat while making his way to the elevators. Now, why did he say that, he thought? It didn't matter, because he felt like his spirit was soaring.

Melissa had made tea with honey before going to bed and had popped a Cold-eez. For two days, it felt like a sinister virus lurked in her head and her throat. By cleverly stalling its progression, she wanted to prevent an exacerbation of her asthma. But she woke at 4 a.m. coughing and lay awake for half an hour, her breathing getting slightly more laborious. She turned on the light, clutched her Albuterol inhaler from the nightstand and took a puff. On the second puff, she knew she'd exhausted the canister. She fell asleep after a while, but slept restlessly, turning the sheet into an uneven mess on one side under the lightweight comforter. When the alarm rang at six-thirty, she thought about skipping morning classes, but she had to hand in an English paper and hated the catch-up consequences if she played hooky, so gradually made her way to the bathroom.

Melissa quickened her steps to the kitchen to find Sara tying shoelaces, which meant her mother would be hitting the pavement after driving Nancy to school.

"Good morning. You sleep okay?" Sara asked.

"Not that well, Mom." Melissa opened the refrigerator, poured some orange juice, deliberated over the fruit bowl and selected a banana.

"I'm sorry, sweetheart."

Melissa put the banana down and shoved books into her backpack, but could not find her English folder. "No. What an idiot!" she exclaimed. "I've left all my English stuff at Pop's and my paper is due in the first class."

Sara questioningly glanced at Melissa.

"Mom, I wrote it there the other night after Mary and I got back from Wellington's. Now I have to run by Mary's and don't have time to pick up a refill on my inhaler."

"I can drop by the drug store this morning for you."

"Thanks, Mom." Melissa finished, tossed the peel in the garbage, and picked up her blue hoody, cell phone and car keys while Annabel and Nancy both bumped into each other going through the doorway.

"Annabel, you better hustle," Sara said. "Karen's mom will be out front any minute to give you a lift. And Nancy, grab a granola bar and something to drink, you're running late. I'll pull the car out. Meet me in the driveway." She waved her keys and flung her shoulder bag up her arm.

Melissa gave Sara a quick kiss. "Love you, Mom. I'll call after school to let you know if I'm not coming right home. Maybe I'll get more info from Wake Forest today. I can't wait to know about dorm assignments." She beamed, cleared her throat, and then coughed.

When Melissa parked her white 2002 used Acura in the driveway, Mary backed out from the garage, and braked alongside her.

Mary rolled down her window. "I'm just running to the store. What'cha doing?"

Mary's dark red hair was pulled tight to keep it away from her face, in preparation for starting a Center Hill Lake scene. She wanted no morning interruptions, like grocery shopping, once she began the painting.

"I forgot my English stuff," Melissa said. "I'll lock the door when I leave."

"Talk to you later then," Mary said.

Melissa ran to the front door, rummaged through her backpack and inserted her keys. She opened the stately door, locked it and placed the keys and bag on the entryway table next to a dried floral arrangement made by her grandmother. She hurried to the kitchen, coughing, stopped a moment to catch her breath. She started to wheeze, slowed again to stop, to clutch the counter, for a deeper breath. Looking around, she didn't see any of her schoolwork. Her chest began to feel tight;

she went upstairs aiming for her second bedroom, holding the banister as breathing became more restrictive. Sucking in, she could hardly do it. It felt like breathing through a straw. Exhaling gave her more comfort; it was a lot easier and took longer.

Melissa slid down the wall, upright, in the hallway, pulling, pulling. Her pulse quickened. Working her suprasternal and neck muscles for accessory help, she tried desperately to yank oxygen into her lungs, but it seemed as if nothing went in and nothing went out. Moisture pooled in the corner of her eyes. She pulled her cell phone from her pocket, her hands changing color, turning blue. Think, she needed to think. But thoughts became foggy.

Melissa dialed the ER number. “ER,” someone said.

“It’s Danny Tilson’s daughter, Melissa. Can you send an ambulance?”

It seemed forever. Voices and noise in the background. The lady said something to someone else about Danny Tilson’s daughter. “What’s wrong?” the woman asked.

“Asthma attack,” Melissa said faintly.

“Where are you? Someone will be on the way.”

“At my Pop’s,” she said.

Casey finished jotting down times and events on paperwork, holding a clipboard outside the emergency department. He had just brought in a fifty-four year old man who complained to his wife of double vision, became confused, and fell hard on the kitchen tile. The ER doctor and staff were busy seeing the three hundred pound man who needed acute treatment, then stabilization of his brittle diabetes. Casey enjoyed the shift; the spring day smacked of summertime.

The automatic door opened behind him. “Casey, you’ve got a run.”

Casey knew the ER nurse. She held half a donut while taking a break, but volunteered to flag him down and deliver the message. She seized the opportunity. He smiled at her as he quickly went inside to the desk.

“Dr. Tilson’s daughter called in,” Mrs. Garner at the front desk said. “She needs an ambulance. Asthma attack.”

Casey flinched, then a surge of adrenaline escaped into his bloodstream. “Melissa?” he asked. “Where is she?”

“At her dad’s.”

Casey spun around, still holding the clipboard. He had to get his partner, Mark. Down the corridor, Casey peeked into the small supply room, at the coffee pot machine and small refrigerator in one corner. Mark sipped from a Styrofoam cup. “Let’s go,” Casey said. They exited to the now-turned-sour spring air. Casey ran to their ambulance in the circular ER spot.

“It’s Dr. Tilson’s daughter. She’s got bad asthma.” Casey pressed the accelerator, turned on the siren lights. Mark took a new clipboard and began scribbling details on their run. Smack in the thick of commuter traffic, Casey could hardly contain his anxiousness, as the ambulance sped around a congested intersection. Traffic snarled because of a red light and Casey’s approach with the ambulance. Drivers didn’t know which direction to veer out of his way. Past the light and down the next street, he had to slow, a yellow school bus had half pulled from the curb, cautioning Casey to the presence of children. He pushed away thoughts about the actual run. Poor Melissa. He couldn’t understand how any situation at home would require her to need an ambulance, unless it was critical and she needed a shot of epinephrine. All he could do was hurry.

Ten minutes later, Casey and Mark sped the blaring ambulance straight into the driveway. They both ran to the front door carrying medical bags. Casey rang, and then held the doorbell. He anxiously looked through the door window panel on the side, but readied to use his own key. They heard the lock turn, the door parted, to a startled Sara. She had a towel wrapped on her head and she tightened the yellow robe she wore.

"What …?" she said, her eyes wide.

Casey became momentarily confused. "Where's Melissa? She called us, having an asthma attack."

Sara felt her heart flutter, like drumbeats not belonging to her. "Omigod. She went to Dad's, I mean Greg's house. Mary's. On the way to school." Panic shot through her as Casey and Mark ran.

"I'll be there," Sara shouted. Using her finest sprinting ability, she bounded up the stairs, threw on clothes and remembered her daughter had absolutely no aerosol.

Casey and Mark shot westward, flying through red lights. Casey turned south on Green Hills Pike. Turning right, the vehicle bounced over the corner curb and they jostled in their seats. Casey tagged a garbage can; it fell, smashing aluminum on concrete. He swerved, avoiding a car pulling out of a driveway.

He checked his watch. Damn it. A full ten minutes. He contorted his face, upset. Right now, he had no control over helping Melissa. Mark leaned to latch his black bag, whose contents were spilling on the floor mat. Casey slowed slightly on Greg's street. Two children were getting into a vehicle. He yanked the wheel into the long driveway. Melissa's car blocked the entrance to the front circular drive.

To the right of the Acura, Casey turned off the ignition, grabbed an emergency bag and swiftly ran to the door. Mark followed as Casey reached it, rang, and tried the handle. Locked.

"No," Casey shouted. He rang again; nothing. He smashed his right shoulder into the unweilding wood. "No," he screamed. "I'll try the back. Mark, get something, to break a window or door."

Mark wiped perspiration from his forehead. "Casey, we can't break and enter."

"She's my responsibility, Mark," Casey yelled, peeling around the side of the house. In the yard, he jumped over the cement wall onto the patio, rang and looked in. Nothing. He dropped the bag and with two hands, threw a ceramic-potted plant into a window. He kicked, creating a big enough hole, and squeezed through with his bag. Nobody. Straight to the entryway, looking in both directions, he didn't see her. He unbolted the front door, saw her keys on the table, and flew upstairs, full of panic and perspiration.

On the last step, Melissa came into view. She was slumped on the floor with her head tilted.

"Melissa, Melissa!"

He took her face into his hands, picked up her arm, felt her wrist for a pulse.

"Melissa!"

Casey flattened her on the carpet and put two fingers on a non-throbbing carotid artery as Mark tailed him and checked respirations. As Casey compressed her chest, Mark's mouth covered her blue lips while he forcefully exhaled.

"Melissa, breathe," Casey commanded.

Mark kneeled erect while Casey thumped her chest. Mark touched his partner's biceps. "Casey," he whispered.

Casey grasped her hand, looking into her ethereal face, her hair softly falling into her blue hood, and then tenderly kissed her cool hand, as lifeless as her opal bracelet.

Chapter 9

In his line of duty, Casey had never before been involved with a personal tragedy; he meekly let his partner carry out their duties. Mark called the hospital, their base station, to relay the situation to a medical doctor. The distant physician received the transmitted EKG and concurred; abort further attempts at resuscitation.

Something wasn't right, Mary was sure of it. Narrowing her eyes, she could make out the ambulance down the block in the driveway, right next to Melissa's car. She pulled behind them, pushed open the car door, and ran into the house after ignoring the full white plastic bags in the back seat.

"Hello? Melissa?" Mary cried loudly from downstairs while scouting each room. She took two steps at a time upstairs when she heard Casey's voice. She stepped over paramedic supplies in the hallway. Mark kneeled by Melissa's head, but Casey crouched over her, his weeping musculature like putty. Mary slinked alongside her niece, next to Casey.

They didn't hear Sara arrive. She rounded the top of the staircase, her eyes bulging, her uncombed hair densely matted, her sweat pant strings hanging untied. Sara dropped to her knees on the other side of Casey and Mary, enveloped her daughter, and tried to wake her up.

Mark left them for some time, but finally guided Sara, Mary and Casey to the living room. Sara pressed her fists into her lap while squeezing the wad of tissues Mark had given her. She dotted her cheeks, absorbing the moisture. Her two tear ducts were too small for the avalanche she felt would ensue. Now she knew about a mother's pain, what it felt like to lose a child.

"We have to call Danny," Mary said.

Casey's mouth trembled. He raised his eyebrows and looked up, considering this. How could they? He dropped his head back down into his hands.

Sara waved a tissue near her face. "How are we going to tell him? His daughter."

Mary pushed the ottoman aside and embraced her sister-in-law. "I don't know if we should call the office, the hospital, or his pager," she said.

Danny had a long list of patient's to see, but today it went like clockwork. Plus, that pretty Rachel had put zip into his steps. Mr. Donaldson seemed so relieved that his surgery was in the past tense, that he now saw humor in it all. Since it had been a rare operation, he had even become a conversation piece in the hospital wing, the attention flattering him.

"Dr. Tilson," he said, "I sure feel lighter getting rid of all those freeloaders living in my head."

Danny laughed. "Any time, Mr. Donaldson. Now just be careful of human being spongers. I won't be able to help you with them."

"Okay, Doc. And thanks again." Danny left the room while Mr. Donaldson resumed eating his scanty bowl of corn flakes.

There were several more patients to see. Danny had also agreed to see one of Bruce's patients, a simple discharge with instructions for him to follow up with Bruce in the office. He sat at the nurse's station writing a note in the chart while looking forward to heading to the office with a to-go cup of coffee. His pager blared, his dad's house number. He rolled his chair and reached across open charts for the phone.

He called to hear Sara, her voice broken-up. "Sara, what's wrong?"

"Danny, it's Melissa," she sobbed. "She was alone and had an acute asthma attack. She didn't make it."

Danny had to park on the street. The driveway and front were cluttered with cars: an ambulance, Melissa and Sara's car, a police car and some strange Honda. He held onto denial like holding a boulder. He had to go inside to wake Sara from her strange dream.

But the cascade of embraces when he entered the house was real, as well as the crumpled faces filled with sorrow. Dr. Neatle, the girls' pediatrician for many years, stood over Melissa's unmoving body, signing a medical death certificate.

Danny stood near the casket the last night of viewing, talking softly with Casey before the funeral home closed. Pastel flowers surrounded them, draping from baskets and stands and heart shaped wreaths. Adults streamed into the funeral chapel, offering him and Sara their condolences. They acknowledged the steady tide of teenagers, who forlornly paused at her casket, her popularity evident. Ivory silk caressed Melissa and a white and red rose lay on her abdomen atop the peach button-down dress she'd planned to wear for graduation.

"Here, I want you to have this," Danny said when all the guests had departed. He reverently slid Melissa's opal bracelet off her wrist and placed it into Casey's hand. Casey held it momentarily. He took Danny's hand, placed it there, and wrapped his hand around it. Leaning forward, he pulled his friend and embraced him firmly. "No. You keep it, always."

Danny, Sara, Annabel and Nancy decided to bring half the flowers home that night and the remainder the next day, the day of Melissa's funeral. They sprinkled the house with gladiolas, mums and carnations. Danny put a mixed arrangement of yellow baby breath orchids in Melissa's bedroom. He quickly exited her room, wanting to visit it again later. He couldn't bear to remember that a few days ago she'd slept there for the last time.

Pulling Melissa's iridescent bracelet from his black suit jacket, he crossed the hall. In the bedroom, he crouched to his bottom dresser drawer. As he took out his leather case, he couldn't believe his mother and daughter were no longer alive. What a cruel world. He must make the pain of Melissa's death subside. He opened the leather flap and took out Einstein's masterpiece. "Mom," he said, ".....your granddaughter .... she's gone. I don't know about anything. Maybe she'll be joining you." Danny reflected on the book and Melissa's bracelet, then slipped them into his burgundy case, and nestled it under his clothes.

At midnight, Danny still lay awake while Sara curled at the edge of the bed in a ball, her breathing irregular, like she was sobbing in her sleep. He wrapped his thoughts around the last time they had all hiked, the weekend his dad was in the hospital from his stroke. Melissa had been as vibrant as spring but as compassionate as a Calcutta nun. He closed his eyes and began at the beginning …

Autumn always proved to be the best time for Sara and Danny to hike in Tennessee, not just the state park trails, but also the ones that Danny and Sara knew from dating, when they disappeared together for hours with nothing more than tattered maps and water bottles. Danny carried two bottles of water in a backpack, one zip lock bag of trail mix, packets of handi-wipes and his cell phone. After ten minutes of walking, Danny realized that burying himself in nature for the morning had been a wise decision. What better way to spend beeper-free time than to be with the family. In any case, they wouldn't have accomplished anything hanging around Greg's hospital room while his stroke workup was in progress.

"Mom, you've got shoes on," Melissa said.

"How about that? Ankle boots for the occasion." Sara held a branch from slapping back onto Melissa.

Leaf colors had not yet peaked, still some trees blazed with yellow shades of fall. They had chosen this particular path because they would veer off on a one-mile circular loop. The byway was less traveled and they were privy to its rocky ridge with a breathtaking view of a gorge.

"Aunt Mary may be coming home for awhile to help Pop-Pop, Melissa. You can ask her about marine life in Alaska."

Danny slowed, wondering if their pace was too fast for Nancy, but she took the opportunity to hurry past him, walking on aged dried leaves posted to the narrow path. A breeze filtered through the woods, subtle near the ground, but swaying tall deciduous trees at the top.

Sara tightened the sweatshirt tied around her waist and slapped an itch on her arm. For a moment, she waved her hands, as if with delight, passing Annabel.

"Just because you're a runner," Annabel said, jokingly.

Sara noticed a fine distinction in the trail ahead. "Is that our turn-off?" she asked Danny.

They got closer. "That's it. Narrower than this path. Single-file," Danny said, leading the way, their mouths quiet, their minds busy.

"Just be alert," Danny remembered. "It's rutting season."

"What does that mean?" Nancy asked.

"It means it's more magical here in the deep woods than the woods in the back of our house. It means the bucks aren't cautious and are moving freely, looking for receptive females, to mate and have babies."

"I'll show you deer tracks when we see them," Melissa said, "they're all over."

"Grandpa showed them to me in the back yard," Nancy said.

"Look, stop," Melissa said, crouching down. "Deer poop."

"Ewww," Nancy whined.

Sara, Danny and Annabel huddled by the ground. "Pop told me that deer can poop thirteen times a day and that naturalists learn things from it," Melissa said.

"Like what, know it all?" Annabel asked.

"She's right, Annabel," Sara said. "And that's not polite."

Annabel rolled her eyes. "Well, I know it's not called deer poop. Grandpa told me they're woodland nuggets, deer droppings or deer pellets."

"These are round droppings," Danny said. "This particular deer must be eating leaves and acorns."

"I want to see," Nancy said. She slithered next to Sara, plopped into the leaves and rolled the pile around with a stick.

"Gross, you idiot," Annabel said.

"Melissa, this is like a biology field trip. Maybe you can be a white-tail biologist," Sara said.

"Maybe, Mom. But I want to learn about marine biology, too." She sighed deeply, catching her breath, and then coughed.

"Okay, let's go girls," Danny said.

They walked again in silence as the temperature warmed, their clothes getting heavier. When they approached their secret ridge, they detoured and stood on the rocky cliff alongside baby white pines. The small evergreens jutted from the bluff beginning their ascent toward sky, like the towering trees behind them. "Beautiful," Sara said. She stepped next to Danny and touched his hand.

"Very beautiful," he said, smiling at her. Danny perched himself on a boulder, Sara sat next to him and the girls stretched on groundcover jutting between rocks. They drank more water and shared dried fruit and smokehouse almonds. "We better head back," Danny said. They resumed their trek, walking a half hour in seclusion.

"What's that smell anyway?" Annabel exclaimed.

"I smell it, too," Sara said.

"Lots of pellets," Melissa said, pointing to the ground.

Danny looked closely at the ground, large deer tracks obvious. He stepped into the brush and woods, the smell becoming stronger.

Sara gasped at what came into view by Danny's feet. A mammoth white-tailed deer lay in the leaves, a slick lengthy arrow protruding from its chest. From where they stood, it was difficult to make out its neck and head.

"Is this some new hunting sport? To kill and not take the venison?" Sara asked.

"How awful," Melissa said.

Danny scanned the area. It couldn't be dead that long; there weren't any flies or vultures around. He agreed with Melissa. "Such a magnificent creature. It won't be running free anymore."

Nancy pinched her nose.

"Girls, that musky smell. It's coming from here." Sara pointed to the fallen animal's back inner legs. "During the breeding season the males pee on these glands. It sits here and mixes with bacteria, making that stink."

Melissa took a twig and rubbed the patch, while Sara continued. "Biologists study these things. Perhaps each deer has its own distinct odor to communicate and attract does."

"Why don't they teach me biology at school?" Nancy asked.

"They will, sweetheart, soon," Sara said. Nancy pouted, kicking leaves underfoot.

"I'll be back in a minute," Danny said.

"Where are you going Dad?" Annabel asked.

"To the restroom."

"What restroom?"

"The woods."

Danny stepped upward onto the mound, parted brush and tree limbs and took a leak. He turned around and came back, picking up a cane-size tree limb to begin clearing the organic matter off the front end of the deer. Finally, everyone had a view of the mutilated animal. Sara's arms tucked Nancy and Annabel into either side of her and the girls nestled their heads into her chest. The slayer had carved the antler rack out of the buck's head.

"Damn poachers," Danny said.

Melissa crumpled to the ground. Salty water pooled, the tears slinked down her cheeks and moistened the corners of her mouth.

Thinking about that day was all Danny could stand. He finally willed himself to fall asleep, the heartache accumulating like the falling petals in Melissa's room.

"Wait, Danny," Sara said. They entered Wellington's Life Care several days later, and she tugged on Danny's shirtsleeve. "Mary left the same time as us. She'll be here in a moment, so let's go see Greg all together."

Annabel plopped into a chair she thought dated back to the 1800's. She dug into her cargo Capri pants and pulled out Melissa's holy card. *Melissa Susan Tilson 1991-2008*. She read the prayer while chewing the gum she'd been harboring under her tongue, occasionally embedding it behind her crooked tooth.

Nancy passed her looking out the window for Mary and mumbled. "Why do we have to wait here anyway?"

Mary hurried into the front lobby after seeing Danny's car in the parking lot and they all steered down the hallway to Greg's room. Greg stared into the hallway, surrounded by his walker.

"Dad, you must be expecting us," Danny said.

"Yah, right." Annabel rolled her eyes as Danny shot her a glance, warning her as to her inappropriateness.

"Dad, look, we brought you oatmeal cookies," Mary said. If Greg got any skinnier, his frame would slither out the bottom of his brown pants. Greg's eyes locked onto Mary's face. Was there recognition there, or a total absence of who she was?

"Sara, why don't we take Dad for a spin?" Mary asked. "Outside, around the fountain. Get his circulation going. We can't complain about his care here, but certainly no one takes him outside."

Greg's jittery hand reached towards the cookie. Mary and Sara guided him by the elbows into a wheelchair and steered him out the door as Mary split the small cookie in two and put one piece into Greg's mouth. Nancy folded Greg's quilt and Annabel poured sunflower seeds in the feeders outside his window.

Danny sat in the rocker reflecting on the last seven days. Melissa had died on Monday and the subsequent gatherings had flown by. He had not thought of work, but had told Bruce he would return on Monday. Surely the next day would be hectic. Even though Bruce and Harold would have seen some of his office patients, his surgeries were rescheduled to him. In the morning he'd do a surgical resection of a single metastatic cancer lesion to the brain.

Mary and Sara came back with the wheelchair – Greg like a fragile, handle with care package propped on the black leather seat. "I'm going to leave in a few minutes," Mary said. "Casey will be off at three o'clock. He's coming over to cover the broken window with a wood panel until the window is repaired. I've had plastic hanging there all week."

"That's nice of him," Danny said. "Say hi."

Casey arrived at Mary's straight off his shift. His entrance made her gasp. She'd seen him in his uniform before, under worse conditions. Now, he wore a half smile; she practically wilted.

"Let me see the damage I did," he said. "I didn't stop to think about neatness at the time." His face soured after saying it, bringing back the memory of last Monday, like a bad dream.

"I swept away the glass. The clear plastic has worked fine, but if you board it, that will be better. Especially if the window company doesn't show for a few more days. You know how that goes."

Casey surveyed the damage, then brought in a piece of plywood from his Jeep and nailed it in place. Mary observed from her perch on the arm of a chair. She knew he was the same age as Danny, but he seemed more spirited. Maybe he manages his time better. Besides his forty-hour workweek, there must be gym time, plus who knows what else. She wondered if he was currently dating a gorgeous Vice President of a bank or an attorney hotshot in Nashville.

"Would you like something to drink?" Mary asked when he finished.

"Sure, whatever you've got." Casey moved a pillow and parked himself on the couch.

She looked in the refrigerator. He occasionally drank beer, so she brought him a Miller and fetched a glass of water. She partially tucked her legs under her at the other end of the sofa. Silence temporarily filled the room. Casey snapped at the tab of aluminum and put the beer down on the side table as Mary took a sip and turned to him.

"You know," he said, "things might have turned out differently. If only I hadn't…"

"No. Casey. Don't ever think that." Mary extended her hand and placed it on his forearm.

Casey looked down at his lap and shook his head. .

"No. Really, Casey. You did your job. What happened …" She slid over toward him. "Please," she said.

They sat quietly. Casey detected Mary's lingering body lotion, like being inland near a coast, teased by the salty ocean smell. He began letting go of the guilt he had carried all week.

"I'll try," he finally said.

Casey took a small sip, but put the can down. He thought of a better pastime than drinking a beer.

"Mary, I bet we haven't had a decent meal this week and I haven't been to Downtown Italy in a long time." He hesitated; surprised at something he had not done before. "Simply put, how about an evening together?" He sat tall and smiled. "Would you like to go to Downtown Italy next weekend?"

"Casey," she said delicately, "is this invitation for a date or to pal with your best friend's sister? Your answer will be the clue to what I wear."

"Absolutely as a date. Your being my best friend's sister as well as being a good friend stays intact no matter what. Deal?"

"Deal."

Chapter 10

Todd Summer's physicians extensively consulted with each other. The origin of the unwanted mass came from his kidney, a renal cell carcinoma, but not all cerebral metastases warranted surgical treatment. Management depended on the clinical situation and outcome probabilities. The internist and oncologist would treat him long-term, and Danny would excise Todd's solitary metastatic cancer lesion in his brain.

Danny leafed through Mr. Summer's chart in the preop area, familiarizing himself again with the medical background of his patient's diagnosis. Mr. Summer still had hematuria, or blood in his urine. That had been the initial symptom landing him in a doctor's office, besides constant pain in his back, below his ribs.

As Danny hurried to OR 5, he wondered if there would be a perk to his case. He wouldn't mind seeing Rachel's eyes or being the center of her attention. Maybe that would alleviate the drudgery of the operating room's four walls, the drone of anesthesia machines and the routine familiarity of drilling into someone's head. It would keep his mind from wandering to the fresh pain of Melissa's death. Something squeezed his heart when he thought of his oldest daughter.

The CRNA and his anesthesia attending staff had Danny's patient intubated and the table turned forty-five degrees. Danny donned a mask and walked in, placing his beeper on the aluminum table under the wall phone. He turned to look at the scrub nurse. Hallelujah, there would be a bright side to his case.

Everyone gave Danny their condolences while Rachel counted instruments on her table. After a speedy start, Danny spied the tumor in Mr. Summer's brain.

"Dr. Tilson, I'm so sorry about your daughter," Rachel said. "I cannot even imagine how you must be feeling."

Danny glanced quickly, making eye contact. "Thank you," he said.

"Is that the only one to remove?" she asked, pointing at the odd looking mass with a scalpel, then handing the scalpel to Danny.

"Only one," he said. "And in the course of treatment for his kidney cancer, this basically comes first."

"Why?"

"Because they are going to treat him with interleukin-2. If this lesion stays here, the chemotherapy will cause cerebral edema. So we have to remove this metastasis before treatment."

"Maybe sometime you can further explain that to me. It's a mystery. The pathophysiology of brain edema."

Danny slowed his hand. Her voice, her tone, was so soothing, she almost purred.

"So what's his name?" he asked, changing the subject.

"Whose name?" she asked.

"That super dog you have."

Under the mask, Rachel smiled widely.

"Oh, him. Dakota," she said, bobbing her head with enthusiasm.

"Hmm. Solid name. Big dog?"

She chuckled. "Dr. Tilson, do you know the breed?'

"My wife and I haven't owned dogs. We've concentrated on kids." And now my daughter is gone, he thought.

"I can tell you all about dogs. Hopefully, you can educate me about brains."

Annabel found her mother in Melissa's bedroom, the door ajar. Sara sat on the bed, her thin legs uncrossed, her sandals firmly planted on the rug. Her face still looked puffy, her eyes narrow and drawn. Her movements had slowed as if arthritis and old age had taken root overnight.

"Mom, you okay?" Annabel asked.

Sara turned to her daughter, teary eyed. "No, Annabel. She's supposed to be here right now. It isn't fair."

"I know, Mom." Annabel sat at Melissa's desk, arranging pens in a pencil caddy. "Can we leave Melissa's room the same, until we have the heart to go through her things?"

"Yes. You're right, we'll do that." Sara wiped her cheeks.

"Let's not be late, Mom. It's not like every day I let some man attempt to straighten my haphazard tooth." Annabel got up and reached her skinny arm around her mother's neck, lightly bumping her forehead, forcing Sara to grin.

"Okay, let's leave things well enough alone," Sara said. "Until I come in here again tomorrow. And cry."

"Mom, let's visit Melissa's grave again this weekend."

They left the bedroom door open. Sara pulled a sporty jacket from the closet and Annabel slid on her sister's hoody as they left.

"Have you decided yet?" Sara asked, when they got into the car.

"On what Mom?"

"Clear or color?"

"Hmm. What would Melissa do?"

"I can guess, but whatever you decide, tell your orthodontist before he starts putting wires in your mouth."

After Danny's surgeries were finished for the day, he rounded on several hospital patients, including Mr. Summers who slept groggily in his room. Danny scanned his head dressing for bleeding then lightly roused him. On morning rounds, he'd learned not to ask patients how they slept, otherwise, he'd hear, "I would've slept fine without someone waking me at 4 a.m. to see if I had a blood pressure or to ask me how I was sleeping."

"Mr. Summers, you did fine," Danny said. "I'll be by to see you tomorrow."

Danny left the hospital thinking about Greg, especially since it had been a few days since he had seen him. His father couldn't understand why the family grieved or why there had been a funeral. Otherwise, the blow would have been heart wrenching.

He undid the top button of his blue shirt while walking along Wellington's main hallway when he arrived at six. He passed residents with cruel Alzheimer's, fading their previous vibrant minds into another sunset without time or place. Every time he entered a senior facility, he vowed to avoid them for Sara and himself. Even some of his Iraqi war vet patients were dependent on others, but most of them lived with family and not in a nursing or assisted living environment. It had to do with loss of independence and not how great the care.

Danny felt confused, and he didn't even have dementia. He missed his daughter; there would never be a day that he wouldn't wonder what Melissa would be doing if she were alive.

Greg was rocking gleefully in his chair. He wore a light plaid shirt with matching trousers that Sara had bought him and his right hand cupped an applesauce container. He waved it toward Danny, plunked it on the nightstand, tapped at it with his index finger.

"Dad, let me open it for you and I'll get you a spoon."

Greg resumed pounding the container and grimaced as Danny noticed a pile up of other single unopened servings from the last few days. Greg hollered his frustration and before Danny could console him, he began to cry.

"Dad, I'm sorry. I wish I could be more helpful."

Danny hurried down the hall to the nurse's station to ask an evening nurse for a spoon. "Please," he asked, "can you make a note for someone to help my Dad late in the day? One of the few things my Dad likes and eats anymore is applesauce. He needs it, he's so skinny. Plus, the irritation of not being able to peel off the foil triggers his anger."

"Dr. Tilson, I'll pass that through to the other shifts."

"Thank you."

In his room, Greg ignored Danny while he slowly shoveled applesauce from two Mott's cups into his mouth.

"I stopped by to see Dad. I asked them for extra assistance with his snacks," Danny said to Sara at home, forging a stale effort at enthusiasm. "Bet the sunset was pretty enough to have sat on the deck tonight."

"It seems warmer than usual for April," Sara said. "This evening I finally pounded the subdivision again. I ran two slow miles."

"That's a warm up for you." Danny sat on a stool with a glass of wine. "Where are Annabel and Nancy?"

"They're both upstairs. Annabel had clear braces put on today. Nancy finished homework. I suspect she's on MySpace."

The family's automobile insurance policy lay before her as she wrote out a six-month check. "I simmered two large cans of beef vegetable soup. There's some left in the pot."

Danny ladled the chunky broth into a bowl and resumed his perch at the counter.

"I talked to Mary this afternoon," Sara said. "I think your best friend's eyes have sprung open. He's noticed your little sister."

Danny contemplated that. "Hmm. That will take some getting used to. But she's not that little, she's the same age as you."

"I know. You dirty old men. There may not be much to get used to though, if it's Casey's conventional six-month relationship."

"Best to stay out of this," Danny commented. "Sisters are sisters and friends are friends. Don't want to jeopardize that."

But Sara's attention had drifted. She gazed out the window where she would never see Melissa on the porch rocker again.

When Danny and Sara went to bed at nine-thirty, Sara brought a section of *The Tennessean.* She laid on her side, facing her husband, but never turned a page. Her eyes scanned the same sentence. Danny read his political terrorist novel without absorbing a paragraph.

"Sara?" He glanced at Sara holding moisture in the pockets of her eyes and a pillow to her chest after closing the newspaper. Sara put her hand lightly on Danny's.

"She'd be hiking and fishing this summer. Her enthusiasm before leaving for college would've been infectious."

"I know. I miss her too."

Soon Sara's lids closed so Danny slid her hand back on her pillow. The room folded into itself like a deep space vacuum. A hollow feeling settled in his chest and a vision unfolded of a small child in a front passenger seat. An adult stopped the car, took the boy's hand and deposited him at an intersection with a cemetery on each street corner. The car drove off as the little boy turned in each direction, scared, abandoned.

Mary chose a thin, dark brown headband to let her hair fall softly but to keep off the angle of her cheeks. She softened some coconut oil into her palms, and then ran it through her hair. Her pale green top plummeted in front but white cotton ran horizontally, as if she wore a white blouse underneath. She selected a linen camel skirt, perfect with low heels. For her, wearing higher, spikier heels accentuated her toeing in. For the grand finale, she chose her favorite orchid summer lipstick.

Casey arrived promptly at six-thirty. "Madam," he said, "you look lovely."

"Thank you, handsome prince," she said, returning his smile and closing the front door.

Casey opened the passenger door of his new Jeep. "Nice car color," she said, when he started the engine.

"Thanks, it's called Serengeti sand."

"I must admit, the last date I had drove me away in a rusty sedan with a broken door handle."

"That's more common in Tennessee than this new baby. You didn't hold that against him, did you?"

"Not at all. I own a rusty pickup truck in Alaska. It's heartbroken for me." They glanced at each other and laughed.

Angelo seated them at an intimate round table at the front window. The only change Casey could detect because of the new owners was a missing room divider, knocked out to make room for several more tables.

"How is your PaPa?" Angelo asked Mary.

"A slow decline, Angelo. Maybe Gianni can fix one of his light pastas so tomorrow I can bring Dad a small container."

"On Italy," he said softly. He handed Mary and Casey a long butterscotch colored menu. "Tonight's special is very nice. Escalope of veal sautéed in marinara sauce. Fresh sautéed vegetables on the side."

Mary nodded at Casey and Angelo. "Make that two," Casey said. "And Mary, shall we order wine?"

"A Cabernet?"

Casey nodded.

Mary unwrapped the linen napkin from the warm bread Antonio had left. "Casey, thank you in advance for the date. The timing is perfect. I needed to dump the smeared-paint-on-my-face look." A couple peered in the window, deliberating whether to dine there. Mary spoke softly. "So, what made you choose to be a paramedic?"

"I knew I wouldn't have lasted with a nine to five desk job," Casey said. "I love what I do, whether it's CPR in a roadside ditch, starting an IV on a teenager pulled from a burning building, or evaluating someone's airway in an overturned car. Lucky for me, I wasn't born fifty years earlier."

"Why's that?"

"For two reasons, but now I'm really going to bore you."

Mary shook an emphatic no. "That's not possible," she beamed.

"The concept of emergency medical services began in the early 1960's. Since then, it's evolved into a successful public service field, including the ability to just dial 9-1-1. It all began due to two innovative anesthesiologists. Both doctors worked independently, but they both saw the need for airway management and CPR to reach victims outside the hospital. And there you have it, the training of paramedics began."

"And what's the second reason?"

"If I was born fifty years earlier, I wouldn't be sitting here with you."

"Casey Hamilton, if you aren't the flirt."

"A subtle flirt. Maybe if your dark blue eyes weren't aglow like this candle, I wouldn't have said that to you."

Mary tried to will her cheeks from flushing, but she couldn't stop them.

"What about you?" Casey asked "You aren't in a nine-to-five job either."

"I was always outdoors, toting around sketch paper, so that was the remotest of possibilities. And Dad and Mom always taught Danny and me that we had to build on the unique gifts we had. It would serve others as well as us to the best advantage."

"I think that's why your parents were so successful. Their business was an offshoot of what they loved to do."

"They weren't afraid to work, either," Mary said.

Angelo placed two warm plates down and left them to taste their entrees.

"Excellente," Casey said when he returned.

"Ottimo," Angelo said.

When they rounded off their dinner with a cappuccino, Casey suggested a movie. They saw an action-adventure film at a nearby theatre. It was midnight when they drove into Mary's driveway. Mary thought the moonlight did justice to Casey's gregarious smile.

"Did the glass company restore the window?" Casey asked at the front door.

"Good as new. And your board held up well in the interim."

"I apologize in the first place for smashing it," he said warmly.

Mary touched his forearm. “No, thank you. You were trying to save Melissa’s life.”

Casey touched her back then slid his hand up to her shoulder. They kissed gently.

Chapter 11

Danny leaned against the wall dictating. Mr. Summer had been discharged from the hospital on Monday, donning a robust smile ever since, grateful for "a new lease on life," even after Danny referred him back to the oncologist. Danny told the office staff to send all his neurosurgery records to the other involved doctors, and then closed the chart. He had to hurry to attend the monthly medical staff meeting.

"Socializing is a prerequisite to gather patient referrals," Bruce would say. Danny had also been reminded by Bruce and the OR staff, including Rachel, that prior to the meeting that night there would be a gathering for the hospital CEO's fifty-fifth birthday.

Danny left the physicians' office building and drove the short distance to the back entrance of the hospital, forgoing the doctors' lot. He entered the first floor public cafeteria and went into a private large room where a spread of hors d'oeuvres, a blue flowered sheet cake and bowls of red punch covered the center conference table.

Mr. Summer's primary oncologist approached Danny. "Dr. Tilson, from your neurosurgical standpoint, how is Todd

Summers?" he asked with a slight stutter. "Will I be seeing him soon?"

Danny shook Mike Carlson's hand. "I saw him for his postop visit this afternoon. His head is clear and he's ready for you. You should be receiving his surgical record."

"Great."

"I'm glad for the CEO's birthday party," Danny said gazing at Mike's hand. "I could use one of those plates."

"It should tide us over our boring meeting," Mike said.

Danny shook his head and took a step towards the covered pans. He tried a Melba round after spreading it with a creamy artichoke dip.

"You must try this," a warm voice offered.

Danny turned sideways to Rachel's outstretched hand with a speared Swedish meatball. The red and gold sleeveless blouse she wore matched her russet silk pants and the ends of her blouse were tautly tied in front. If there was a beauty pageant under way, she'd steal it.

"Really," she said, "they must have an authentic Swedish cook in the kitchen."

"I should. Before the rice wiggles its way to the floor."

Rachel laughed at his comment as she guided it to his mouth with her right hand, her left palm shadowing it, ready to catch anything from falling. They both giggled at her risky method.

"Very tasty," he said.

"Dr. Tilson, shall I get you a piece of cake? I want to indulge since this is also my birthday month. I won't be having marble cake with butter cream frosting like his."

"You must be turning twenty-five," Danny said.

"Really, you are a gentlemen. I'm going to be the same age as you, thirty-seven."

"Really, you are a lady. But I'm a whopping forty-five."

Danny selected appetizers here and there, enough to pass for a light dinner, as Rachel slid slivers of cake onto two plates. She handed Danny one after he finished. On the far side of the room, Harold mingled but looked for his colleagues. .

"Let's switch," Danny said. "I think the rose adorned slice is yours. It's the least I can do." He trailed off with his gregarious laugh as Rachel's eyes held.

Harold weaved his way through hospital staff and acknowledged Danny. "I'll see you over there," he said, and left.

Danny and Rachel both threw their plates in a can. "See you in the OR," Danny said.

"I'm leaving, too," Rachel said. "I don't like walking across that busy street to the employee parking lot, though. It seems like every month another pedestrian gets hit, especially after hours."

"My car is right out here and I'll be reparking in the doctor's lot on the northeast corner. I'll drop you off. After all, I wouldn't want you on my operating room table tonight."

She jabbed his arm and kept up with his long stride. "Dr. Tilson, what a lovely thing to say. We just couldn't have that anyway, because then, who would scrub for you?"

Danny opened his Lexus door for her and threw a newspaper and empty coffee cup in the back seat.

"Thank you, Dr. Tilson."

"Please call me Danny." He went around the other side, slid behind the wheel and sprang his engine to life. She looked like a trophy from a luxury car commercial. She had elegant long fingers, her hands resting on a petite shoulder bag lying on her crossed legs.

"Will you be discussing OR block time at your meeting?" she asked.

"Probably. We address it briefly every month."

"Dr. Tilson, I mean, Danny, it seems to me that you and your two colleagues could schedule block time more effectively."

"I'm listening," he said. "Do you have a suggestion?"

She uncrossed her legs and edged sideways. Never before in Danny's car had a front seat passenger felt that close.

"Right now, the three of you have three half days blocked for your cases. Two of those days include two rooms. But sometimes when your block time ends at one p.m., you can't start a new case at say, twelve, because it would run into the next surgical specialty's time."

Danny nodded, creeping through rows of parked cars.

"Well, if you traded in at least two half days for a full day, you'd have less wasted time, or down time. Between the three of you, cases in that room would flow. And with the amount of business the three of you have, I don't see how the hospital wouldn't allow it. It would just mean rearranging the present schedule."

"No surgeons have been given a full day before," Danny commented.

"No one has tried since the new OR's were finished last year. Plus, even for the neurosurgery equipment your group uses, it would be easier for the OR staff."

Danny rolled her idea around. It would mean rearranging the office schedule also, but that wouldn't be a big deal. "Hmm. I'll discuss that with my partners and toss it around at our meeting."

Danny went through the intersection then slowed into the employee's parking lot. Rachel pointed to a back aisle and Danny stopped behind her vehicle.

"Nice CRV."

"It's configured for my Chessie," she said.

"What do you mean?" Danny asked, not being able to see through the tinted back window.

"The back seats are folded down and a large rubber mat covers the back. I've never been married and don't have kids so I give the space to my big dog."

"Ahh. Yes. Your working therapy dog." Danny searched for his name. "Dakota."

Rachel's smile broadened. "You remembered," she said softly, slowly. "Thank you Danny for your courtesy. For the lift, that is." She leaned over the middle console to plant a momentary kiss on his cheek. Danny turned his head as the left side of her moist lips landed on the side of his mouth, startling him.

She got out and flashed a smile.

Danny tried not to make noise opening the conference room door. The meeting had started; he had no valid excuse for being late. He signed the attendance sheet and joined Bruce and Harold in the back of the room. Bruce scowled at his tardiness, so Danny waited to ask him in a whisper his opinion about an extra long OR day. Bruce liked the idea and by the end of the meeting, a genitourinary surgery group considered trading slots. Later they would discuss it with the OR committee, which was as good as a done deal.

"Wait for me, Mom," Annabel said as she laced a new pair of striped Nike's.

"You're serious," Sara said.

"I told you when school finished I would run with you."

"This is going to be fun. Your age will compensate for my experience. But I thought you canned the baseball cap."

"But you're wearing one, too, Mom. While I run or fish, it's allowed."

"You're right, sweetheart. We'll keep the rays off our sun sensitive skin but absorb the vitamin D." Sara opened the back door, stepped to the porch rail and stretched. She was glad for the sunshine and weather getting warmer; if she had to face a bleak winter after Melissa's death, she didn't know how she would've survived.

Nancy sat rocking, holding her first summer book. "Have fun," she said, looking at Annabel. "I bet Mom will beat you."

"I don't know about that, but I know I could beat you."

"You wish. Like everything else." She stuck her tongue out.

Past the brush line, twigs crackled with the fleeing of a single deer as Sara stepped down the steps. The hummingbird and finch feeders whirred with activity; the flighty gluttons hovered in mid-air and the finches pinched seed between their beaks and stole away. She had overstuffed a feeder deep in the yard, hanging from a tree hook, which was attracting a variety of species. Tree-clinging red-bellied and redheaded woodpeckers ran up and down the tree busily grabbing black oil sunflower seeds. They were easy to see without binoculars from the house. She marveled at the detail of a full bellied male scurrying up the trunk, proudly holding a single seed in its beak.

"Mom, if I like running and practice with you all summer, I could join a track team in college."

"Are you thinking about college already?"

"A little. I haven't told you or Dad, but I may want to be premed or prevet."

"That's a big commitment," Sara sighed. "You have plenty of time to think about it."

"Mom, so does Nancy."

Sara secretly would dislike it if either girl embarked on that difficult career choice. She wanted Annabel and Nancy to have worthy professions but not give their lives to them. Life was too short. Danny's training had taken forever. But she'd support her daughters if that's what they wanted. They rounded the street corner and jogged in the middle of the street to avoid cars and trucks. The construction workers building a nearby log cabin had nowhere to park except on the side of the road.

"How far we going to run?" Annabel asked.

"Just a few miles."

Annabel caught the flirty look from the foreman's young son and hastened her pace to show off. She avoided further conversation with her mother; something about talking made it easier to loose her breath.

Casey had to work Saturday night so he declined a Friday night poker game to take Mary out instead. Casey and Mary ordered Thai curry and rice and decided to skip a movie. They kept unveiling silly or surprising things about each other and those discoveries were better than any Hollywood story. Mary confessed she clued her parents into searching for Danny and Casey when they were fifteen years old and were sneaking cigarettes in the back yard. Casey had often slept over and Mary had aroused her parents from sleep one night by pretending to be sick. Casey admitted to Mary that he and Danny had hidden her fishing pole when she was little, preventing her from tailing them to their fishing pond.

They slouched on porch lounge chairs at Mary's after returning from the restaurant. Casey opened a bottle of wine. Sipping slowly, they appreciated the lush view over the hills. It had been a wetter spring than the last two; thick carpets of green grass blanketed the areas between Donna's trees.

"Do you still employ the same gardening crew your mom and dad used?" Casey asked.

"For some things. They're fantastic. It's as if they remain loyal to Mom and Dad."

"There are two dead trees down there," Casey said. "Your dad has a chain saw around here. I can cut them down for you one of these days."

"I'd appreciate that." Mary slipped her sandals off. "I suppose it's official," she said. "Barefoot with wine in Tennessee."

"Why is that official?" Casey tipped the bottle into her stout glass.

"I let my friend in Alaska rent with an option to buy. We confirmed her purchase this week. And she's buying my boat, to boot."

"Are you sure that's what you want?"

"I'm sure. It's important that I continue to monitor Dad's finances and affairs. And I can't justify selling this place either. It's too big for me, but for the time being, it's where I belong."

"Danny appreciates what you do. But he's not the only one who admires you."

"Really?" Mary edged forward, anticipating what he would say.

"You make a wonderful aunt to Annabel and Nancy."

"Is that all?"

"You make a pretty good date."

She pouted, pretending to be hurt. "Like I said, is that all?"

Casey left his chair and sat on the edge of hers. "I'm sorry." He took her hand. "You are by far the easiest to talk to, and loveliest woman that I have ever dated."

"And you are the most sure of yourself conceited male I've ever dated." She met his glance, a big smile erupting. "Who is somehow unsure of himself with me."

Casey growled a masculine rumble, placed her wine on the aluminum patio table and enveloped her in his arms. He kissed like a bottomless abyss, making them forget the day, the time, the place. When they surfaced, they eased off the chair. Mary left her sandals, tiptoed alongside him into the house, peeled off a gabardine vest inside and dropped it onto the counter. Casey unbuttoned his shirt on the way up the stairs, and Mary's lavender skirt slipped to the carpet outside her bedroom. They locked into each other's arms inside her room, against the wall, ridding each other of their half-buttoned shirts.

Casey carried Mary's featherweight to the bed where their remaining clothes ended on the floor. Mary's hands kneaded the muscle of his back and arms as they laid sideways and explored. They rolled over where Casey caught the gleam of Mary's eyes as they melted into one.

Mary pulled the sheet around them as a barrier to the cool room air settling on their moist skin. Casey's arm embraced her, his head almost awash with her silky hair, as they lay wrapped alongside each other.

"What made you so independent?" Casey whispered into her ear.

"You mean minus a man?"

"I suppose."

"It wasn't my grand plan, it's just how it worked out. I love my independence, but more than that, I like to make solo decisions. I've been happy with every single thing I've done, and have kept out of trouble." She paused. "Along the way, no one has surfaced who truly enamored me."

Mary rolled flat. "What about you?"

"If you asked your brother, he'd say I'm too picky. It's easy for him to say since he has the perfect marriage. Plus, the two of them should get medals for the way they raise those girls."

Mary raised her eyebrows. "You're right about his marriage."

"I've had several special relationships, but I'm not on the prowl and I don't force things. There have been reasons for relationship failures. Try women who are ready to get married. Period. Women who are ready to have a baby. Period. Meddling women who encourage me to work a nine to five day and dump the shift work. Women who don't want to meet me half way with dating schedules, women who are so beautiful, they flirt with other men when I go out with them, women who expect me to be their front man to their auto mechanic by the end of our second date. And as time marches on, the list grows like a swelling tsunami."

Mary thought about this. "I can understand your disappointment. It's difficult finding a partner who doesn't have an agenda, let alone one you can admire and care about."

"Well, as for us, we had a magical evening. And to think I would've been winning at poker."

"Casey Hamilton."

He ran his fingers along her long smooth hair draped in front of her neck. "I've played many hands, but it's not every day I realize I knew someone special for a long time."

Chapter 12

Harold and Danny chipped away at elective Saturday cases. They prodded at and relieved several patients' cervical and lumbar degenerative disc disease problems. Harold went home in the early afternoon, leaving Danny to remain on call and to round on patients later in the day. Danny stacked a croissant with ham and cheese in the doctor's lounge to bring to the call room in the rear-most hallway. It had been built along with the new ORs and lounges a year ago, and looked like a high-end hotel suite. It harbored a large bathroom, a queen bed and a flat screen TV as well as stashes of fragrant soaps and musky after shaves. Going home before making rounds would be a waste of time, so he had placed his briefcase and small duffel bag next to the desk. Danny occasionally did paperwork there, but mostly passed the time watching sports channels not available at home.

He ate the sandwich while flicking the remote but stopped when he found a golf tournament on the west coast. Crashing waves made more noise than the hushed crowd mesmerized by Tiger Woods on the green. Danny leaned back on the headboard of the queen bed and intermittently dozed. Later, he called Sara, then strolled in and out of patient's rooms and amended orders at nursing stations.

When Danny's pager beeped, he wondered if the ambulance sirens he had heard outside were for an inbound neurosurgical case. Things hadn't changed since residency. Most Saturday night ambulances brought in heart patients or general surgery/trauma patients.

Danny called the busy ER. "It's hectic in here," said a physician. "EMS is wheeling in a sixty-five year old woman with a head injury. She's an MVA with a Glasgow coma scale of six."

Since a total Glasgow coma scale of fifteen was normal, Danny knew the patient would land on their service. "I'm in house. I'll be there."

When Danny got to the ER, he passed one of the MVA patients without significant injury. He looked around eighteen years old, maybe a new, now scared, driver. The young man fumbled through his wallet as a staff woman from ER admitting tried to procure his health insurance information.

Danny found Casey and Mark buckling the strap to the ambulance stretcher. They had moved their patient to another gurney and an ER doctor was alongside the female patient.

"She and her husband got rear ended. Hit the car in front of them," Casey said. "Her husband was driving. He's alert. He's in a room around here somewhere, but he told us his wife is on anticoagulants for atrial fib."

"How long we out?"

Casey nodded, knowing the importance of Danny's question. "An hour."

The frail woman disappeared into the CT scanner after Danny finished his assessment. Danny found her husband, almost in tears, with his arm in a sling and his other forearm being drained for a few vials of blood.

"I'm waiting for CT pictures of your wife's head," Danny said. "I may need to take her to surgery."

"It's all my fault," the man said. "It may not have happened if I hadn't taken my eye off the road. I was pointing out a llama on a farm we were passing."

Down the corridor, Danny slipped into the small room to scout for coffee. Casey and Mark leaned against the counters while fresh brew trickled into the round pot. A female x-ray technician thumbed through a magazine at the table, glancing intermittently at Casey.

"Are you two concocting the coffee?" Danny asked.

"We'll vouch for it," Casey said. "We need it as much as you."

"So? Do I dare ask?" Danny wore an extra-wide grin. "About my sister's recent social life?"

"Our dating is going along fine. Very fine." The young woman at the table frowned.

Danny wasn't offered any more information, so he didn't press to weed it out of him. They were having a good time. For now, anyway. As long as Casey didn't break her heart. "In the meantime," Danny said, "Annabel, even Nancy, has surprised us. They're considering premed."

Casey rolled his eyes. "Since when have they been type A personalities?"

"I don't know. We'll have to hike and fish this summer to cloud their heads with great memories in case either of them go ahead and bury their future."

"You two just going to stand there?" Mark tilted the glass pot over a Styrofoam cup and dumped in one sugar packet.

Casey poured three. He handed one to the technician and Danny. "Thank you," she said, investigating the color of his eyes.

Pauline Macke's CT showed an acute subdural hematoma, and what Danny feared, greater than one centimeter. He called the OR to book his emergent case. The critical wheels started turning; so far, Mrs. Macke abided by the 'four hour rule.' Getting to surgery within four hours of her injury would increase the chance of her survival. She did have a complicating factor, though - her anticoagulant treatment. Danny proceeded to the OR to talk personally with Dr. Lucas, the anesthesiologist on call. He decided to forego an exploratory burr hole. He had his diagnosis of an intracranial bleed and a burr hole would probably be too modest for a surgical evacuation. He found Dr. Lucas in the recovery room, told him the initial pertinent details about the case, then walked to the OR front desk. Rachel and another nurse both held a blue wrapped packet and checked off a list of supplies on a clipboard.

"Miss Hendersen," Danny said, "I didn't know you were working today."

"Three to eleven, Dr. Tilson. Nurse Ratchett here and I are going to pull equipment for your case."

Linda, the circulator, thumped Rachel with a desk magazine.

"Then I won't disturb you and Miss Linda," Danny said turning to leave.

"He's so awesome," Rachel told her coworker.

The time on the wall clock gave Danny an extra level of comfort for Pauline Macke. He'd be getting the job done within three hours of her injury. Dr. Lucas was up and down in his anesthesia chair, making notes, adjusting tubes, and taping things while Linda still scattered around the room doing her paperwork and retrieving items for Rachel and Danny. Danny worked on a large craniotomy flap wondering how tricky it would be after removing the thick coagulum to gain access to the actual site responsible for the bleeding.

"Suction," Danny said, darting his eyes toward Rachel, who closely monitored him and handed him the catheter.

"Linda, did your boy go on the camping trip this weekend?" Dr. Lucas asked.

Linda stopped at the foot of the blue draped OR table. "He did. Bet they're knee deep in ghost stories right now."

"I doubt that," Rachel said. "They're probably downloading porn on a laptop."

"I disagree with both of you. They're bragging to each other about things they've never done," Dr. Lucas said.

"Rachel, you wouldn't know about kids anyway," Linda said.

Danny's drill interrupted them. Dr. Lucas took an empty plastic container from Linda and drained the foley bag.

"I will know someday," Rachel said.

"You? Who bashes the institution of marriage?" Linda asked.

Rachel handed Danny a lap sponge and aligned her steel instruments in a straight line.

Conversation waned as Danny removed the blood causing pressure on the brain and suctioned the active bleeding site. After a few harrowing minutes, he repaired the vascular tear while Dr. Lucas transfused a unit of blood, monitoring vital signs closely and keeping ahead of serious hypotension.

Danny peeled his latex gloves and surgical gown off while Linda counted lap sponges with Rachel and Dr. Lucas peered at the patient's pupils after untaping her eyes. The anesthesiologist's plan was to keep the patient intubated, breathing on a ventilator overnight. He decreased the inhalational agent and administered a trace more of a neuromuscular blocker.

"Dr. Tilson, you look tired," Rachel said as he retrieved his pager.

"Nothing another cup of coffee won't cure."

A short time later, Danny sat at the long recovery room desk, coffee and snack in tow. His patient looked stable with all monitors attached and still under the remaining spell of the anesthesiologist. The smell of microwave popcorn lightly wafted in the air, coming from the nurse's lounge, as he left for the back corridor a few minutes after eleven. He prodded off his sneakers and turned on the television in the call room. At present, sipping coffee and munching on peanut butter crackers seemed more appealing than being in his usual rush to get home.

He heard a knock. "Hello? Who is it?" he asked, getting off the bed. He padded to the door without shoes.

The door opened. Rachel slid inside and closed the door softly. She held a list of patients. "You forgot this."

"It's not mine," he said, glancing at it. "Maybe it belongs to Dr. Lucas." A sportscaster in the background recapped the golf Danny missed late in the day.

"Nice room." Rachel took another step, deeper into the room. A silence swallowed the distance between them. Danny moved to the side but she leaned towards him slowly, testing his approachability. She closed her eyes and kissed him gingerly. He tasted kettle corn, salty and sweet; better yet, the fullest, moistest lips. That's all, he thought. But the soft kiss was a precursor, a forerunner to her voracious appetite. She pressed into him; thin scrubs couldn't mask the fleshy contour of Rachel's body. She felt as exciting as she looked enticing. She dropped the paper on the dresser and they landed on the bed. As she straddled him, they deeply kissed, sinking further into the submissive bed. He had to stop now. Maybe in a moment.

She untied his scrubs. Danny's mind spun. Where did she learn that? If he had been standing, he would've reeled from ecstasy. And it was unbelievable. What a talented mouth.

Except for faint solar lantern lighting in front, the house was shrouded in darkness when Danny arrived home. He went straight upstairs after going in, took off his shoes and got into bed wearing his scrubs. Anything to not wake Sara.

"That you?" she said. "You don't have to be that quiet, my husband isn't home."

She giggled and turned over.

Danny's heart pounded. That wasn't funny. It added to the uncomfortable feeling that he'd crossed the line.

"Sorry, I had an ASDH. Been working all day, except for the peanut butter crackers I just stayed to eat."

"That's weird, I smell popcorn," she said, and closed her eyes.

Casey hadn't used a chain saw since last summer. He had to admit … satisfaction came from the roar of the motor. Revving a power tool was simply a guy thing. Toppling the dead trees helped Mary with the endless care of the property and made him shine at the same time. He cut a long spindly deadwood into eight pieces and assembled a woodpile nearby.

Casey waved to Mary to let her know he'd finished, so she stepped back inside and packed a duffle bag with clean clothes to bring Greg. Everyone had agreed to meet at Wellington's for a Sunday family visit after Greg's nap.

Mary and Casey rounded Greg's doorway to the smell of floor disinfectant. Greg sat in his rocking chair, wearing a fresh, open collared shirt. His eyebrows slid upward when they entered, his furry brows a more dominant feature of his face since he'd become so gaunt.

"Dad, you look wonderful," Mary said. She crouched and gave him a kiss. "Look who I brought. Casey removed some dead trees today in your old backyard."

Greg focused on Casey. His head bobbed enthusiastically. "Good man," he said.

Mary put her father's laundry into his drawers and replaced a toothbrush in the bathroom with a new one. She slid on his absent shoe, pulling the Velcro strap taut. "If your leg gets any skinnier, Dad, it'll be a walking stick."

"Grandpa, we're here, too," Annabel said, buoyantly coming in. Greg patted her hand, studying it.

"It's me Grandpa, Nancy, too."

Sara took a tissue and wiped Greg's nose. "Dad, do you have a cold?"

"He does look a little flushed, Sara," Danny said.

"Grandpa, we brought you oatmeal cookies." Nancy took one out of a plastic bag and handed it to him.

"Casey," Annabel said, "would you like one? We made them yesterday."

"Absolutely. And let me see those teeth. Aligning properly so soon?"

"Absolutely," she echoed, displaying a wide smile.

"How's our acute subdural from last night?" Casey asked Danny. "Any word today?"

"Harold rounded today. He never called, so she must be fine," Danny nodded. "How was the rest of your night?"

"We had a few more runs. A sleeping pill overdose. A meth overdose. And two smoke inhalation patients from a small blaze in a downtown bar. How about you?"

"Fine. I mean, things simmered." Danny grew uncomfortable. He had not given it any thought, but it would be awkward if Rachel strolled through Wellington's on a volunteer visit with her dog.

Danny heard voices in the hallway. A quick stepping twenty-something year old woman walked in, her white shoes as spotless as Greg's floor. "Dr. Tilson, anything I can bring your father before I leave?"

"I don't think so."

"I have to hurry. I have another part-time job," she said reaching near Greg for an empty juice container.

"I worked part-time once," Greg stuttered. "I was a Chippendale."

The woman stared stupefied at Greg, but continued without dropping a beat. "Why Mr. Tilson, I bet that's how you became a wealthy man. From the dollar bills the women slipped you."

"Except their fingernails hurt." Greg's eyes flightily followed a cardinal outside his window.

"What on earth?" Sara whispered to Mary. Danny and Casey shook their heads while the young woman left stifling her chuckles.

Greg glanced back into the room. He rose from the rocker with Nancy stabilizing him. He walked along as they cleared a path, wobbly, to the door. His back arched forward, there was no flesh left on his rear end.

"Mary, has he been getting his Ensure?" Sara asked, shaking her head.

"As far as I know. The doctor even wrote it as an order. One with lunch, one with dinner."

Greg stopped at the doorway. Two silver haired women scuffled along the corridor; heads huddled together, in chatty conversation.

"Turn that phonograph off," Greg said, glancing back to Danny.

"Dad, what are you talking about?"

Greg mimicked bird beak movements with his hand. "Yack-yack. Somebody needs to change the record." He gestured toward the two women residents.

"Dad, you are in rare form today."

Greg settled again into his rocker, his energy spent, and quieted.

Subdued family conversation continued, and after an hour, Annabel was the first to get up. "Bye Grandpa. We love you."

Mary watched the good byes, memorizing the details. Greg might not have known for sure who they all were, but she liked to think he still understood the concept of family, that the people in his room cherished him and respected him. She loved the values he passed to her and Danny and how her parents had raised them, showering them with attention and strict discipline.

As Annabel and Nancy left, lagging behind their parents, Annabel turned to her sister. "What's a Chippendale, anyway?"

"I thought you'd know. Must be something old people know about."

Chapter 13

Danny's week dragged like a thick mist that wouldn't blow away. Rachel recuperated his spirit every time she scrubbed for one of his cases, especially the morning she invited him to her place on Sunday, smoothly dropping the remark from beneath her mask. Danny carried his pager on call Sunday. After late morning rounds he detoured to the address she had given him, which was southeast of the hospital, and almost fifteen miles south of home. Her townhouse resided in the middle of three buildings with six units each. Woods flanked the structures and behind, the lawn sloped to a picturesque pond.

Danny stopped on the first floor deck. If he rang the bell, he'd be bridging a river. But hadn't he done that already? He pressed the doorbell and scanned the crowded cars jamming the street. Two doors down, flashy real estate banners hung on railings announcing an open house.

The gray wood door opened to Rachel's smile and she parted the screen door. She wore a loose fitting tee shirt, khaki Capri pants and sandals. Danny began entering, but plastered himself against the screen door when he saw what barreled toward him. A sorrel, eighty-pound Chesapeake Bay retriever came galloping to the entrance and bolted past.

Down the steps the dog ran. Within seconds, he zipped up the front steps to the neighbor's extravaganza, whizzing past a shocked man holding a wine glass on the deck and sporting a cigarette.

Rachel shrugged her shoulders. "I guess that's why they call it an open house." She walked down the steps, her sandals flip-flopping underneath, as Danny followed at a respectable distance. She reached the bottom of the neighbor's stairs. "Did my dog just go in there?" she shouted.

"Yeah, he sure did," said a realtor.

Rachel held the handrail to go up just in case her dog rushed past her. She shook her head, acknowledging to the realtor that she would reprimand her best friend.

Another man, an inside greeter, stood in the foyer. His eyes bulged and he gripped his glass because the dog had zoomed past him and up the second flight of stairs. He pointed upstairs to the bedrooms.

Rachel followed the upheaval to disappear inside. When the Chessie exited while ignoring her, she reversed her path. "Home," she yelled, "and don't do that again."

"I guess introductions are in order," Rachel said, offering Danny a cushioned wicker chair after they had gone inside. Danny planted himself into the bowl shaped seat. Rachel sat on the matching ottoman and grabbed her dog by his green collar. "This is Dakota."

"Hey, Dakota." The dog nuzzled him, turned sideways, and swiped his tail.

"Sorry. Mostly, he likes his butt to be petted."

"Are therapy dogs always that precocious?" Danny asked.

"His inquiring mind sometimes overshadows his good manners. In any case, it's his job to tour novel places."

Danny rubbed his fingers into Dakota's curly top coat. The dog peered around giving Danny a look of approval with bright amber-colored eyes.

"What can I get you? A Coke?"

"Sure."

Rachel went to the small kitchen while Danny looked around. Dozens of CD's and DVD's lined shelves in the wall unit next to him and old bottles lined the top shelf.

Dakota sat erect, his eyes glued to his master. Rachel poured Danny's soda into a clear plastic glass and came back. She sipped Danny's Coke, and then handed it to him.

"Danny, you did a spectacular job this week," she said. "Saving lives by drilling into people's heads. Such responsibility." She moved onto the ottoman cushion next to an end table with several medical field pamphlets and a visitor guide to Knoxville. Dakota laid alongside her, exhaling a sigh. "Do you ever get frightened by what you have to do?"

"Actually, what seems easy to others may terrify me the most," Danny said and paused. Rachel sat engrossed with every word. "Like a brain biopsy. To insert a thin, exceptionally long needle into a nail-size hole in a skull, deep into the brain or even the brain stem can require nerves of steel." Rachel's left hand rested on the dog's head. "All it takes," Danny said, "is misjudging a major vessel or not accurately identifying the specimen needed for the pathologist. What if I send him a noncancerous specimen that's adjacent to the cells wreaking havoc? What if the patient dies eight months later? After all, the specimen I send is extremely small. And sometimes the pathologist wants me to probe around more, increasing the patient's risk, and get more samples."

Rachel grimaced at the thought and leaned back. She took her foot out of a sandal and smoothly slid it into Danny's crotch. Her toes massaged his conceding manhood.

"I'm beginning to enjoy my scrub nurse." Danny said quietly. "Is she taking any days off next week?"

"No sir. I'm too enamored by the hospital's neurosurgeon, so I'll be in his OR."

In a short while, the growing bulge in Danny's pants couldn't be restrained. Rachel led him to the bedroom, shutting the door on Dakota.

Danny's pager stayed quiet the remainder of the day. When he went to bed that night with Sara, he said good night but she didn't hear him. She fell asleep quickly; with no novel, no newspaper. She's a good mother to the girls, he thought. After awhile, Rachel infiltrated his thoughts. Her body, her scent and the things they had done that afternoon.

Danny fell asleep for only a few hours, and monitored the long black minute hand of his bedside clock after four. He finally got up at five and showered, uncluttered a coffee cup and newspaper gathering in his car, and went to the office early. To the dismay of staff, a pot of steaming coffee awaited them when they arrived. Danny wasn't the normal early bird to start the coffee machine.

Danny took a quick look at his first patient's MRI on the view box. He knocked on the door of the exam room and entered for the second appointment with a thirty-eight year old female who had complained vehemently two weeks ago about a multitude of symptoms. Susan Dexter's problems "reappear whenever they want to," she had said. "Last week my arm could barely lift a mug, and two months ago I had stabbing pain in my feet and weakness in my legs."

"Good morning, Mrs. Dexter." Danny shook her hand to evaluate her reach and purpose of grip. "How have you been?"

"You know, I don't mean to be a whiner, but I just don't sleep these days. And I swear my eyes did something weird the other day. And you know, I've got a damn headache today. Do I have brain cancer?"

Not the most compelling case to start the day with, Danny thought. Maybe she needs a shrink, not a neurosurgeon. "Mrs. Dexter, the lab work we did is negative and more importantly, your MRI is clean. You don't have to worry about cancer in your brain."

Mrs. Dexter stopped swinging her legs. "Oh. Well, that's good. But then it doesn't explain what's wrong with me."

Danny wrote a short note in the chart. "A nonsteroidal anti-inflammatory may alleviate your headache. Do you have a favorite that is over-the-counter, such as ibuprofen, or would you like a prescription?"

"Is Advil the same thing?"

"That will do."

Danny smiled and handed the office slip to her for the front desk. "You call if you ever need us again."

Bruce ducked into the viewing room with a cup of coffee and several charts. He slipped films from a stack on the counter to the X-ray box and snapped on the light. His patient's surgery had gone well a month ago, and sure enough, no residual tumor appeared on the MRI. He swung around to lean against the counter and to indicate in the progress notes that he had seen the new film.

Bruce adjusted his vision with his bifocals as he approached the brain MRI which Danny had left on the opposite wall. An MRI with clear white matter abnormalities. He looked closer to detect another fainter plaque. Now that's something we don't see in our office often, he thought. He wondered which patient had multiple sclerosis.

Nancy sprayed the porch windows with ammonia cleaner and rubbed it off in circles, as Danny hammered a loose nail onto a floorboard. Annabel held open the door for her Mom, coaxing her to start their run, while Sara adjusted her baseball cap to block the sun.

Annabel had pointed out to her mother that it was the most perfect Saturday afternoon, and the absolute reason they needed to take advantage of it and run together.

"Mom's going to beat you," Nancy said.

"Whatever," Annabel replied.

"I've fixed salads to bring to Mary's when we come back," Sara said to Nancy and Danny. "Casey has some ribs simmering on the grill."

"Then we're going to visit Grandpa," Annabel said.

"I'll meet you at Mary's. I've got a few errands after this porch work," Danny said. "Nancy can go with you."

Nancy put the spray bottle down and sat glumly. At least she only had one weekend chore left, to clean her room. Maybe if Danny left soon, she could disappear to her room and MySpace on the computer.

"Okay, see you later," Sara said. She almost approached Danny to kiss him, but he rambled around in the toolbox. She couldn't tell if he intended to close the lid or get another tool. Annabel and Sara sprang off the deck and jogged away.

Danny snapped the lid shut. "I'll be leaving in a short while," he said to Nancy. "See you later." He changed into a fresh cotton short-sleeve shirt, tucked it into his shorts, and dabbed subtle lime aftershave on his face. Rachel said she would be home that afternoon. He yearned for a quick visit since OR conversation and glances during the week hadn't sufficed.

Danny parked across the street from the townhouse. He rang the bell, but when Rachel didn't come to the door, he walked down and around. The grass smelled from fresh clippings along the slope to the pond, where baby ducks paddled determinedly after their mother. Two children threw a Frisbee at the water's edge.

Rachel hurried up the hill carrying a red leash. She wore a tangerine colored sleeveless tank top and looked spectacular except for the frown she wore in pursuit of Dakota. He galloped ahead toward the adjacent building as Rachel and Danny waved toward each other. Danny got close then waited.

The Chesapeake's butt and tail disappeared as he dashed through the dark entryway of an open door. Rachel stopped, as if wondering whether to walk into someone's staircase or ground floor garage, because maybe no one was home. A vehicle was parked in the garage; she tiptoed onto the concrete slab. Danny and Rachel heard screams as chairs scuffled along the floor upstairs. In a few moments, Dakota flashed by them and a lady came through after him. In her right hand, she held a flat knife. She busily licked her left index finger.

"I'm so sorry," Rachel said, frantically. "He's never done anything like this before." She paused. "No. I take that back. My dog never did anything like this before except for last weekend. He darted into the neighbor's open house."

"Well, did he buy?" For a woman who just had a chesty bulldozer run through her condo, her face unexpectedly beamed a smile.

Her humor caught Rachel off guard. She couldn't help but laugh. "No, he didn't," she said. "Again, I'm so sorry."

"That's okay," she said. "We were just having birthday cake."

"You mean you're having a birthday party?"

"Yes. He wanted to appraise the sheet cake," she said, waving the knife toward Dakota.

"Omigod," Rachel said. "Happy birthday."

Both women turned their respective ways. Rachel to face her sorrel friend an arm's distance away, who proceeded to play bow as if to taunt her.

"I'm so glad you're here," Rachel said to Danny. " Let's go inside." Rachel smiled and they walked together. "Just ignore his antics."

They reached her unit, while Dakota maintained a respectable distance behind them to avoid capture, but going up the steps the dog reversed the order and paved the way. When they slipped inside, Dakota ran into the bedroom, sprang onto the bed and circled multiple times while raking the comforter into his own private nest.

Rachel and Danny spied from the door. "Guess I'll be remaking my bed," Rachel said. "Unless you and I want to mess it up some more."

Danny put his hand on her waist, pulled her in and kissed her. They made love while still in the doorway, then slid to the floor. Shortly, Rachel laid with her head on Danny's lap, as Dakota maintained his perch where he wasn't supposed to be. He had no desire to leave his post just to investigate.

"You smell good," Rachel said.

"You, too."

"The mousse in my hair smells like a palm tree."

"By the way, the one full day schedule in the OR that you suggested is working out well," Danny said. "We're sprouting more business and now we're squeezing in a few more elective cases because of it. It's made the guys happier."

"Dr. Garner probably favors the increased revenue. More money to give his underlings a raise. Or will that never happen?"

"Rachel, I make plenty. And Bruce may have shrewd business sense, but he's a good physician who deserves his fine reputation."

"You're right. He can be terse with OR personnel but we all do respect him."

"Your place is quiet," Danny remarked as he ran his fingers through her hair. They ignored the clothes scattered around them and lingered.

"Dakota rarely barks unless it's important. I'm lucky the owner let me keep him here because I just rent."

"Has your landlord ever seen the size of him?"

Rachel grinned. "Why? You think I'd be on the street if he did? Then we could get a secret love nest somewhere." She chuckled, kneeled alongside him and gave him a tender kiss.

"I do need to leave," Danny said. They both slipped clothes back on; Danny used the bathroom and peeked in the mirror. "I'll see you on Monday," he said. Rachel walked barefoot with him to the door.

"I'll be waiting." She laid her hand on the doorknob. "Really, Danny, I can't stop thinking about you." Her soft words floated in the air.

Danny touched her hair again. "I know. Me, too."

Sara and Mary lined casseroles along the counter. Annabel poured iced tea and looked for another beer for Casey while Nancy continued her glass cleaning, this time on her aunt's back windows.

"I really do appreciate the help," Mary said, puttering out the door.

Casey turned over a slab of ribs and brushed them with barbecue sauce. "Mary, you must have paid the butcher under the table, because these are falling away from the bone like they came off Texas cattle this morning."

"I know." Mary put a clean serving plate next to the grill. "But better than the ribs is the man preparing them."

"I just feel great after spending the night with my lady," he said quietly.

"And getting to the gym and barber shop this morning," Mary said. "You can't stand it if your hair isn't true to its short cut."

"You noticed."

"Like, don't you two ever stop goggling over each other?" Nancy asked, plopping into a chaise lounge chair.

Danny stepped onto the patio from the kitchen door. "Greetings everybody."

"Good timing, now that the cooking's done," Casey said.

"We thought you would beat us over here," Annabel said.

"I went for a drive-through oil change." He took a water cracker and cheese square from a plate on the patio table.

"Okay," Casey said, "let's eat." He slipped the meat on the serving platter where juicy drippings began to pool at the bottom.

"Let's go inside, Casey," Mary said.

Everyone took a plate and served themselves from the kitchen island. Danny sliced a baguette then sat across from Nancy.

"So do those oil change places rotate tires?" Nancy asked. "I didn't think they did that."

"I don't think they do," Danny said.

"Why, Nancy?" Casey asked.

"Dad and I went to that place, like two months ago for his oil change." She looked at her father. "You said you were going to the dealer next time, Dad, because your tires needed to be rotated and whatever else."

Danny's fork teased the pork from the bone. "Nancy, I totally forgot I had that oil change so recently. I'll get those other things done at the dealer next time."

Sara started to say it was unusual for him to make a blunder like that, but thought better.

Chapter 14

A waist-coated nurse, Mrs. Ryder, stepped quickly from behind the nurse's station when she saw the Tilson family and Casey veer into Wellington's ground floor hallway. "Mrs. Tilson, Doctor Tilson," she said compassionately, halting in front of Mary. "I just left you a message on your recorder. We've called hospice."

Mary nodded, her face wilting.

"He doesn't recognize anyone and he hasn't had anything to eat or drink today," Mrs. Ryder said. "You still don't want him to have a central line for TPN, correct?"

"That's total parenteral nutrition, Mary," Danny said, putting his arm around Mary's shoulder. "No Ma'am. No prolongation of the inevitable."

"Sometimes families change their minds at the last minute," Mrs. Ryder said. "They can't bear to watch a loved one die when they think they're assisting it."

"We are sure," Mary said. "And thank you."

After Annabel slightly elevated the head of her grandfather's bed, she sat on the edge of the cranked mattress. Greg's white sheet made a neat border folded over the top of the quilt. There was barely a rise in the covers from his shriveled body underneath.

"Grandpa is all blue and blotchy," Annabel said imploringly to Danny.

"And his hand is so cold," Mary said, embracing it between hers.

Danny sat on the rocker, immediately behind them. Greg's other hand picked at the top of the sheet. His eyes looked distant, staring into an unknown abode that did not include his family.

Danny leaned close. "Dad, it's Danny. And your daughter Mary. Your grandchildren, Annabel and Nancy are here. And Sara and our friend, Casey. We all love you."

"You've been good to all of us, Dad," Mary said. "We want you to know, it's okay to leave us when you're ready. We'll always love you and we'll never forget you."

Tears slid down Annabel's cheeks. She brushed them away with her fingers. Greg's chest rose several times. "He's breathing better now," Nancy said.

Greg's body stilled again for almost ten seconds. Annabel gulped her own air waiting for him to breathe again. The next respirations were noisy, a rattling from the tomb. The unlit room became more somber. Casey turned the bureau lamp on the lowest setting and resumed his post. Mary squeezed Greg's hand. He tilted his head and he looked at his family. For at least half a minute, they could swear that Greg's expression registered recognition and love, as well as acceptance and farewell. Danny felt so choked, he couldn't utter a thing.

No one was aware that Mrs. Ryder had come in. "The hospice nurse will be here tomorrow. If any of you would like to stay, we can bring in a cot." She stepped next to the rocker and whispered to Danny and Mary. "Your dad could die tonight, or in a day or two. Please, anything we can do for all of you let us know." She walked out, her white shoes as quiet as tiptoeing on slipper socks.

"I'm staying," Mary said. "Perhaps we can take turns over the next few days?"

"Mom, can I stay tonight, too?" Nancy said. "I can curl up in the chair. Please, Mom?"

"Danny, what do you think?" Sara asked.

"Okay. We'll be here first thing in the morning."

Mary leaned out of the way so Casey could press Greg's hand. Greg's dried fingers surrendered in his palm. Casey nodded goodbye to the family and left.

Danny sagged on the bed. "Dad, you're going to join Mom. She's waiting for you. You've been the best father."

Danny, Sara and Annabel didn't exchange words until they turned onto their street. "Grandpa's only seventy-one. That's not old anymore," Annabel said.

Sara turned around to face her daughter. "You're right, Annabel. But many people die too young as well."

"Like Melissa," Annabel retorted. She turned her head away from Sara and stared out the window. "When I was little, everything seemed easy. Now it looks to me like life kicks the wrong people in the butt. It isn't fair."

Mary arranged the portable cot alongside her father's bed, spread linen on top and fluffed a pillow. She resumed holding Greg's icy, wrinkled fingers. Nancy took the other set of sheets and plastered them on the mint green upholstered chair. She sat sideways, dangling her feet before turning out the light.

Mary knew her father curled further into the fetal position as the night wore on, with faint light streaming through the blinds.

Something ironic about that, she thought, to terminate life in the position we start with. We become what we were.

The long nightly stretch approached 5 a.m. Mary anticipated that sounds from the hallway would soon infiltrate the room: carts in the hallway, aides scurrying to help residents dress or guide them to bathrooms for sponge baths, the business people rushing to the cafeteria kitchen to grab coffee supplies for the front office. She sat up, planted her feet on the floor, and held her father's wrist. "Nancy, are you awake?" Mary asked.

"I've been awake most of the night."

"Grandpa barely has a pulse."

They took a place on either side of Greg. His mouth parted, almost smiling, his eyes glossed over.

"We're born crying while everyone around the newborn smiles," Mary said almost in a whisper. "We die looking pleased, everyone around us crying."

The last remnant of Greg's blood flow dissipated and Mary no longer felt a thready pulsation underneath her fingers. She took a very deep sigh and wept.

Greg's casket stood waiting to be lowered into the ground. Annabel and Nancy stood alongside each other, their arms touching.

"Why don't you just ask your orthodontist next time for black braces?" Nancy asked.

"I plan on having these braces off, not changing their color again," Annabel said sullenly.

"Come on girls," Sara said, linking her arm in Danny's.

Danny removed Sara's arm, took several steps and crouched. His mother was buried here. One single physical spot on earth for his parents. A black hole to house them.

As they headed to the car the sky further darkened. "It's going to rain," Sara said, waving upward.

Danny couldn't agree more. "Happy is the bride that the sun shines on and happy is the corpse that the rain rains on." Sara stared at her husband. "I learned it from him," he said, and mustered a baby smile.

Danny stood in a Nashville office building, the large windows facing north, as a tugboat towed a barge in the brackish Cumberland River below. The attorney he and Mary waited for had taken care of his parents legal matters for years, and Danny recalled visiting his office as a young man and waiting outside in the lobby, just as Annabel, Nancy and Sara were doing.

Tom Werner tapped on the conference room door and entered. Since the last time Danny had seen him, more gray weaved through his black hair and he had grown a goatee. But his wearing suspenders hadn't changed; today's were Valentine red.

He gave Danny a strong handshake. "I'm sorry about your Pa, Danny. Mary, did you have any difficulty with the funeral arrangements since we talked?"

"No Mr. Werner."

"We're on a first name basis here," he said. "I took care of your mom and dad for years. And Mary, you and I haven't been strangers since you've been overseeing your Dad's funds for quite some time now."

He gestured for Danny to sit, and pulled a chair out for himself. As he spread the will and trust papers before them, he agreed that the girls remain in the receptionist's area. "I would like to bring them in at the end. We can inform them, briefly, what will happen when they turn eighteen, if that's okay with you, Mary.

"That's fine."

"A lot of this is moot," Tom said. "Danny, as you know, your sister and the bank will implement the details of Greg's estate." He looked at Mary. "Mary, take care of residual funeral bills, don't forget to notify all financial institutions of Greg's death and recheck those lists you prepared on his assets and liabilities. You will also be responsible to pay the bequest he made to the American Cancer Society."

"The only debt left will be forthcoming bills from the nursing home," Mary said.

Tom read the basic will to them both and highlighted the trust sitting on the table.

"Mary, I can take care of the real estate legal affairs if you'd like. Transfer the house deed to your name."

"That would be fine," she said.

Tom leaned back into his chair and crossed long legs. "Danny, as you know, your dad felt strongly that your financial security was a given. He's handing over most of his liquid estate to his grandchildren. The bank will manage that trust, which starts for each of them when they turn eighteen. They will receive half their trust the first four years, and then the rest in biannual increments for twenty years. Your father essentially wanted to pay their entire college or higher education, that's why the big payoff up front. Any questions before I simply explain it to the girls?"

"No Tom," Danny said. "There are no surprises here."

Annabel and Nancy came in and sat at the far end of the table, not expecting to be part of the remaining conversation. When Tom gave them details about their eighteenth birthday, Annabel's goal became that much more attainable. Now she wouldn't drop any future medical school from consideration because of tuition. And if she earned a scholarship, any money she earned from part-time jobs would be straight savings, or better yet, she could put it towards a college fishing club fund.

"Wow, Dad," Annabel said. "I wish Grandpa were alive. So I could thank him."

Sara dabbed her nose. She smoothed her fingers on her lap. Her father-in-law had been a gem.

Danny clasped his daughters when they left. "Do you mind that Dad gave most of his estate to Mary and the girls?" he asked Sara.

"Danny, he left us almost everything. The girls are an extension of us."

Chapter 15

Annabel pushed the turn signal down and slowly crept left onto the street. She couldn't wait until the spring when she'd turn sixteen and get an intermediate restricted driver's license and the use of Melissa's Acura. For now, she considered herself lucky to have Sara with her while she drove with a permit.

It was the fall semester in her second year of high school. This term she studied at a consistent pace; no more staying up very late for cramming subjects at the last minute. She wanted to develop mature study habits for college and hopefully medical school. She dedicated more time to her advanced placement English class, maintaining a consistent A with a constant flow of essays. Polishing her writing skills would be beneficial no matter what she did, medicine or not. If she topped it off by refining her spoken words, that would be even better. In college, she wanted to join a debate team.

"Nice job," Sara said as Annabel coasted the car into Mary's driveway. Annabel shut off the ignition.

"Thanks, Mom."

"Have fun tonight. I'll be outside school tomorrow."

"See you then. Tonight I'm going to edit a paper and study for a math test."

Annabel unclasped the seat belt and picked up her olive knapsack. Lately she resided at Mary's at least half the time. Annabel had splurged on a shopping spree, officially converting Danny's old bedroom into her second bedroom. She'd bought a paisley bedspread, bought accessory sham covers and curtains and hung a younger rocker than the U2 poster Melissa had framed. She liked a poster of John Lennon that Danny had left on a closet shelf so she resurrected it to hang on the closet door. She had a second home and second set of parents, since Casey also lived there part-time as well.

Sara changed seats and drove to Nancy's school where Nancy already stood on the sidewalk with a group of girls. Nancy wore a Capri pink zipped hoody and denim skirt over black leggings, making her legs look like toothpicks. No doubt, Sara thought, her baby was in the throes of adolescent hormones, her height springing skyward like a germinating tulip. Sara liked Nancy's new hairstyle, parted right down the middle, flattened with a curling iron. It bluntly stopped at her shoulders and she used a therapy product to shine it like silk. Today she wore a thin zebra print headband, almost unnoticeable. All told, her hair still fell along the side of her face, nicely masking her troublesome-looking ears.

Sara waved when Nancy looked towards the blue CRV and parted from her friends. Nancy opened the passenger door, threw in a book bag, followed by her skinny legs.

"Guess Annabel's at Mary's," she said, noting her sister's absence. "You're going to have to run by yourself, Mom."

"That'll work."

At home, Sara stirred a crockpot concoction while Nancy spread cream cheese on a cracker. "Guess I'll go change and run," Sara said, putting the utensil down.

"Dad going to be home for dinner?" Nancy asked.

Sara tried to recall what he'd told her that morning. "I can't remember if he's on call today or if he said he'd be late."

Nancy grinned and slapped more spread on the next cracker. "It's all the same these days," she said.

Sara winced, expelling the words from her mind as quickly as she had heard them.

Casey's seven-to-three shift finished quietly while he sat in the ER. He hadn't seen Danny in days, so he took two steps at a time to the OR and looked in the doctor's lounge. Danny sat at a side table rolling a mouse in front of the computer, gathering lab results. Casey tapped Danny's shoulder as he walked by, lowered the loud television and sat at a round table where Danny joined him.

"I'm waiting on a case," Danny said.

"One I brought you?"

"Not all my cases come through you." Danny said, kidding him. "This one comes from an internist who did a superb medical workup. Geriatric medicine at it's finest."

"Why? What did they find?"

"Normal pressure hydrocephalus."

"Refresh me," Casey said.

"It should be a consideration for every doc practicing geriatric medicine. Someone in the family will bring grandpa in with urinary incontinence, memory impairment and gait disturbance. Everybody writes it off as Alzheimer's, but if it's NPH and it's treated timely, symptoms improve."

"So are you going to do a lumbar drain?"

"A VP shunt. Ventricle to peritoneum. Then I'll follow him with CT's." Coverage of the approaching presidential election caught their attention. A speech from a major contender at a prominent university ended and the newscaster returned.

"Are you heading out?" Danny asked.

"I'm going to the gym, then to Mary's. Annabel is staying the night there, too," he added.

"I've noticed women admirers around here are becoming impatient with you," Danny grinned. "They aren't making headway snatching a date with the ambulance driver."

"Hey, watch it. I'm a highly trained EMT. A paramedic. You, you're just a brain mechanic."

"Shut up, Casey."

After a momentary silence, Danny and Casey cracked a smile.

"Come on, Casey, are you and Mary serious?"

"So far, so good. Better than good."

Danny took an apple from the fruit bowl in the center of the table and bit in. The lounge door opened. A surgeon entered, followed by a woman in scrubs who approached their table. "Dr. Tilson," she said, "excuse me, but your case is going to the room. I won't be scrubbing for it and won't be staying over my shift. I have a guest visiting later, so I have to get home."

"This is Rachel," Danny said, gesturing. "Casey."

"Nice to meet you." She turned her attention back to Danny. "I better get going. Good luck with your case, Dr. Tilson. I hope it doesn't take you that long." She picked an apple from the fruit bowl in the center of the table, took a bite and left.

After Casey left for the day, Danny called Sara. "Are you on call?" Sara asked. "I've made one of your favorites and Nancy and I are going to eat around six. We're wondering if you'll be joining us."

"No, I'm not on call," Danny said "But I have an add-on case shortly. If I'm very late, please don't wait up for me."

"Okay," Sara said despondently.

Danny scrubbed and started the add-on surgery. He remained aloof to conversation and had no opinion as to musical selections. Despite trying to concentrate, the medium pressure valve he chose just wouldn't cooperate. "Damn quality control," he said, flinging it. "Can you get me something that works around here?"

The anesthesiologist and the circulator exchanged glances as the nurse went to hunt for another one. The next shunt seemed to appease Danny, and to the satisfaction of everyone in the room, the case finally finished. Danny zipped out of sight as though he peeled out of a fire.

Danny rapped his knuckles on the door at Rachel's townhouse. She opened promptly, and looked like the picture of relaxation. She smiled, eased Danny's jacket off and hung it on the back of a seat. Dakota cantered to them as they embraced, and finding no one paying attention to him, he clutched a fringed throw pillow off the couch and galloped away with it.

Danny peered around the couch after they sat down to see the Chesapeake's head resting perfectly on the white cushion. "I'll acknowledge you now," Danny said.

Dakota went to Danny wearing a motorized tail and turned his head in approval of Danny rubbing his hind end.

"Would you like me to make you a sandwich?" Rachel asked.

"Please," Danny said.

Rachel stocked her refrigerator with Danny's favorite cold cuts. She dolloped mayonnaise and butter on wheat toast, piled on mesquite turkey and Monterey Jack cheese, then poured him a soft drink. She placed them on the cocktail table, sat beside him and flipped off her squeaky house clogs.

"Did your case go well?

"Fine, except for malfunctioning hardware." He downed the sandwich quickly, being hungrier than he had realized, then eased his back into the couch, propping his feet to the side, on the wicker chair's ottoman. Rachel tucked into the corner of the couch, laid her head on his lap and stroked his leg. She clicked on the remote, and handed it to him.

They stopped channel surfing when Danny found a familiar spy movie, the agent impressed with his own slick gadgetry. Danny's hand sought the soft skin beneath Rachel's pearl turtleneck. Dakota couldn't separate them when he nosed into Rachel so he taunted her by dangling a pillow. "Actually, thanks," Rachel said, pulling it from his mouth and easing it under her hair. A relaxed bliss descended on both of them, which paved the way to closed eyelids. An hour and a half later, their sleep progressed to a deep REM.

Nancy closed her notebook and rolled off her bed. She stretched, changed into cotton sleepwear and stared out her front bedroom window. With the half moon's illumination, she saw few leaves dangling from trees. A fine parade of them blew across the pebbly cul-de-sac. It was eleven o'clock, later than normal for finishing her homework, but she had hung out with her mom in the evening longer than she thought. A melancholic mood had enveloped Sara, so much so, that she did not swing her arms in their normal melodramatic flare when she tempted Nancy with a newly rented DVD or discussed an upcoming mini-marathon for the Children's Hospital.

Nancy looked in the mirror to swipe some acne cream on the bulge forming on her chin, then sat down to her laptop and clicked onto MySpace. Several new messages appeared. She decided to change the video insert on her page, so began searching for clips by her favorite music artists.

Sara missed previously frequent movie rental nights with Danny when she'd lie on the couch, her head on his lap. He'd stroke his hand through her hair. She made herself a wide mug of hot chocolate and tucked her feet under her, although her toes were toasty warm in thick blue slipper socks. The bulk of the late night monologue focused on the presidential election. Each guest inserted his or her two cents worth about their favorite candidate but the talk show host craftily kept his impending vote choice neutral. By eleven thirty, she'd drained her cup, and stared blankly at the ads following the show. She channel surfed and stopped at some sci-fi with a bad music score; as amusing as the late night show, but she wasn't in the mood for humor. She clicked off the television, rinsed the pottery in the sink and went upstairs, leaving the hall light on for Danny.

Sara passed her wedding picture in the hallway. She loved the memories of that day, how consumed they had been taking their vows after an impeccable courtship. She had never seen Danny wear a tuxedo; she had gulped for air when she saw him waiting for her at the end of the church aisle.

The light was on in Nancy's room, next to hers. The door stood ajar. "Nancy?"

"Hey, Mom," Nancy said. Sara pushed the door open, went in, looked at the computer screen, but then sat on her daughter's bed. Nancy closed the website, and shut down her computer.

Sara absently mindedly smoothed the bedspread then wrung her hands on her lap. Nancy slithered off the hardwood chair and nestled beside her. Sara glanced toward the window before darting her eyes to her daughter. She thought about taking Nancy's hands into hers, but she couldn't move. Sara pushed away the stone wall of denial and knew her husband was with another woman.

A snout pushed Danny's elbow. He gently tried to swipe it away, but as he moved, he remembered the family didn't own a dog and his heart ticked faster. Jeez, he thought, rubbing his eyes. Rachel stirred, propping herself up from his lap.

"This isn't good," Danny said, "what time is it?"

Rachel saw the wall clock. "One o'clock."

They both got up. Rachel slipped on her clogs while Danny used the bathroom. He came out, walked to the front door where Rachel joined him, and shook his head. She planted him a kiss.

Danny could see lights on when he pulled the car into the garage. The light upstairs came from Nancy's front bedroom; the downstairs light, maybe Sara had purposefully left on for him. What could have professionally detained him? Countless things.

He gripped his keys after turning off the car and headed to the door. Quietly he went in. He took off his jacket and draped it on a chair instead of hanging it in the closet. All was silent so he went to switch off the hallway fixture.

Danny felt his wife's presence and turned. "You awake?" he asked in a whisper. "I'm sorry I got delayed."

Sara fixed her eyes onto him. Right through him. She unveiled his adultery like breaking open a vault of hidden atrocities.

Danny knew no explanation would be acceptable. It would make matters worse. At least he had that good sense.

"Go ahead," Sara's voice creaked. "You can turn that light out. Only if you think you can find your way to the couch without it."

Chapter 16

Sara knew deep in her heart that Danny's unfaithfulness hadn't been a one-night stand. It had been more serious than that, involving repeated escapades with someone. She had no clue as to who that someone was. She needed to think about the future before they discussed the situation together. The marriage was over. He knew what he was doing while he was doing it. Perhaps at some level she could forgive him, but not in the role of wife and husband. Besides her children, he had meant everything to her.

After 6 a.m., Sara heard the water running downstairs. The garage door opened and a vehicle pulled out. She washed, brushed her teeth and changed as she heard Nancy in her bedroom. In the kitchen, she slid two frozen waffles into the toaster for Nancy, but after they popped up, she absent mindedly pushed the lever down again.

Nancy reluctantly came into the kitchen and sighed to find her father gone. She took a double take at the plate, but it wasn't the right time to talk to her mother about her toaster skills. "Thanks for making these, mom."

"You're welcome. We deserve it this morning." Sara swirled a spoon repetitively in her coffee cup. She drove Nancy to school, each absorbed in silence except for comments about early pedestrians. "I'll be here after school," Sara said, "with Annabel."

Danny first used the call room down the corridor from the OR. He pulled his toiletry bag from a shelf, freshened up, made rounds, and went to the office. He had skipped through the hospital lounge quickly, so poured his first dark roasted blend in the office kitchen. Bran muffins sat on a tray in the middle of the table. He took a butter container from the refrigerator, slid out a chair and sat as his nurse, Cheryl, walked in.

"Good morning," Danny said. "Do I have you to thank for these?"

"Yes. It's a new recipe. No better way to test it than at the office."

"Your husband can always try them on for size."

"He says he has to loose fifteen pounds and I don't help him."

"I think you just like to bake for us anyway." Danny eased the tray toward her. "You too," he said. She cut one and gave Danny the other half.

"Sara called a short while ago," Cheryl said. "She asked me for your schedule today. Then she asked if we could fit her in around lunchtime, when there's a lull in your appointments."

Danny dictated the pertinent facts of his last morning patient into the transcription record and went to his office. He saw Sara's crossed legs through the half-open door. Her left hand was in motion between the armrest and her brown jeans. He remembered she had called those pants UPS brown. He was confounded that he already recalled something she had said, looking back as if it were a distant past and what they had shared was a remote memory.

She heard him and turned in the chair. Danny pushed the door closed behind him, took off his white coat and sat at his desk. He guessed Sara's morning activity from the puffiness under her eyes.

"It's best that we don't prolong this," Sara said, resting her hand on the armrest.

"Sara, I'm sorry," Danny said, but couldn't look her in the face.

"I bet you are."

The telephone rang, then stopped.

"When would you like to gather your things from the house?"

Danny's heart flip-flopped in his chest, like a coin toss. He looked out the window but couldn't grasp this errand she was giving him. He was supposed to schedule a time to go to his own house?

"I'll take the girls out to dinner between six and eight," Sara finally said. "Clear out what you need then." Sara shoved the tissue she grasped in her right hand into her purse and got up.

"I'll let you know where I'll be," Danny said.

"Leave us a note. Not only will the girls want to know, but that's information a divorce attorney will need."

Before Danny could utter a word, Sara tore off out the door.

Annabel sprinted to the blue CRV where Sara handed her the keys and Annabel put the car in drive. "Mom, I got so much done last night at Mary's. I finished half tonight's homework already and wrote a fantastic paper. And you can't believe the watercolor Mary finished. It's so simple but so creative. It's a woman with a sunhat sitting on a hammock leaning over. Mom, she is so good; like she should have her own art exhibit in a museum."

Annabel kept a motor on her mouth driving half the distance to Nancy's school but eventually slowed down. Her mother had not contributed anything, not that she had given her the opportunity. Finally, Annabel realized her mother looked downright distraught.

They slowed outside Nancy's school. Nancy approached them quickly when they parked. Once inside, she leaned toward the front seat, gave Sara a tiny hug and kissed her cheek. "Mom, are you okay?" she said.

Sara gave her a tiny affirmative nod.

After office hours, Danny stopped at the hospital because Bruce had asked him to see one of his surgical patients. He had to find Rachel to tell her what happened, but the OR front desk told him she had the day off. He called her apartment but there was no answer.

At seven o'clock Danny parked his car in his garage. He took two suitcases from the garage, unlocked the door, and went in. He stacked a few medical books and clothing from the front closet into two shopping bags from the kitchen. He slid his laptop into his computer bag and began assembling the items in the hallway. Most of what he needed resided upstairs in the bedroom. He took his photographs off the dresser, Sara and he would have to figure out family pictures later. The two expandable suitcases bulged by the time he finished packing.

In his bottom dresser drawer, he removed one sweater. Underneath, he clutched his leather bag to take it out. He slowed his tasks, opened the case and smoothed his fingers over the rich hardbound book. He flipped the pages, confirming that the book was in fine shape. He groped for the other content, the plastic bag holding Melissa's bracelet. Danny placed it in his palm and kissed it. He replaced the book and bracelet in the monogrammed case and tucked it into an outer zippered compartment of the larger black suitcase.

He put everything into the car trunk, then reached for his phone to call Rachel again. This time he'd try her cell phone, but he pulled out of the driveway cursing himself. He rarely used her cell phone number; it was on a scrap of paper in the top drawer of his office. Focusing on placing the call made it easier to peel away from his house. His eyes remained glued on the cul-de-sac, the porch, the bedroom windows and then the rearview mirror as he turned onto the main street of the subdivision.

Danny parked at an independent pricey coffee joint. For fifteen minutes over a steamed milk coffee, he pondered his situation. They'd probably be cramped in Rachel's townhouse if they both lived there for any length of time.

He headed to an apartment complex that he often passed, but the front office was locked. He went next door to the clubhouse, where, luckily, the on-site manager attended a potluck dinner gathering.

"We rent by the month," the old man said, holding a plate of food. "A two month deposit, too."

"Do you have anything furnished, as well as available?" Danny asked.

"We rent unfurnished. Only the model apartment has furniture."

"I'll pay you more if I can rent it," Danny said. "Doesn't it make more sense to rent it to me than leave it unrented as a show piece?"

"Yah got a point."

"I'll take it right now," Danny said.

"Don't yah wanna see it?" the man asked, putting down his plate.

"No."

"Then let's go. I'll get the keys, take your money and give you the rental agreement. Read the fine print."

Danny fell asleep in a new bed. With his shoes on.

Their headway through a large pizza was slow going. Annabel couldn't finish the last piece, especially the crust. She went to the cashier's counter, found a toothpick, and then sat delicately fishing crust out of her braces. Sara and Nancy glumly exchanged glances.

"Just because I haven't been told what's going on, doesn't mean I don't know something's going on," Annabel said, dancing the toothpick at them. "So, what's going on?"

A smidgen of a smile crept over Sara's face. "You're right," Sara said, grasping her daughter's hand and squeezing it.

"Your dad won't be staying at home. He's romantically involved with someone else."

"You're kidding. Really, like, that doesn't happen to our family," she stuttered. They left the pizza place. Annabel leaned against the glass exit door. "How could he do this to us?" she snarled.

Danny slept solidly and awoke in a semi-strange environment with ample time to get ready. He found a small stack of towels in a linen closet and showered, then tautly wrapped a towel around his waist and put the two suitcases on the bed. After unloading all the clothes into dresser drawers and the closet, he unzipped the outside pockets.

What to do with the burgundy leather bag? No dresser drawer this time.

Danny peeled the corner of the luxury resort looking bedspread, flipping it to the top of the bed. The box spring was thick and solid, the mattress thinner and clean white. He pushed up the end of the mattress at the foot of the bed. "Here you go Mr. Einstein and Melissa," he said, placing the monogrammed case between the box spring and mattress and smoothing the bedspread back to normal.

The apartment was long and narrow, with the bedroom at the end of a corridor. Rent was on the hefty side, but last night it had solved his problems. Behind the ginger bedroom curtains, he found a sliding glass door to a covered patio, and in the living room, a flat screen TV probably took the place of an interior designer's picture over a small fireplace. Not too bad, Danny thought; a fifteen hundred square foot bachelor pad with a loft upstairs.

After dressing and before leaving, Danny scouted the furnishings in the kitchen. Besides condiment containers and a toaster, an automatic coffee maker graced the counter. He had what he needed minus a bag of ground Columbian.

Rachel skillfully handed Danny his instruments from the instrument tray. She seemed to know what to deliver before he asked. The last two days had been hectic as hell. Hearing her voice and catching her eyes glimpsing at him would suffice until he could whisper pleasantries to her in bed. 'My wife and I have separated," Danny said at the beginning of the case, almost in a whisper. He poised a blunt instrument in his right hand; he couldn't make out Rachel's expression due to the mask.

Rachel nodded. "We'll have to talk then," she said.

Their OR door swung open while Danny operated. Bruce held a mask on his lower face. He stepped to the side, at the counter below the telephone. He picked up Danny's pager. "The floor has paged you twice, Danny," he said. "Your pager is off!"

Danny startled. He never heard Bruce come in. "I thought I turned it on."

"You need to go upstairs between cases. Sounds like your normal pressure hydrocephalus patient from the other day has a shunt obstruction, a shunt infection, or both."

Danny turned his head but Bruce was already gone.

By the end of the morning, Danny finished two surgeries and started his shunt patient on an IV antibiotic for a simmering infection. Rachel found him while on her lunch break. They decided she would visit him in the evening. Danny called Tom Werner's office at 5 p.m., talked to his secretary and scheduled an appointment late in the day for Monday. He would have to jockey around patient care to get to his attorney.

So rarely did Danny drink beer, that when he did, he bought the most expensive six- pack, attributing price to quality. He took two cold ones out of his refrigerator that evening and handed one to Rachel. When she sat, she slipped off her shoes, curled her legs under her and took a sip. She had a thin white turtleneck on underneath a classic V-neck sweater. Her eye color matched the aqua sweater; it wasn't just the beer that swum around in Danny's head.

"Is this what you want?" Rachel asked.

"I think so," Danny replied. "The marriage is over. It's you I'm in love with." Danny nestled his lips into her neck, then they kissed tenderly.

"Why don't we see each other often, spend time at each place," Rachel said. "Then we can decide which one suits us better."

Danny also took off his shoes. Rachel put down her beer to knead the bottom of his feet.

"I must say, I'm used to Dakota hanging by your side." Danny mused.

"The poor fellow. I told him I'd be back tonight. Told him I'd be with you, but he cocked his head and growled." She dug her fingers into his foot, laughed and ran off into the bedroom. Danny followed so they could christen his new bed.

It was so cold and dreary the next Monday, that Danny thought the clouds had the potential for snow. Far north of the Cumberland River, the clouds were thicker; maybe those Kentuckians were in for their first taste of winter. He already waited on Tom a half hour; a half hour which could have been useful in the office. Finally, the conference room door opened and Tom Werner walked in.

He put the palm of his hand out in front of him. "Danny, I am so sorry. Not just for being late. I had no idea you had an appointment, otherwise I would have called you myself."

Danny had started to sit again, but stopped.

"I can't represent you. It would be a conflict of interest. Your wife has retained our firm. I didn't feel comfortable with it myself, since I've known you both for years. One of the other partners will be representing her."

Tom put his large hand on Danny's shoulder and patted him. He smiled sincerely. "You just let me know if there's anything else I can do for the family."

"I suppose she's told you all the sordid details."

"Even if she had, I wouldn't have listened. We don't care what goes on behind closed doors, nor will a judge. It has nothing to do with the case. But to tell you the truth, that's often the business that brings us the business."

Chapter 17

Annabel and Nancy compressed school assignments into their backpacks. It had gotten easier to go back and forth to Mary's whenever they wanted because they kept extra clothes and school supplies there. They carried their new digital audio players in their purses.

"Your dad said he'd be at Mary's around six," Sara informed them as Annabel drove. Sara took the wheel after the girls got out. "I'll see you tomorrow afternoon," she said and drove away from her sister-in-law's.

Danny left Tom's office and aimed toward his sister's. He hadn't seen the girls since leaving home, which he had done on purpose. If his girls were upset with him, a few days distance would simmer down their immediate resentment; even Sara's, in case he crossed her path.

He parked in Mary's driveway, tapped on the door and entered. No one was downstairs, but Danny took a few minutes to appreciate Mary's watercolor leaning against the fireplace. The twisted cords of a hammock had incredible clarity for a watercolor and the woman sitting on it wore a white sunhat shielding sunshine from her face. Although he had Mary's ability to concentrate and he possessed skilled hands, he had not inherited one morsel of creative talent.

Mary flopped behind him wearing slippers. Her painting smock and the tapered artist's brush in her hand smelled of fresh oil paint.

"Really nice," Danny said.

"Thanks. I've sold it already. To the county mayor and his wife. It's their second piece from me." She sat on the edge of a chair, eyeing it. "My art is finally supporting me in Tennessee. I'm going to inch up my prices, too."

"Now I'll know where to get a loan," Danny joked. "Are the girls here?"

"Upstairs," she waved. "But you're not getting off the hook yet. What's going on, Danny? I'm hearing details from everyone but you."

For a few seconds, an uncomfortable silence breathed between them. Danny hadn't thought of what to tell his sister. He slid off his jacket and held it.

"But the last thing I want is to get in the middle," Mary said. "Sara is like a sister to me. I'm going to stay neutral. Especially for the girls."

"I don't expect anything else." Danny half-smiled while slipping into a chair. "I've been seeing a scrub nurse from the hospital. I spend so many hours there, Mary. She's at my side. Assisting me. It just happened."

"I can't morally judge my own brother…" She frowned. "But …" She stared hard at him and clamped together her lips.

Facing the topic wasn't as bad as Danny thought it would be. He sighed with relief.

"Go see your girls," she said.

Danny always liked visiting his old room, now taken by Annabel, but getting there disheartened him. Walking through the upstairs hallway, he never failed to ache for Melissa; it had been months since her death, but only yesterday in his mind. He stared at the floor as if her presence lingered on the carpet and she awaited oxygen and CPR. If only …

When he peered around the bedroom corner, Annabel's head bobbed in rhythm with her music, black wires dangling from her ears. She had a textbook and spiral notebook in front of her on the bed, but looked out to the backyard.

Danny went in and stood near her. Her legs crossed at the ankles, dangling up in the air. She popped out an ear bud.

"I used to do the same thing," Danny said.

Annabel yanked the other earpiece out. She rolled from her position and sat up. "What?" she said.

"Look to that peaceful view while I was supposed to be studying."

"It didn't hurt you. You got what you wanted. Or who you wanted."

Annabel's sarcasm hit Danny as if it came from a mature boxer. Since he was the adult, he thought he'd be the one in charge of the conversation, not the other way around. He searched for words.

"So you and Mom are getting a divorce?"

Danny nodded.

"Are you going to marry the other one?"

He looked to the side, pursing his lips. "That's not the issue right now."

"So leaving all of us is? So you can do whatever it is you do with her? Like getting the President's under-the-table?"

"That's enough," Danny said, putting parental authority into his voice. This generation knew it all and wasn't afraid to talk about it. Sex had simply become water fountain talk, as casual as the previous evening's NCAA scores.

A minute elapsed. "Annabel, your future is important. Please, let's not lose sight of your college goals. Or your wanting to be a doctor. Don't get tangled in your parent's problems. Or criticize us. We've done the best we could for both of you."

"Who said I'm criticizing Mom?"

"I'm going to see Nancy," he said and kissed her forehead.

Annabel pulled away from him as a tear escaped from the corner of her eye.

Nancy sidetracked from homework on MySpace using Mary's computer. *Divorce sucks*, she typed. *Anybody's parent having an affair like mine*? She swiveled in the chair and looked down at her TN Lady Vols shirt. The chest bulges made her smile. Her new habit entailed checking on their ascent routinely.

Danny rapped on the almost closed door. Nancy swung her foot, pushing the door wide open. "Hey," Danny said.

Her face soured. She wanted to continue with her on-line bantering. Anything but to talk to him.

Danny tried leaning on the doorframe but he wasn't up to the relaxed pose. He tugged at his Henley shirt neckline to give himself some more air. "How was school today?" he ventured.

"Why?" Her eyes swiveled to the ceiling.

"I've asked you that many times. I've never gotten that question as a response."

"That's because you and Mom have never split up before. I don't even know where my father lives, so why do you care about my school day?"

"Nancy, marriages don't always last forever. It doesn't mean I love you any less; it doesn't change our relationship."

She lowered her eyes and picked lint off her black stretch pants.

Danny continued to stand there, feeling worse by the second. His daughter diverted her eyes to the computer screen as if he were a pop up window she wanted to close.

"Come downstairs to help Mary as soon as you're finished. We'll all eat together."

"Nothing fancy, Danny," Mary said as he joined her in the kitchen. "I'm only microwaving Idaho potatoes." Annabel and Nancy padded down the stairs fifteen minutes later.

"We'll load 'em up," Mary said, grabbing cheddar cheese and sour cream from the refrigerator. Danny got bacon bits and butter and Nancy put utensils and napkins on the table. "Casey'll be here after the gym," Mary said. "He worked seven to three."

"I haven't had a chance to talk to him." Danny said, as he held potholders to slide hot potatoes out of the microwave. "Does he know?"

"I told him," Mary said softly as Danny narrowed his eyes. "Only a sentence or two. Facts only. Most of it should come from you. You are his best friend."

At the table, Danny reached for the tub of coleslaw, which Nancy hadn't passed to him. He scooped only one spoonful; he'd lost his appetite. "I'd like to take you girls to dinner this weekend, and show you my apartment." The girls remained distracted. "I'll ramp up efforts to see you," he added tentatively.

Annabel peered over at Nancy. "We'll see, Dad. Maybe."

Danny saw Mary sigh with partial relief. She finished putting dirty dishes into the dishwasher. He said good-night to the girls and walked through the hallway with Mary hobbling behind him. "Listen," he said turning to her. "I love you, sis."

"I love you, too."

He opened the front door to see Casey's Jeep pulling along side his car.

Casey had left the gym and detoured into a liquor store on the way to Mary's. He paced the wine aisle, trying to decide whether to bring a Riesling that she liked or surprise her with something different. Once he had bought her a white Russian in a bar lounge, which she had raved about. He'd get her a bottle of Kahlua. He spotted the yellow and red label between the Irish Creams and Amarettos, paid the cashier and left with the bottle in a flimsy paper bag.

Warm air blew from his Jeep vents. He cut if off, but left the fan on. The workout had made him sweaty and although he had showered in the meager locker room facilities, he still had a fresh, pulsating feeling from the cardiac conditioning. He decided to crack his window as well as to unzip his jacket.

Casey turned into the driveway, next to Danny's car as the motion lights over the garage doors flicked on. He shut off the engine as Danny exited the house. Casey stepped out, pushed his hip against the door and halted at the front bumper of Danny's vehicle.

"Danny, we need to talk. I'm the last to know."

Danny dug into his pocket, feeling around for car keys. "I'm sorry. It's been hectic."

"I bet it has."

"What the hell is that supposed to mean?"

"Just because everyone else is pussyfooting around you, doesn't mean I'm going to be an enabler."

Danny felt blood boom through his arteries, fueling the anger welling within him.

"It's her, isn't it?"

"Who?"

"The nurse."

"Yeah, so," Danny said and looked at the garage door panel.

"You know, you aren't the brightest light bulb in the cafeteria, are you?"

Danny's vision shot right back to Casey, piercing him. "What are you talking about?" he shouted. "Melissa would still be alive if you hadn't gone to the wrong house."

Casey's muscles rippled like steam in a glass tube. With a single sudden movement, Casey's right arm wielded a blow straight into Danny's face. The garage door pinged as Danny's body crashed into it, then Danny slid to the ground. A curtain of colorful stars danced before him as a perilous pain stabbed him in the middle of his face. He fumbled to get up as blood escaped from his nose.

Casey's arm muscles twitched for more. He could beat Danny to a pulp for what he had said. He could plaster him right into the cement if he wanted to. Instead, he used the minute to compose himself as Danny tried to straighten himself. Casey stepped to reach into his car for Mary's liquer and his small duffel bag. He ignored Danny's misery while he went into the house.

Mary watched the encounter from the glass panels along side the front door. She passed Casey. "What's wrong with you two?"

Casey shook his head. "Ask him. He's lucky I didn't kill him."

Danny hovered near the hood of his car, a small pool of red accumulating on the ground as he continued leaning forward. The pain was agonizing. His nasal bones must be pulverized and projected up into his brain.

Mary ran to him. "You're going to need ice. Are you still going to leave?"

Danny nodded and Mary hurried inside for a cold compress. When she came back out, Annabel and Nancy trailed her.

Annabel eyed Danny skeptically as she pulled her sweater together. "Do you need to go to the hospital, Dad?"

Danny ever so slightly shook his head no and held out his palm, stunting further discussion. Mary handed him a cloth with crushed ice and he drove off. To hell with him, he thought.

Before bed, Mary emerged from the master bathroom swinging a toothbrush in her right hand. Casey had stripped down to sleeping attire, a white cotton brief, and sat on the edge of the king bed, burying his head. Mary put the brush on the dresser and nestled along side him. She took his hands, uncovering his face.

"I know how thick you both are. You can't stay mad at each other forever."

Casey lightened his sad expression. "You're a ray of sunshine, Mary. Just like your artwork." He smoothed his palm along the peach satin pajamas she wore then kissed her upper lip. He kissed her bottom lip; then both of them together.

She closed her eyes, catching herself from drifting under his spell. "I've been wondering," she said. "I'm almost afraid to ask you. There is so much room here; it doesn't make sense for you to rent an apartment. Should we try a trial run of living together?"

"An excellent idea if you let me pay the utility bills." A smile crept across his face, inching seductively into a flashing white beam. "And make love more frequently with the woman who mesmerizes me." Mary's cheeks flushed to the color of her nightwear. "I love you," he said.

She locked onto his eyes. "I love you more."

Mary never used her toothbrush. Two hours later, Casey arose after falling asleep and switched off the bathroom light.

By elevating his head to reduce swelling and popping six-hundred milligrams of ibuprofen, Danny thought he would get some sleep. But even when he nodded off, strange dreams slithered their way into his mind. A green gremlin rummaged through his nose discarding osteoclast and osteoblast cells, responsible for bone resorption and bone formation. In the early morning, he panicked looking in the mirror to see a misshapen and swollen nose, the area under his eyes puffed up like dough, and the mid-facial color of the day … fresh purple.

This was going to make a memorable office day. By the looks of things, he would have to see an ear, nose and throat specialist within a day or two. On top of that, he still had to hire an attorney.

"What the hell happened to you?" Bruce said, as Danny passed him and Harold in the office hall.

Harold saw some humor and almost blurted "husband abuse for finding him cheating." Instead, he looked at Danny wide-eyed, as curious as his boss.

"A guy thing. An altercation."

Danny offered no further explanation. He went straight in to see a patient, whose jaw dropped. She stared fixated on his face and couldn't remember the speech she had prepared regarding the history of her headaches. "Ouch, that must hurt," she said.

Danny wrote for her to get a CT of the head, and went to call another attorney's office. This lawyer knew of the Neurosurgical Group of Middle Tennessee. The only way he agreed to see Danny on short notice was for a casual dinner at the end of the day. Another night Danny planned with Rachel shot to hell. Then he called the ENT doc in their medical building. “Charlie, its Danny Tilson. I took a punch in the face last night. Can you fit me in this afternoon?”

“Sure, we’ll page you later when I can see you.”

Three patients still had appointments with him late in the afternoon when Danny’s pager beeped. One thumbed through magazines in the waiting room and another talked on a cell phone in front of the please turn off cell phones sign. He saw Harold come out of an examining room.

“Can you do me a huge favor?” Danny asked.

“Depends.”

“I have to leave. ENT Charlie has to examine my nose and then I have an attorney’s appointment. I haven’t even hired a lawyer yet.”

“I’ll see your remaining patients, if that’s what you’re asking. You better get seen.” Harold took a patient’s chart from the plastic inbox on the wall. “I’d expect the same if I looked like you.”

Danny thanked his partner, hung his white coat and took the elevator upstairs. A nurse ushered him into an examining room and after several minutes his old med school colleague walked in. Skinny, bronzed and wearing the shaved head look, Charlie traded ENT for a guitar on the weekends. They shook hands while Charlie eyed the right and left profiles of Danny’s face.

“You could deemphasize your face if you wear psychedelic purple clothing.”

“Thanks,” Danny mourned.

Charlie pressed Danny’s surrounding orbital area then gently touched the outside of his nose. He used a nasal speculum and peered into his nostrils. Danny cringed.

“The bones and cartilage in your nose have been rearranged so I have to manually realign them,” Charlie said. “We’ll have to schedule a closed reduction of your nose within ten days of the fracture. The good news is you probably don't need surgery, but the bad news is you need to go to the OR anyway, for a general anesthetic.

"How about Friday?" Danny asked. "It's going to wreak havoc on our office and surgery schedule."

"Outpatient surgery. Don't eat or drink, etc. etc. Get your blood drawn for labs before you leave." He shook Danny's hand again. "Somebody did a nice job on you," he said as they both exited the room.

Danny could spot a lawyer anywhere. Mark Cunningham paced the restaurant lobby talking on a cell phone.

"I bet that smarts," Mark said, then introduced himself.

He looked to be sixty and Danny wondered why he still punished himself by practicing family law. The waitress escorted them to a wooden bench, Mark Cunningham following her with quick baby steps. Mark had the thickest brownish-grey hair Danny had ever seen.

Mark slapped a small tablet from his briefcase on the table while they waited for their appetizers. "How many years have you been married?" Mark asked. "What does your wife do? I need all the pertinents first."

"We were married in 1989."

"Almost twenty years," Mark said and scribbled the numbers.

"My wife taught biology until our third daughter was born. Since then, she's been at home."

Three girls, Mark wrote. "Names?"

Danny tried to swallow some ice water but it was as if an ice cube sneaked into his mouth and prevented it. "We lost a daughter."

"I'm sorry," Mark said. Danny gave him more facts as they ate.

"So for the divorce decree," Mark asked, "do I record 'irreconcilable differences' as the reason for the termination of the marriage?"

"I don't know. Is there a list of categories or options?"

Mark raised his eyebrows at Danny.

"What about falling in love with another woman?"

"Infidelity?"

Danny squirmed in his chair. Mark picked up his pen and wrote. *Irreconcilable differences*.

The waiter took their soup bowls as they continued. They leaned back while he placed steaming entrees before them. "As far as wrapping this up, the simpler the better," Danny said. "I don't want a drag out fight and I'm sure, neither does my wife."

"But just be prepared to lose most of whatever you've got," Mark said. "That's going to happen with or without prolongation. And with or without a shark as an attorney."

Danny hired the straightforward Mark Cunningham, went home to his apartment and called Rachel to say goodnight.

Chapter 18

Casey turned the key, poked his head into the hallway and shouted, "Hey, honey, I'm home."

Mary peered around the kitchen corner. "Wise ass," she said.

Casey planted the stuffed moving container on the kitchen island. Besides other personal possessions, he had moved a few favorite pieces of furniture, hi-tech gadgets and books to Mary's. He began finalizing his bills from the apartment, even forsaking his gym routine, and sealed the deal with address change notices.

"And don't you look dreamy," Casey said. Mary's long off-white popcorn sweater mirrored her creamy complexion.

"Likewise," she said. He still wore his uniform and leather jacket, having stopped at his apartment after a day shift to pack the remainder of his things. His steel arms embraced her; he swept her off her feet. Mary kissed him while he rooted her back to the floor.

She dripped honey into hot green tea. "I just finished stretching a canvas for my next project. Nice timing for a break." She sat on a stool, her hands wrapped around her mug. "Did you rescue any one today?"

"I like it when that happens. But no, not today. There weren't any major highway accidents or fires. We brought medical patients to the ER, mostly senior citizens noncompliant with their meds."

"How you love your work."

"We both have that in common." He took her hand, brought it to his lips, and kissed her fingers.

"Don't forget," she said, "this place is huge. Pick an area of the house when it's your turn to host poker. As long as you let me spy on a game."

"Absolutely."

"By the way, Danny is having his broken nose fixed tomorrow." She read his gloomy face. "I offered to take him home afterwards, but he declined."

"Hmm. I hope straightening his nose straightens his head."

"When are you two going to repair your friendship?"

Casey let the silence stretch. "Words can go too far, Mary. Like tottering on the end of a diving board. Danny took the plunge, now he can't undo it."

In the morning, Danny's stomach growled. He couldn't eat or drink before his impending trip to the OR. The sedation of his own OR patient before him had waned after Danny had numbed his scalp for incision, which would be the only painful part. Skull and brain have no sensation, so while the man lay totally awake, Danny planned to electrically stimulate his brain. The man would then have to look at slides and name the pictured objects.

"Just like you, I sure missed coffee this morning," he said to his patient, looking at his brain, as well as to Rachel, who fiddled with pointed instruments.

"Can't hardly going to be able to answer 'yer questions, doc, without drinkin a mud cup, either," said the man.

"You'll be fine, I'm sure," Danny said. "I'm going to tell this pretty nurse here what we are doing, if that's okay with you."

"Shure."

"Mr. Shane, here, has intractable seizures," Danny said. "We're going to do language mapping. He'll tell us what he sees when I stimulate areas of the brain, but once I stimulate the site responsible for language, he won't be able to."

"Then doc Tilson can treat me the right way," Mr. Shane piped through the drapes. "Like cut a little hole there to take out the bad part or something. But I saw a movie once, doc, they took a whole chunk of a guy's brain out. Maybe it was that there Stephen King guy who rote it. But, you ain't ganna do nothing like that to me, are yah?"

"No. But we need to get to work here, Mr. Shane. I'm going to surgery today, too."

"Good thing you're cutting on me before your brain gets split open like a watermelon, too. I'll try and shud up unless you want me to name them there pictures."

"That would be helpful, Mr. Shane."

Rachel had a major smile under her mask. "Dr. Tilson, I do plan on taking you home after your surgery later today."

"Hey, can yah take me home, too?"

Danny zapped him and he said, "That? That there is a fine basketball in that picture."

"Basketball is all you need to say," Mr. Shane.

Danny hurried through Mr. Shane's post op orders. He told his patient to schedule an office appointment in a week or two; Danny wouldn't take him off anti-convulsants for a few months. As Danny crossed the street to check himself into outpatient admitting, he despised his own upcoming procedure … one more rock in his shoe. An orderly threw him a flimsy gown to wear after he filled out forms and a nurse anesthetist started an IV. He used an adjacent wall phone to call Sara.

"The girls must be in school," he said. "I promised them dinner this weekend. Can you tell them not tonight? I'll be recuperating from having my nose fixed."

"I heard about that. Hope it's not scaring away your girlfriend." Sara bit her tongue too late. "But, I'll tell them. Should they expect you tomorrow night?"

"Yes. I'll pick them up at 5 o'clock."

When he laid on the stretcher, the nurse anesthetist crouched over him, slipped drugs through his IV and then they wheeled him to a room where he marveled at the strong overhead lights and saw Charlie's face magnified above him. Within a minute after the blood pressure cuff, EKG pads and pulse oximeter were attached, Danny was given an anesthetic cocktail. He heard someone say he'd gotten whacked by a paramedic as he drifted away.

Danny shivered on awakening in the recovery room; he tried to shake the strange images he had dreamed, of people lining along the stretcher to laugh at him. A familiar and pretty face came into view with a partially unbuttoned gold blouse and a rust v-neck sweater. "Hey, handsome," Rachel hummed.

"You're just saying that," he whispered.

"Except for the Easter colors, and the bandage, you may have a new and improved profile."

A recovery room nurse stepped between the drapes. "Dr. Tilson is doing fine. He'll be ready in thirty minutes and you can pull your car around."

"We can get your car in the morning when I have to go to work," Rachel said. She took his postop orders and went to get her car.

"I went home after work, changed and brought Dakota over to your apartment so I could spend the night," Rachel said when she opened the car door for Danny. "We'll drop him off at my place in the morning."

The middle of Danny's face throbbed; nausea tickled his throat, and he ducked from noticing Rachel speed beating yellow lights. He sunk his head back and only opened his eyes when they arrived. He expected Dakota to knock him over when Rachel unlocked the door, but Danny didn't see him. He beelined for the couch as a stealthy reddish figure slinked to the floor from the corner armrest.

"Hmm. Making yourself at home," Danny said.

Dakota performed a few figure eights, slapping Danny with his tail. Rachel brought a ginger ale, set it on a thick ceramic coaster then decided to get one as well. She took a sip after sitting on the floor next to Danny, who had laid down and centered his head into a plush corduroy pillow.

"You don't look so good yourself," Danny said.

"Oh, it's nothing," Rachel said, "just a little stomach virus." Danny furrowed his eyebrows, concerned. "I thought some ginger ale would help."

Danny laid his right hand on her neck, lightly rubbing it. "Glad my nose dilemma is over with."

"I agree." Rachel let more soda quench her queasiness. "Your case this morning was magnificent. I've never assisted for an awake crany."

"I thought your last job covered comprehensive big city neurosurgical cases?"

"You must be more skilled and advanced than many neurosurgeons, Danny."

He and Rachel channel surfed and stopped on a weather story. "I'll be back," Rachel said, grabbing Dakota's leash. "I'll take him for his last walk."

There were plenty of trees and shrubs behind the complex, so she guided Dakota to the back of the building. He lifted his leg several times on vertical growth, trumping the scent of previous stray male dogs. His tail and head bobbed with the excitement of new territory.

When they'd gone far enough, Rachel yanked him and headed back. A man came toward them, from a lighted breezeway near the clubhouse. "Ma'am," he said loudly into the cold air. "I don't know which unit you are in or if you are visiting someone, but dogs aren't allowed."

"I wasn't aware of that," she said apologetically. "I'll take care of it."

The man had run out without a coat, so wrapped his arms to his chest. His right arm rose, he waved to acknowledge her understanding, and hurried through the passageway. Rachel and Dakota disappeared around the building corner and ran to Danny's unit.

Inside, the Chessie's energy popped like a cork. He thoroughbreded into the back bedroom, pounced onto the bed and circled, digging into the bedspread. Part of it clumped into a central bird's nest. Rachel wrapped her arm around Danny's shoulders, and they followed the dog's path. Dakota lay in his newly created bed.

"Dakota," Danny said, "off."

Big amber eyes keyed to the direction of Danny's voice. The dog sighed and took a jump, then lay down with his head between his front paws.

"You'd swear I hurt his feelings," Danny said.

"You have. Now he'll do anything for you."

"I'd like him to play dead for a change." Danny straightened out some comforter to sit on the edge of the bed.

"Anything to make you happy." Rachel moved to gain eye contact with Dakota.

"Dakota, dead dog!"

Dakota shimmied his body to gain momentum, flipped and laid belly up.

"Damn," Danny said. "Sometimes I think that dog is a lot smarter than we give him credit for."

"No doubt."

Late the next afternoon, Danny crunched along pebbles in the cul-de-sac after stepping out of his car, not wanting to park in his old driveway. He headed toward the front door, but stopped instead when the girls came out. Nancy readjusted a bra cup deep through the top of her wooly jacket, not noticing her father's bewildered expression.

"What on earth? Are you wearing Ramen noodles?" he asked.

Nancy paused, one hip higher than the other and tilted her head. "That's not funny," she said. "It's my new hairstyle. It's called a perm."

"Well, your light brown curls are … very becoming."

"So is the new green," she smirked.

"Oh, that. My face hasn't decided what rainbow color to wear."

Danny drove to Downtown Italy, stupefied by his third daughter's alterations. Sometimes girls were a mystery to him. But, he felt some relief; the atmosphere seemed less thick than the other day.

Inside the restaurant, the aroma of Italian red sauce and pasta crept over Danny like awake electrical neurostimulation, reviving his memory of Downtown Italy's scents. His father had languished over their family business, he had depended on the restaurant's sustenance during med school, and …

A mature teenager reached for elongated menus. "How many?" he said.

"Three," Danny said.

The teen showed them a table, unfolded napkins for the girls, lingered his eyes on Annabel.

"Is Angelo here tonight?" Danny asked.

"Yes. Would you like him as your waiter?"

"Would appreciate that," Danny said. The young man poured them ice water and left.

Annabel slid her coat off her shoulders, exposing a ribbed camel sweater with mid length amber beads lying against her chest. His girls were becoming young ladies under his eyes.

"Dad, we've figured out Thanksgiving," Annabel said, placing a breadstick on a plate.

"Dad, are you listening? We're all eating early at Mary's, Casey, too. Later in the day when Mom goes home, you can come over. We'll have plenty of leftovers. Casey can go upstairs or something, if you want." She ran her tongue over her braces after nibbling away at her bread straw.

"Why doesn't Casey just go home?"

"Dad," said Nancy, filling in for her sister, "Casey and Mary are living together now."

"At grandpa's?"

"Well, yeah, you mean Mary's."

"Bon jorno." An exuberant Angelo bowed his head. "So pleased to see you."

"Angelo, you too," Annabel said.

"You girls are getting lovelier." He smiled at Nancy's locks. "Those waves are lapping against the sunshine of your face."

Nancy straightened from slouching. "Wow, thanks, Angelo."

"Now, where is your most beautiful counterpart?" Angelo asked Danny. "Shall I ask Gianni to make her favorite appetizer?"

"Mom and Dad," Annabel said, "are getting divorced."

"Dad doesn't live with us any more," Nancy said.

"I am sorry to know this," Angelo said, crestfallen. "But sometimes adults don't match together."

"No," Annabel said, "that wasn't it."

"Like, not at all," Nancy added.

Danny frowned, hid his face inside the menu jacket, and carefully avoided reading descriptions of Sara's favorite entrees.

Chapter 19

"I'm giving Dr. Tilson five more minutes," Mark Cunningham said to his secretary, "then I expect you to be gone and me not far behind." He slapped a file folder into her inbox for the morning just as Danny huffed and puffed his way through the double door, having taken the stairs two at a time instead of waiting for an elevator.

Danny heard a guttural "good evening" from Mark and followed him to a rather small and messy office. He sat in one of the two chairs in front of the desk while Mark plunged into a rolling black leather easy chair across from him. Silver plated bowling trophies lined the top of the bookcase behind his attorney and a studio photograph of Mark and his wife jutted out from the clutter on his desk.

"You're in vogue, going green," Mark said. "And ouch, that must have hurt."

Danny wanted to roll his eyes like a teenager. "It's fading," he said. "So what happened with my wife's attorney?"

"Her attorney, Jim Dorsey, is a babe just hatched, maybe hasn't even rolled a shaver over his face yet." He laughed, amused at himself. "Must've known somebody for Tom Werner's group to have hired him." Mark unpeeled a miniature piece of gum from a fancy square box and popped it into his mouth.

Mark quickly rolled and leaned forward as if the gum had an energy boost in it. "I've talked some sense into him, though. Told him he can experiment with his other cases, but this is how I see it: bicker, fight and spin paperwork for a few years or just get all the money dealing flat squared right off and you both sign divorce papers as soon as possible."

"I'm listening," Danny said.

"Child support." Mark scrambled through a paperwork pile and opened a yellow pad. "Figured from straight charts and your pay, give or take other info, comes to … both girls … thirty-two hundred a month. If your wife isn't a mall cruiser and takes care of your girls, she'll bank it for their college."

Danny gulped. "Whoe, slow down. I forgot to tell you something. My Dad left almost all his assets to my girls. They have a huge trust, payment starts when they turn eighteen. College is already taken care of. We can decrease payments to Sara."

"Every time I think I've seen it all, I haven't," Mark said. "Your girls are in for a big caboodle, but you're left out? I take it your father never dreamed his son would bail out of his marriage?"

Danny nodded, dumfounded. His lawyer had a talent to cut to the core.

"Your misfortune. Sorry, it won't change payment to your wife." He turned a yellow page. "Alimony," he said.

"My father gave Sara and me our house. Now she's in it, so she gets my only part of my father's inheritance to me. Why should I have to pay her alimony when she doesn't even have to pay a mortgage?"

"Doubly not smart family planning on your part," Tom exclaimed. "We can go back to the drawing board if you want to argue for the house. All this historical family info, again, probably won't impact the outcome."

Danny bit his tongue. It would take too much time, too much money in attorney fees to argue about it. He just wanted to ditch divorce conflicts and get on with a new life with Rachel. "Okay, tell me what they have up their sleeve regarding alimony."

"Jim Dorsey and I contemplated two scenarios, your choice. Big payments for ten years, then stop. Or, medium payments until your wife turns sixty-five. I made a point that she could always return to teaching and make her own living."

"What are we talking here?"

Mark looked at scribbled notes. "Twenty-eight hundred a month for ten years, or fifteen hundred a month for twenty-two years."

Danny's head spun. What would be left for him and Rachel?

"Each way has its advantages and disadvantages," Mark said lifting the pad towards him. "Your wife prefers bigger payments per month for ten years, but overall she'll get less by not going the sixty-five route. What would you like to do?"

Danny took a pen and calculated, taking his time, getting the number crunch correct. "I want to get this over with. Tell them ten years of payments."

Talk of tender turkey, pumpkin pie and NFL tradition circulated the OR as Danny began closing a patient's back the day before Thanksgiving. Harold and Danny had flip- flopped OR rooms all afternoon, rotating a lumbar laminectomy schedule that would have taken two days if he had been a resident. Besides conversation, the ventilator droned, a CD played and his beeper intermittently blared. All dependable sounds; the day had been smoother than any he had had in a few weeks. Maybe that night at Rachel's place he would bury himself in a novel. He looked forward to Thanksgiving Day off, except that he'd only see the girls and Mary later in the day.

Rachel had several days off. She left Nashville in the afternoon to go to her sister's in Chicago and had invited Danny to stay at her place. "Perhaps you could mind Dakota, so I wouldn't have to kennel him," she had said. "He would be in familiar surroundings."

Danny planted a large surgical needle into the patient's back, ready for the last, outer layer skin suturing as the room door swung open. Bruce held his hands out in front, signaling the scrub nurse to gown and glove him.

"You need to go to the office. I'll finish this," he scowled under his mask. The suture in Danny's hand poised in mid-air.

"You're being served," Bruce said.

Danny couldn't fathom it; Sara wanted an expeditious split as much as he did. Why would she be serving him with some kind of divorce papers unless she had reconsidered the settlement? He stepped to the side, gave Bruce medical and surgical details of the case, and left.

A uniformed man rose from a chair in the office waiting room. He walked to Danny, shoved an envelope with a face-slip into his hands. "Wet out there, Doc," the man said, sliding on a black jacket with a slender furry collar. "Sign there."

Danny went to the seclusion of his office. Behind his desk, he glanced between the serenity of the fishing print on the wall, and the white stuffed envelope. Finally, he slit it open.

Susan Dexter, Plaintiff, vs. Daniel Tilson, M.D. and The Neurosurgery Group for Middle Tennessee, Defendant. A shudder slinked under his shoulders and ran down his arms. A medical malpractice suit; virgin territory. He couldn't remember names of patients from one week to the next. Who was Susan Dexter?

Danny trudged through the papers, every sentence causing panic and dread. Incriminating words scolded him: *said doctor caused the patient's delayed diagnosis; he mismanaged, he delayed treatment, he misdiagnosed, patient suffered severe pain and complications*. And worst of all, a core shattering accusation: *Dr. Tilson practiced negligently*.

The lawsuit charged him with flagrantly dismissing Susan Dexter's symptoms and diagnosis. He had ordered an MRI; the radiologist's report clearly described images of plaque denoting myelin loss, consistent with multiple sclerosis, or MS. Yet, he had told the plaintiff her MRI was negative, and that nothing was wrong with her, preventing her from seeking further medical treatment and self care. *The patient's continued symptoms caused great dysfunction, pain and suffering. Treatment with steroids, intravenous drugs, physical therapy, appropriate self-care etc. was delayed because of Dr. Tilson.*

Danny put the legal document on his desk and sat staring at *Grandpa and Boy Fishing* for a long time.

Dakota pulled a throw pillow off Rachel's couch, placed his head on it after dropping it, and lay intermittently opening his lids to monitor Danny. Danny didn't feel as comfortable as the dog; the lonely holiday afternoon magnified his problems. He had flicked through every station and drank as much apple cider as he could stomach.

"Come on, Dakota," Danny said. "I'll walk you before I leave for a few hours." The dog jumped up, got the leash off a kitchen island hook and dragged it across the floor.

"Good boy," Danny said, snapping it on. He couldn't believe he was talking to a dog. Thanksgiving Day, no less. When he brought Dakota back in at five o'clock, he left for Mary's.

The dog walk had warmed Danny against the chill; the strange day hinted at mixed seasons. Cold and damp, then crisp and sunny. He left his jacket unzipped after getting out of the car in Mary's driveway, and went straight in the unlocked door without knocking, especially since Sara's car wasn't around. Casey was midway in the hallway, almost to the stairs. Each of them waited for the other one's move.

"You don't have to disappear," Danny said.

The somber look on both their faces relaxed. "Your family deserves more from you," Casey said, "but you've been my best friend forever." He extended his right hand. Danny clasped it, their torsos briefly embraced.

"Happy Thanksgiving," Danny said.

"You too," Casey said.

Both men walked to the kitchen where half the assortment of pots, pans and dishes still littered the counters and where the smell from Mary and Casey's cooking intensified. Annabel poked Nancy, throwing her eyes in the direction of the two men. "You and I don't even make up that fast," Annabel whispered.

"Hey, Dad," Nancy said, giving Danny a small hug. "My hair's the same."

"I notice that. It's growing on me," Danny said. "Happy Thanksgiving everybody."

"We've got a feast for you," Mary said. "And we're ready for a turkey sandwich."

Parity Medical Malpractice Corporation sent two attorneys. Bruce and Danny had set the meeting for 4:30 p.m. in their small conference room. Only a week later, their malpractice carrier wanted the facts and wanted to meet the physician in question: what kind of believability, credibility, and sincerity did he have as the defendant in a courtroom? The plaintiff's attorneys would waste no time initiating discovery, and if depositions were forthcoming, the Parity attorneys wanted to get their client ready.

Danny thought they would send a senior and junior attorney. But that wasn't the case. A female and male attorney, who had both worked for Parity for almost twenty years and seen their share of medical litigation, sat with Starbuck cups and legal paperwork. They cracked small smiles and shook hands robustly when both doctors entered.

"Ms. Stewart," Bruce said, "thank you for the prompt visit."

"You are welcome," she said. Call me Stewart; it's my first and last name. And Mr. Argon, here, will tell you to call him Richard."

According to Annabel and Nancy, femininity was back in vogue, but that wasn't obvious with the business-like female before them.

Bruce nodded. "First a few questions," Richard said. He asked Danny for his full name, the number of years he trained and practiced, and whether he was board certified. Stewart confirmed the information she had or wrote on their forms. "What is your address?"

Danny told them. "It's different than what we have," Stewart said. "Have you moved? And are you married?"

"It's a relatively new apartment. My wife is in our house. We are separated and filing for divorce."

"Defendant going through divorce, left residence," Stewart mumbled while writing.

"What does that have to do with anything?" Danny snapped. He expected a reply but they ignored him. The attractive woman slid her eyeglasses along the bridge of her nose with polished nails.

"Danny," Bruce said, "Richard asked for Susan Dexter's chart, which you are leaning on."

Danny slid the chart across the table; the chart went from one attorney to the next, as if they had done it hundreds of times.

"Your note from the patient's last office visit," Stewart said, "clearly reads: MRI negative. Impression, it states: patient's symptoms not neurological, perhaps psychiatric. Plan: no further evaluation, patient to return prn." She looked at Danny. "That means to return when and if needed, correct?"

"Yes," Danny said.

"The MRI radiologist's report is also here on the chart, which I am sure you have read since the allegations."

"But, usually we read the MRI or CT independent of the radiologist. We are experts reading these, and since we deal more thoroughly with the brain than they do, we can read them better. I had the MRI before the radiologist's report, which is often the case."

"So Dr. Tilson, let me get this straight. If you are smarter than a radiologist, then why weren't you smart enough to make the diagnosis based on radiologic evidence?"

"Look, whose side are you on anyway?" Danny said, rolling a pen along the table.

"Just trying to play devil's advocate here," Richard said.

"Just trying to see how composed you would be under cross-examination," Stewart said.

"This isn't a neurosurgeon's arena anyway, this case," Danny said. "We don't operate on or treat for MS, so it wasn't my job. Patients with multiple sclerosis are treated by neurologists."

"But certainly, like you said, neurosurgeons are savvy with head images," Stewart said. "It was your job to at least suspect

MS by the, err, what do you call them, plaques, and refer the patient immediately to a neurologist."

"But you were busy leaving your wife of how many years? Because of irreconcilable differences?" Richard asked. "Or at least we hope that was the reason."

Danny shot up from his seat, and leaned over the conference table.

Bruce, Stewart and Richard stared blankly at him then Stewart tapped her pen on the polished surface. "Like we said, Dr. Tilson, we are ascertaining what the plaintiff's attorney can do to you."

As Danny gathered his brief case and coat from his office an hour later, Bruce appeared in the doorway dressed in a long dark coat. "Good night," he said.

"Good night," Danny replied. Bruce scowled.

"The cost of our malpractice policy better not go up."

"I know. We've had clean records until now." Bruce had already told him twice.

On the way home, Danny called Rachel. "I'm going to my apartment. Will you come spend the night?"

"I'll be there, Dakota in tow."

Danny straightened his bed sheets while waiting for her, and then ripped open two day's worth of mail. One envelope had the return address of his attorney. Mark Cunningham had forwarded correspondence he received from Tom Werner's office.

You are maliciously late in child support and alimony. You are proving yourself noncompliant right away; you risk a motion for contempt of court. We will garnish your wages if payment is not received in this office in several days. Blah,

blah, blah to the bottom of the eleven-inch white page, barely leaving room for Jim Dorsey's signature and name.

Danny snapped open a beer can, slugged some down, and paced the room. Why did they have to mail such a mean letter? All Sara or her attorney should have done was to ask him or remind him.

In the meantime, Rachel gathered a shoulder bag and an overnight duffel bag from her front seat. She took Dakota's leash in her free hand and quickly spun him for a walk around the building, avoiding landscape lighting. Several bushes made ample fire hydrants and Dakota readily cooperated, but before she could sneak away, the man who had cited apartment pet rules to her had exited the office door.

"Miss, I thought I told you before, dogs can't stay here."

His proximity was too close to act deaf, she could see his cold breath. "I'm just walking him," she said, offended. "I'm leaving."

The man pulled a cap over his ears; he walked away in a different direction. With Dakota's leash held taut, Rachel quickly pranced the two of them into Danny's apartment. Dakota bumped Danny, pressing him for acknowledgement, while Rachel placed her bag on the counter, unzipped it and slipped her leather gloves inside.

"What's wrong?" Rachel asked. "Nothing's gone sour with your business partners, has it?"

"No," he said. He unsnapped Dakota, curled the leash and put it next to Rachel's bag. He kissed her while pressing his palms behind her head, reining her in for the moistness of her lips and juicy curves.

"Let's just cozy up together on the couch," Rachel said as they parted. "I'm so tired, you'll have to do all the channel surfing."

Chapter 20

Rachel counted instruments and lap sponges with the circulating nurse, while Danny finished the surgery closure, his last case before afternoon patients. The office was closing at 3 p.m., a considerate gesture from Bruce, to give staff an early day for mall shopping the last Friday before Christmas day. Danny wanted to shop for the girls and Mary, as well as Rachel. He had given it much thought; to buy a moderate length chain with a diamond, to sparkle like angel dust around Rachel's neck. He looked over to her aqua eyes.

She glanced at Danny when they finished counting. "It was very nice working with you, Dr. Tilson," she said.

"Why, likewise, it always is," Danny said. He snapped off latex gloves while the anesthesiologist unclutched the table foot brake, and swung the head of the OR table towards her machine and medical equipment.

"Stewart and Richard just called," Bruce said later in the office, while pouring old coffee into the sink. "Your deposition is here next week. Do your homework beforehand, please, and reread the patient's chart." Bruce dumped the used filter caked with coffee grounds into the garbage. “It probably wouldn’t hurt if you read about MS this weekend, either.”

Danny nodded. “I was thinking the same thing.” He fitted a fresh filter into the coffee maker. Both men peeked in the cabinet and agreed on a New Orleans chicory blend; Danny filled the filter two-thirds, poured in water, and pressed the power button.

At sunset, as artificial light poured onto the concrete parking lot, Danny quickly stepped into the indoor mall near Opryland. Red, green and white strung lights hung on artificial trees and Christmas music blared. He passed a line of elementary school children, with tired parents, waiting in line to see a plump Santa Claus. He stopped at a kiosk to admire women’s bags; perfect, he thought for Nancy and Annabel, even Mary. He purchased sporty but functional taupe, sandalwood and navy woven purses. In the next aisle, he bought them each matching wool hats, gloves and scarves, all in a neutral cream color to coordinate with their bags. Casey had taught him how to shop for women after all.

Nearby, he went to the first counter of an international jewelry store, browsing at necklaces. He skipped the beads, pearls and birthstones and found a variety of gold chains and chokers. A woman came to help, telling him her own likes and dislikes. He put his selection on credit, almost five hundred for a flat choker, with a gold triangle in front with a baby diamond. It certainly wasn’t a minor gift. Under his new circumstances, the price was hefty.

Rachel gave Dakota a walk before they piled into her car; she placed him all the way in the back, avoiding boxes, bags and suitcases already there. “Wait here,” she said, and cracked the window. She walked into the townhouse office to take care of business, wished them happy holidays and headed to Danny's apartment. Danny had told her he wouldn't be home until eight that night, but she could make herself comfortable beforehand. He would even bring in a pepperoni pizza; they could unwind with a movie.

Before getting out of the car, Rachel stuck Danny's key into her pocket. She pulled the corduroy collar of her sporty jacket around her neck, grabbed Dakota's leash, and stepped out into a gust of wind. The temperature had dipped to the lowest of the season so far. She'd been a southern girl all her life so she didn't welcome a freezing wind chill, but it was a different story for her dog whose breed hunted waterfowl in icy rugged conditions. They could retrieve in the most strenuous conditions, face wind and swim in tides, break ice with their powerful chests. The colder the temperature, the friskier the dog.

She opened the hatchback to leash him, then hurriedly jogged to Danny's apartment door while Dakota jumped up, trying to grab the end of his red leash. "It's not a good time to try and walk yourself," Rachel said. The dog wanted no part in obeying her; he continued springing up to hold the leash end himself, like the tenderness to hold fowl instilled in his genes. Rachel dug the key out, opened the door, and they went inside where she unsnapped him, ducked back out and ran to her car. She picked up a medium sized bag of Purina and an aluminum bowl.

Dakota considered the thick leash on the chair. He clasped it in his jaw, ran around the table with kinetic energy mounting like a storm. He let go of it when his amber eyes spied a potential raceway - the wooden floor to the back bedroom. His hindquarters tucked lower than his shoulders, and gathering momentum, he lurched ahead. Well-webbed feet zoomed along the hardwood surface, now a formula 1 racetrack, bedroom in sight. Once he hit the doorway there was no stopping. The powerfully built Chessie plummeted into Danny's bed full force, vaulting onto it with such brute muscle that the mattress moved, sliding into the headboard as well as shifting sideways. He pawed at the bedspread, clumping it towards the middle. He circled to survey his efforts, gave it one last raking, and plopped into his berth.

Once back inside, Rachel eyed the red leash strewn over the floor, and placed the dried food bag and bowl on the counter. She cupped her hands over her mouth while exhaling to warm them, found a pen and a pad advertising an anti-seizure medication and wrote Danny a note.

Rachel walked to the rear following the absence of the dog. At the doorway, she chuckled at the sight: Dakota rounded into a ball; intelligently closing his eyes to sway her into thinking he was asleep.

Rachel stepped closer to the corner of the box spring, where the mattress was jimmied off its top.

"What's this?" she said, pushing the mattress up to get a better view of a wedged burgundy leather case. She pulled it out and sat on the tossed bed near Dakota who didn't budge. She ran her warmed fingers over dark blocked monogramming: DT.

Rachel opened the closure then tilted it to slide out the contents: a book and a baggie with a bracelet fell out. A very nice bracelet. She felt the smoothness of the gems; she could live with this color, or better yet, she could save the jewelry for later.

But why would anyone hide a stupid book? It looked old due to its dull binding color; she never saw books made like that any more. She picked it up. *Relativity: The Special and the General Theory*. Opening the cover, she read the title again as well as … *by Albert Einstein*. And right there, could it be? The gigantic genius's own autograph? Now she knew why the slipcase was concealed out of sight. She glided the bracelet onto her wrist, stuck the baggie back inside. She wondered if the book would fit into the deep wide pocket under the brown corduroy flap of her jacket so she stood to align the book to the outside size of the pocket. Yess. The leather case with Danny's initials she correctly placed where she found it.

Rachel walked to the other side of the bed. "Dakota," she said. "I'm sorry, boy. I need to disturb you." Grabbing him by the collar, she coaxed him off, realigned the mattress on the box spring and straightened the bedspread. "Looks like you weren't even here."

She walked out of the back room while Dakota reluctantly trotted after her. At the front door, she leaned over the dog to give him a kiss on his broad skull. "You'll be fine, I'm sure of it," she said. She gave him one more acknowledgement by sinking her fingers into his curly top coat. "And thanks, Dakota, for the nice find."

In the apartment breezeway, Danny unlocked his mailbox and took out advertisements and envelopes and dropped them into one of the Christmas shopping bags. He ducked into the office to pay his rent for next month so he wouldn't forget. A woman ran a vacuum cleaner around a coffee table and smiled over at him as he pulled out his envelope with a check and dropped it in the payments box slot. A sign stood propped on the counter announcing that the office would close for two weeks over the holidays and gave a number in case of a maintenance emergency. Danny waved at the woman as he went back out the door. "If you see that elderly office manager, would you mind telling him that Dr. Tilson said to have a nice holiday?"

"He no here," she said, wrapping the cord around the vacuum. "He go on vacation."

"Good for him," Danny said. "You have a pleasant holiday, too."

With the shopping parcels and bag set down, Danny felt for his key, but could have sworn he heard a few low barks inside. Dakota stopped barking as Danny swung open the door.

He put all his things on the coffee table to free his hands, then sat down to return Dakota's rambunctious greeting. "Hey, boy, are you minding my place?" He patted the dog firmly, scratched the base of his tail as Dakota stretched his neck and mouthed the air in appreciation. "You know, I could get permanently used to you."

The mail jutted out of the shopping bag, so Danny opened the first envelope, just a credit card solicitation. The second was a bulky manila envelope from Mark Cunningham. Much of the contents were typed documents regarding the divorce details they had worked out. The actual divorce papers to be signed were also included with a cover letter stating it was one of the fastest divorces for a surgeon. Danny unzipped his jacket, took a pen from his breast shirt pocket and signed underneath Sara's signature. The last two pages of the packet were attorney bills, but there must have been a mistake. Danny's bill was large enough, but Sara's was inadvertently attached, it being the more expensive of the two.

Danny put the mail to the side, turned on the flat screen TV, and walked down the hallway to the bedroom. Perhaps somehow Rachel had not taken her car and was tucked in his bed taking a nap. But she wasn't there, so he went to the refrigerator for a soda and found the number for take out pizza. He dialed and asked for a large pepperoni. He gave the man directions and his name and spotted Rachel's note.

"It'll be twenty minutes," said the voice on the other end, "and thirteen ninety-five."

Danny hung up and leaned over. Elegant handwriting, as feminine as Rachel herself.

Dear Danny,

I'm leaving Nashville for awhile. Have a nice holiday with your girls. Please take care of Dakota.

Love, Rachel

Danny read it three times, then again as he sat on the couch. He turned it over, wanting to see more words, an entire explanation. But there weren't any. Beyond the paper in his hands, there were two big amber eyes gazing at him. "What do you know, Dakota? Did she go to her sister's in Chicago?" The dog pressed his muzzle on Danny's knee.

The pizza arrived semi-warm but dripping with oil, New York style, the way Danny liked it. He ate the first slice quickly, sipping a beer behind it, and then waved the crust at Dakota. "Dead dog," Danny said. Dakota obeyed, then sprang up, and sat erect. "Gimme five," Danny said. Dakota pranced both paws into the air, and then snapped down the chunk of pizza crust, bonding with Danny forever.

In the morning, Danny walked Dakota and mailed the signed divorce papers. He drove to the hospital late in the morning for rounds; Harold and Danny had split up the weekend call and Danny chose Saturday. After seeing patients and taking care of notes and orders he went to the lounge, poured fresh coffee, and thumbed through papers for the latest newspaper. He read a section of *The Tennessean* and occasionally glanced at television, which showed the newly elected President giving a speech. Would wise change come?

At two-thirty Danny left the lounge and went to the ER, to see if there were any potential neuro cases before he left and to check on Casey's schedule. The ER was busy for an afternoon, but nothing that needed his evaluation. When Danny inquired about Casey's whereabouts, the secretary at the desk pointed outside the glass doors to the ambulance.

The back doors of the truck were open. Casey buckled an empty stretcher, tidying the inside at the end of his shift. "Hey, stranger," Danny said.

"Hey, you coming or going?"

"Leaving. If you don't have plans, how about late lunch, early dinner? My treat when you're finished. Downtown Italy."

Casey beamed. "Sure thing. Mary and I don't have any special dinner plans."

"Meet you there," Danny said.

Inside Downtown Italy, the linen topped tables aligned into several sitting areas for catered parties that evening. The maitre d' showed Danny to a table for two near the entrance. He watched pedestrians walk briskly, sometimes stopping at decorated store fronts.

"Hope you didn't wait too long," Casey said when he entered. "I had forgotten. I promised a patient I would help him at the end of my shift."

A stocky waiter politely interrupted to describe the special of the day.

"What did you do for him?" Danny asked when the waiter left.

"You're not going to believe this one. Mark and I made an ambulance run today. We find this man in his house having a heart attack, clutching at his chest, pain running down his arm." Casey paused, taking a sip of water. "We're extracting as much information from him as we can while hooking him to oxygen, taking his vitals. While he's grasping for air, he's telling us, 'Go to the bedroom closet. You gotta take the women's clothes out of there.' So Mark says 'take your wife's clothes out of the closet?' The man shakes his head no, tells us his wife is away and the woman he's having an affair with left clothes in their closet. His wife will find them if he's taken to the hospital." Casey unsnapped his cell phone from his belt and placed it aside. "I pointed out to him that we wouldn't know his girlfriend's clothes from his wife's clothes."

"What did he say to that?"

"As he was practically having another heart attack on top of the heart attack, he then told us to get rid of all the women's clothes in the closet."

Danny sat stunned by the desperation of it.

"As we're wheeling him out on a stretcher, we told him we couldn't do that anyway. After my shift, I asked him if he had contacted someone to help him with that, like I promised. A friend was going over there. And the patient is next in line for the cardiac cath lab."

"That poor man," Danny said.

"Lately, I'm facing the same lesson in my personal and professional life."

"What's that?" Danny asked.

"Not to be judgmental."

"And my recent lesson," Danny added "is not to say things I don't mean."

The pager vibrated on Danny's waist as he read the menu "It's not the hospital," Danny said, checking the number. "Good thing. I've got a dog to walk by this evening."

"Since when do you own a dog?" Casey asked as Danny pulled out his cell phone and dialed.

"It belongs to Rachel."

"Wellington's Life Care," someone said on the line.

"Yes, someone paged me, it's Dr. Tilson."

"Dr. Tilson, this is Charlotte, at the front desk. We've been refurbishing here, as well as decorating and rummaging through storage cabinets. Someone found a small paper bag with a few of your father's things. Can you pick them up?"

"Sure. I'll stop by later." Danny shrugged his shoulders. "That was Dad's nursing home. Apparently we've left some of his items."

"Thank the chef for us," Danny said to the waiter as they left. Casey and Danny parted outside the door. "Say hi to Mary," Danny said. "I'll bring the wine on Christmas Eve."

Two volunteers straightened lopsided blinking lights hanging in the center foyer while Danny passed them on his way to the front desk. The smell of pine and wintergreen shrouded Wellington's smell of disinfectant. The woman he had spoken with, Charlotte, recognized him, picked up a plastic bag and waved it in the air.

"Thank you," Danny said.

"Hope it's nothing important since it's been sitting here. It has your Dad's name on the masking tape label," she said.

"Appreciate the call," Danny said, turning to leave. He had an afterthought, however, and stopped.

"I don't know how it works, but can someone else bring Dakota here to visit the patients besides Rachel? Perhaps my daughters?"

"Dakota?"

"Rachel's therapy dog."

Charlotte stared blankly at Danny.

"Rachel is a nurse. She has a trained therapy dog named Dakota. They come here."

"Dr. Tilson, we have never had a handler with their therapy dog volunteer here. I wish we did, it's a wonderful idea. But I would know about it, I'm in charge of resident activities."

Chapter 21

The hectic pace in the office kept Danny so busy on Monday that his first opportunity to contact Mark Cunningham only arrived as Stewart and Richard readied with the plaintiff's attorney to take Danny's deposition.

"Mark," Danny said, calling from his office, "I put the signed divorce papers in the mail over the weekend along with a check for your legal fees. But, you accidentally sent me Sara's bill. Want me to send it back?"

Mark cleared his throat. "Jim Dorsey and Sara have requested that you pay it. If you don't they'll just bring it before a Judge."

A cloud of confusion agitated Danny. Hadn't he given them everything they'd asked for? Why did he deserve this? "Mark, why should I pay her bills? I'm already actually paying the bill since I'm giving her most of my income. She can pay it from the alimony."

"It doesn't work like that, Danny."

"Why the hell not?"

"It's called discrepancy of income. You have the income stream and she doesn't."

"Mark. I've been very nice about this. Maybe we should take this one to a Judge."

"Whatever you say. I'll try to counter it at a Monday morning motion hour."

"What's that?"

"Quick motions are argued before a Judge on Monday mornings. The Judge gives snappy decisions, but if the subject lingers, or isn't clear, then actual court time is scheduled for longer arguments before the bench." Mark waited. "Danny is that what you want?"

"Go for it," Danny said. "Enough's enough."

A court reporter sat at the head of the conference room table, catty-corner to Bruce, who thumped his fingers on the table. The Parity attorneys spread folders in front of them, which bordered the scattering of paperwork created by the plaintiff's attorney. If the stack size of legal documents indicated who was ahead in the case, then the plaintiff's attorney had the impetus to win.

As Danny took a seat after an introduction to Susan Dexter's attorney, Mr. Ward, his mind searched for upcoming events that would jeopardize attending the Monday morning court time. He would like to see Mark argue for him, but it would again require rescheduling either office visits or surgeries.

The court reporter busily ran his fingers over the stenotype machine then sat motionless, waiting on Danny. So did the hard staring Mr. Ward.

"Danny," Bruce bellowed. "Please answer the questions."

The plaintiff's counsel introduced Danny into the record by asking personal information, medical education and training, years and sites where he practiced. Twenty minutes later, he asked Danny the first question regarding his client, Susan Dexter. By then, questions from the sharply dressed attorney with the annoying facial tic were as welcome as a pack of preschoolers screeching in their waiting room.

"Early this year you saw a thirty-eight year old female patient named Susan Dexter. Is that correct?" Mr. Ward asked.

"That is correct."

"And for the record, you have her chart?"

"Yes, right here," Danny said.

"On her first visit, what where the symptoms she reported to you?"

"She experienced weakness in her legs, the right one greater than the left. She said she had been fatigued and had experienced one episode of decreased vision."

"What did you write first in the physical exam section of your office note?"

"She pointed to the middle of her back, describing an electric shock type sensation when she bent down or over."

"Dr. Tilson, are you aware of the prevailing age of onset for MS and it's predilection for the female sex?"

"Yes."

"Please state that for the record."

"It's twice as common in women as men and the normal onset is between twenty and forty."

"It states here Susan Dexter is thirty-eight years old. Is it possible she didn't recognize her symptoms for several years, but when she most needed treatment from a doctor, and came to you for help, you failed her?"

Mr. Ward flapped shut his folder and kept going. "Is it true treatments can modify the course of the disease?"

"Yes, but …"

"Can't MS lead to permanent disability?"

Danny looked to Stewart and Richard, who couldn't bail him out. After they broached Danny's misreading of the MRI, but the correct radiologist's report, Danny yearned for the inquisition to be over.

"How long can I trust you to plug your bladder?" Danny said aloud to Dakota two days later, as the dog awarded Danny with his full attention. "I worry how long I leave you. Rachel hasn't even called about you. Hasn't called to talk to me, either. And I get some weird message about a ten digit number when I call her cell phone."

Danny watched Dakota lying on the tweed braid rug in the kitchen, walked over to him and smoothed his fingers along his face to the base of his ears. Dakota's tongue lunged, plastering Danny's nose. "At least your kisses are just wet, not slobbery like some dogs," Danny said approvingly. He took two bottles of Riesling from the refrigerator and placed them in velvet green bags. After wrapping Christmas presents, he put them back in the original mall shopping bags, but left Rachel's necklace. "This is staying here," he said, putting the white satin box on the counter, near Rachel's note, which he had read every day. The dog cocked his head, his loosely hanging ears becoming more alert.

"What the heck, Mary won't mind. You're coming with me."

Dakota sprang up, bumping Danny's legs, and ran to the door.

When Danny arrived, the motion sensor set off the driveway lights. The garage door was open with Casey's Jeep inside. Dakota sniffed his way along the garage floor, Danny unleashed him and they entered the kitchen.

One hundred forty-four letters of the Scrabble alternative, Bananagrams, lay on the table. Casey, Mary, Annabel and Nancy each had their own ivory tiles methodically arranged into networks of words. They glanced over at Danny's entrance while hearing a skirmish on the floor as Dakota bumped Mary's elbow, sending her forearm forward into her puzzle pieces. A strong straight tail swiped Annabel, followed by paws stepping on feet under the table and Nancy's chair being knocked two inches from where she sat. Casey peered under the tablecloth, coming face to face with Dakota. Annabel and Nancy flung out from their chairs and crouched to the floor as the dog swung around to greet them, beating Casey in the face with his tail.

"Merry Christmas Eve," Danny said. "This is Dakota."

"He's got like sprouty reddish hair!" Nancy exclaimed.

"When did you get a dog?" Annabel asked.

"He's huge," Nancy said with dismay,

"He's not mine. He's on loan," Danny said, attempting to grab Dakota by the collar to make him sit, but the dog ducked deeper under the table when he realized Danny's intent.

Casey pushed his chair out, locked onto his collar and guided him out.

"Sit Dakota," Danny said. Dakota sat and everyone began petting him in a closed circle. Annabel tried hugging him and fell against him. He laid down in complete bliss.

"Awesome dog," Casey said.

"Yeah, we're becoming a twosome," Danny said. "Mary, do you mind that I brought him?"

"How could anyone turn away those eyes?"

Like his master's eyes, Danny thought, and wondered when Rachel would call. Danny ran out to the garage and brought back bags of presents and the wine bottles. They had aborted their Bananagram game and everyone sat ogling over Dakota in the great room. Danny broke off a chunk of bread from a baguette on the counter, opened a bottle of wine, and bused three glasses on a tray inside. "Dig into the bags everybody," he said. "And open your Christmas presents."

"Dad, did you get Dakota a present?" Nancy asked. Dakota nudged behind her noodled hairdo to lick an ear. She giggled and locked her arm around him. "Can't he be a new member of the family?"

"Really, he doesn't belong to me, so frolic with him while you can."

Before going to sleep late that night, Danny checked his telephone recorder. Not one message. He put Rachel's Christmas present on top of the mantle and went to bed.

"Hope you had a nice Christmas," Cheryl said, putting a stack of lab work results on Danny's desk before they were filed.

"It was too quiet." Danny said. "But you look rosy. Santa must have been good to you." Danny's extension rang; he picked it up, and waved to Cheryl that he would attend to the charts.

"Danny, it's Mark. Your motion's scheduled for Monday. I can meet you in the lobby of the courthouse if you'd still like to attend."

"I'll be there. How long will it take?"

"It's from eight to nine. I'll meet you at seven fifty-five."

"Okay," Danny said and hung up. He called Cheryl back into his office.

"I must be in court Monday morning from eight to nine. So, I'll be a little late for office hours." He flipped open the first chart. "I suppose I'll have to start hospital rounds by 6 a.m."

"I'll take care of the office," Cheryl said.

Monday morning Danny's alarm screamed at four-thirty. He had to hit the road for the hospital by five-fifteen, but needed enough time to get ready, make coffee to open his eyes and perform the new chore in his life … walking the dog. He grudgingly went through the motions besides taking a to-go cup out the door and sipping as he drove, breaking his long held belief of not talking on a cell phone or drinking or eating while driving. Many of the patients whose heads he had repaired had confessed doing those things prior to their accidents.

When Danny arrived, he thought Mark looked too cheerful, not sympathetic enough about his circumstances. With all the recent legal charades brought on by his now ex-wife, Danny felt inundated. He wanted some compassion and encouragement.

Mark walked briskly, charging ahead into a packed courtroom, turning to hand Danny the several page motion he had submitted. Lawyers stood and sat, some with clients, most without. Uniformed court guards lurked off to the side up front and a black robed Judge already sat adjusting his glasses as someone placed stacks of folders on his bench. Mark tugged at Danny, parting a crowd to find a spot to sit.

Danny finally heard "Tilson vs. Tilson." Mark started talking from where he stood, acknowledging his presence, making his way towards the front. A young man across the aisle also slinked to the aisle, Jim Dorsey, Sara's attorney.

"Mr. Cunningham, Mr. Dorsey, it appears this divorce is finalized. I take it you both have the financial settlement and custody matters finalized without dragging it through family court?"

"Yes, your Honor," Mark said.

"Your honor," Tom began, "my client expressed an interest not to hound her ex-husband for anything more than that which is fair and equitable."

The Judge waved away his small talk. "Mr. Dorsey, spare the melodramatic. This is motion hour. Now," he said, peering over the rim of his glasses. "Mrs. Tilson is requesting Dr. Tilson to pay her nine-thousand dollar and some cents legal bill, to date. Your doctor client has a problem with that, Mr. Cunningham?"

"Your Honor, Doctor Tilson has previously not disputed giving anything to his ex-wife. He gave her the house he inherited from his father, more than adequate child support and alimony…"

"That is very commendable of your client, Mr. Cunningham. Now let's get to the meat of it. Your client makes an income with a number that is followed by five zeroes. His ex-wife makes an income with no real number because it is a zero. Haven't you heard of disparity of income, Mr. Cunningham?"

"Yes, your Honor."

"Dr. Tilson is ordered to pay Mrs. Tilson her legal fees, including any fees to commence the resolution of this issue." With that, he pounded his gavel on its block for the next motion.

Mark and Danny unobtrusively peeled out of the courtroom along the sidewall. "Mark, I'm mixed between feelings of anger and depression. I'm actually glad I went. It opened my eyes further to the system."

"Join the working man's dilemma," he said. "Actually, sometimes these days, it's a working woman's dilemma, too, if she was married to a deadbeat."

Danny wished him a good day and hurried to the office.

Cheryl stalled until ten minutes after nine then put two patients into rooms. After another ten minutes, a man opened his door to look for Danny in the hallway. "I can't understand it," the patient said to Bruce who walked by. "I'm Dr. Tilson's first patient scheduled for nine o'clock. Can you see me instead?"

"I'm sure Dr. Tilson was emergently detained. Would you like for Cheryl to bring you a cup of coffee?"

"Forget it. This is the first and last time I'm going to him."

In the doctor's lounge, Danny scrolled the computer for patients' labs before his scheduled one o'clock case. It was already after one, even though he speeded through seeing office patients to make up for his morning tardiness, but lucky for him, his surgery case had arrived late. The best thing to happen all day, he thought. He small talked with another surgeon then strolled to the front desk.

Staff hurried in and out of the small room, blue scrubs coming and going. One woman sat at the desk facing the open window to the hallway. "Your case is going back right now, Dr. Tilson, just sit tight." She grinned while ignoring the incessant phone.

"It's not that," Danny said. "I just have a question about the scrub nurse, Rachel Hendersen, the one who assists in my cases."

"Yeah, I heard about you two." She raised her eyebrows. "But if you want to know anything particular, you'll have to ask the head nurse. Pat is around here somewhere. Do you want her to stop by your case to talk to you?"

"Sure, thanks." Danny walked to OR 10. He greeted his patient again on the operating room table before anesthesia raced through her IV, scrubbed, and began surgery. The patient had a classic presentation of seizures, but less common was the diagnosis of an oligodendroglioma, which only comprised about two to four percent of primary brain tumors. Rarer still were ones that needed surgery before chemotherapy. Danny isolated the solid portion and talked to the pathologist about it on the intercom, describing its appearance. Although the physician hated to report confirmations on cancerous cells, he anxiously awaited the tissue, as its "fried egg" appearance would be an interesting pathology specimen. Danny told him the specimen would be shortly on its way.

The OR door opened; with a sideward glance, Danny saw Pat, the charge nurse. She held a clipboard to keep track of rooms, cases and surgeons. She peered into the patient's brain as Danny halted the scalpel.

"Dr. Tilson, you had a question?"

"I'm wondering if you know when nurse Rachel will be back to work," Danny asked. "Not that my present nurse isn't doing a nice job." He nodded pleasantly to her.

Pat dropped her clipboard arm to her side, surprised. "Dr. Tilson, Rachel doesn't work here any more. She handed me her resignation."

Danny's hands trembled. The scalpel he held tumbled from his right fingers like a residual drop of water after a faucet is shut.

Pat took a step towards the door.

"Did she leave a forwarding address or job information?" Danny stuttered.

"No. Left cold turkey."

Pat raised her clipboard and started for the hallway again. "Oh, and Dr. Tilson? Rachel Henderson wasn't an RN, but a technician." One side of the metal door creaked closed behind her.

A quiet in the room became dead silence to Danny. He shook with disbelief. He looked down at the scalpel, luckily perched on the edge of his patient's skull which was covered by sterile drape. The sharp edge tottered above the open hole to moist gray brain.

Chapter 22

"A quarter-pounder with cheese," Danny said at the drive through window. "And fries. And a coke. Oh, better make that two."

"Like two what, everything?" asked a young female voice.

"No, just the quarter-pounder."

"With cheese?"

"I believe so. I think dogs eat cheese, it doesn't make them sick, does it?"

"Mister, if you're feeding a dog fast food instead of dog food, I don't think cheese'll kill 'im." Before Danny drove forward, he heard the teen remark to a coworker. "People driving through here just keep getting stupider than my brother."

At the window, the girl with a pierced eyebrow took his money, shoved a large bag at him followed by a monstrously large coke. "Your silver metal ring is very becoming," Danny said smiling.

She cracked a wad of gum. "Thanks."

"Last month's article in the New Duncefield Medical Journal confirmed it though."

"Confirmed what?"

"The gray matter in the brain has a neuro system. You know, electrical synapses, so in essence there is this low magnetic field between the right and left part of your brain. They are called hemispheres. People with eyebrow rings have to balance out the magnetism to even out their brain. In other words, you better put metal on the other side. You'd look good with another color, too."

She stopped chewing. "Hey, like thanks mister."

Danny drove away chuckling, and hoped Dakota had a big bladder like his brain since he had walked him before sunrise. He arrived home at 8 p.m. to a gregarious greeting, the dog spinning around Danny as he precariously put the burger bag and cup on the counter. Danny spotted pooled moisture oozing into the hardwood floor. Below the armrest of the couch and the corner of the area rug there lingered an aromatic smell. By the looks of the puddle, Danny thought it was fresh out of Dakota's dispenser. He fetched a roll of paper towels. It took a dozen super absorbent sheets to sop up the mess. Dakota kept his distance with a sorry expression, his head lower than his shoulders as he laid still.

"It's not your fault," Danny said, extending his left arm to touch his head. "I know you're housetrained. I can't expect you to perform miracles." Dakota crawled toward him and Danny patted his head. "Okay, go get your leash and we'll tackle that stiff wind together. And wait until you taste one of those succulent cheeseburgers you're smelling."

Danny decided New Year's Eve would be the end of a string of lousy circumstances. More than lousy. In 2009, he had to consider prioritizing agendas and straighten out his life. Even his financial situation was dismal. More than dismal. He went to the office considering Mary and Casey's party invitation for that night. His thoughts abruptly stopped when Bruce practically blocked him at the door.

"Stewart and Richard are tacking us on at the end of their day," Bruce said tersely, "so don't go anywhere later. It's nice of them to do that on New Year's Eve."

"Yeah, that's swell of them."

"You know …" Bruce began, but then stopped, turned and stormed away, throwing a chart on the front desk.

All day, Danny played low-key, keeping out of Bruce's way, sneaking coffee when Bruce was seeing patients. Office personnel and patients left at five, a later pre-holiday wrap-up than Bruce had wanted for the staff. Danny finally wrote the check to Sara's attorney, trying not to swear obscenities, which were becoming more customary to his vocabulary. He dated it January 1, 2009, payable to Jim Dorsey for nine thousand eight hundred three dollars. Divorce costs would use up all his January's after tax salary, without paying the rent. He addressed the envelope and put it in his outgoing mailbox.

Danny heard a knock at the door and Bruce stuck his head in. "We're in the conference room," he said.

The two attorneys stood shuffling folders as Danny entered hastily. "Happy New Year tomorrow," Stewart said.

"Thank you for coming so quickly after the deposition. And lots of cheer next year too," Bruce said. "Ditto," Danny said. Stewart shot him a glance, straightened her blazer and sat.

"Let's cut to the chase," Richard said.

"Richard and I have thoroughly reviewed the deposition transcripts from both Dr. Tilson and Ms. Dexter. There is bad news and good news."

"The good news," Richard continued, "is that Dr. Tilson here did not actively do anything negligent to the patient, nor was there any kind of permanent, serious or immediately life threatening action to the patient caused by Dr. Tilson. He was negligent as we know, by other means, minimizing his evaluation of her CT scan, failure to send the patient to a neurologist etcetera, etcetera."

"That puts us in better shape to minimize the amount they're asking for," Stewart said. "The unfortunate news is that Danny does look bad. We would not stunningly win this case, and may even have to fork over more money if we don't come to a mutually agreeable resolution."

"We suggest settling this out of court. The plaintiff's attorney and the two of us have judiciously been beating around the bush."

"Their lawsuit asks for a million dollars," Bruce said, scowling.

"They know, and we know, that's preposterous," Stewart said. She looked at Richard, who sat next to her, both of them at an angle towards each other, like a mirror image.

"Yes, preposterous," Richard echoed. "But you never know the price tag a jury hangs on it. You could have a juror who had a similar situation with a loved one who would like to see Dr. Tilson suffer."

Danny let out a sigh, and ungripped the armrest. Nothing was in his hands any more.

"We think we can start with a figure of one hundred thousand but not go higher than two hundred thousand," Richard said. "We believe the plaintiff will be ecstatic with that kind of money, the damage done doesn't deserve any more, and we don't want to play roulette by suggesting any less.

"Is that all?" Danny said.

"Why, do you want it to be more?" Richard asked.

"No, I didn't mean the settlement. I was waiting for Stewart's half to your half of what you just said."

Richard and Stewart both rose, looking at each other. "Think about it," Richard said. "Give us a call on Monday and we'll try a fast resolution."

"After all," Stewart said, "you don't want your medical reputation to tarnish in the interim."

Bruce coughed. "Danny's taking care of that himself lately."

After rushing home, Danny got his mail. He discarded leafy supermarket advertisements, thumbed through envelopes and dropped the rest on the kitchen counter. He was too tired to deal with junk, even an envelope from the apartment complex. Probably a bill for the rent, which he'd paid already.

Dakota dropped his leash at Danny's feet and stood wagging his tail. "Okay, boy, let's go."

Danny and Dakota ambled through the causeway, towards the back. There was something soulful about taking a dog for a walk. He wouldn't have experienced the apartment grounds, the network of paths or bundled up again to brave the cold; it established a dependable routine. The walks gave him a respite, a means to reflect on the day. Instead of thinking that Rachel dumped Dakota on him, he began thinking it was Rachel's loss. His new four-legged buddy wasn't a substitute for his girls, but the dog made him feel less lonely.

Dakota's nose detected a luxurious scent and he sniffed with enthusiasm, yanking Danny over to a different swatch of brown grass to inhale the aroma. He lifted his leg and dispatched a stream, the balancing act getting more precarious as the seconds ticked by. Dakota pranced along Danny's side occasionally peering up to Danny, occasionally bumping Danny's leg with his snout. "I love you, too, dog," Danny finally said.

Inside, Danny scooped Purina into a dog bowl, spread on the couch with the portable phone and called Mary and Casey. "I'm declining the New Year's Eve invite," he said. "The festivities don't need me. I need to chill, quiet and alone."

"We thought you'd be here an hour or two ago," Casey said. Danny heard glassware and voices in the background.

"Well, I got detained."

"I'm off next week," Casey said. "Mary and I are contemplating a few days out of town, just in case I don't see you before then."

"Okay, happy New Year," Danny said and hung up. He pressed his hand into the warmth of Dakota's wavy double coat on his neck as a nap drew his eyelids shut.

Except for booked surgeries that couldn't wait, the first week of the New Year brought lighter than normal office appointments. Patients were reluctant to hurry in; they carried looming credit card debt from the holidays and couldn't afford shelling out the New Year's deductibles of their medical insurance coverage. Danny and Harold would appreciate the lull, but Bruce hated it. Instead of making more trips to the coffee room, he spent more socializing time in each patient's room, polishing his PR skills. On Wednesday, Danny sprung for the delivery of pepperoni pizzas to the office for lunch. He opened a cardboard box, steaming with melted cheese and tomato sauce. Cheryl and Danny folded triangles and began to eat.

"Thanks, Dr. Tilson," she said. "But not a thoughtful way to start a female dieter's New Year."

"My pleasure," Danny said as Bruce walked in.

"Are you going to take a break and eat?" Cheryl asked.

"I will as I discuss legal affairs with Danny, but you don't have to leave." Bruce took a rigid polystyrene plate, slid on a slice and poured an iced tea. "We have to call Parity Insurance today. Since the group is listed on the lawsuit, settlement comes from all our pockets, so to speak." He took a bite over the table.

"Richard and Stewart," Bruce said, "have given us their professional judgment, which we should agree with. What about starting out with their beginning figure and hopefully the plaintiff's attorney doesn't push it over two hundred thousand."

"I agree," Danny said, silently grateful for the concurrence of their opinions.

"You call them." Bruce flipped the lid open to cool a second piece. "I hope we never have another lawsuit in this group. And if there is, that it's at least defensible." He gave Danny a hard stare.

At 3:00 p.m., Danny called Parity. Stewart congratulated their decision, saying they would propose the settlement to the opposing attorney by 5:00 p.m.

The fortune of leaving early was like a surprise gift. Danny arrived home, changed into sneakers and jeans and threw a ribbed neck sweater over his shirt. Every time Danny had wanted to ask the girls to his apartment, there had been another situation out of control, preventing it. "Get your leash while I call the girls," Danny said.

Annabel picked up the phone. "I'll take you and Nancy to dinner," Danny said. "Then I'll show you my apartment if you'd like."

"Awesome Dad."

"I'll pick you up."

Danny donned his jacket, leashed Dakota and stuck his car keys and cell phone into his pocket. He walked Dakota around the complex then opened his Lexus hatchback for Dakota's entry. When he stopped in front of his old house, he kept the heat going as Annabel and Nancy hurried from the front door towards the vehicle.

"Wow, you brought Dakota," Annabel said, getting in the front door.

"Cool, Dad," Nancy said as the dog's thrashing tail pounded the back door. Nancy turned around to pet him.

"Dad, the orthodontist said my bottom braces are coming off the next visit and it won't be long for the top ones either."

"Good for you." He leaned over for a hug before driving. "Where should I take you? Downtown Italy?"

"We're taking Dakota?" Nancy asked.

"It's not hot like summer when I wouldn't think about it. We can leave him in the car, windows cracked. We won't be that long."

"How about some place not as fancy?" Nancy asked. "Sometimes I get sad to go to Downtown Italy. It's not the same like when we were all together." Nancy changed her tone to continue. "Plus, we're dying to see what you're living in." She stopped petting Dakota and buckled her seat belt.

"How about the barbecue place on the same street?"

"That'll work for us," Annabel said.

The heavy scent of barbecue piped into their nostrils as they clustered into a booth. Danny ordered the pork sandwich plate and iced tea.

"Iced tea doesn't seem like a winter drink," Nancy said.

"Just ignore my sister," Annabel said to the teenage waiter. "That's not stopping us."

"Make it three of everything," Danny said when the girls agreed. "Actually, I'll take an extra sandwich."

"Mom is still running," Annabel said. She studied Danny's face, testing his interest. "I still join her sometimes because I think I'm going to try out for track and field in college. Mom's pretty fast so I have to keep up with her."

"She's a good runner. You have a fine teacher."

"Dad, like Nancy, I'm thinking about medical school after college. Do you think I could tail you around your office next month? See what it's like?"

"There are countless specialties in medicine though, Annabel, you would only be seeing a neurosurgeon in an office."

The young man came back with three plastic glasses and a pitcher of iced tea with lemon wedges floating on top. He smiled at Annabel, displaying two hollows at the edge of his mouth.

"Cute dimples," Nancy said to Annabel when he left.

Annabel turned to Danny. "I understand that, Dad. I still want to do it."

"Okay. Call the office and correlate a few hours after school when I'm there."

Danny handed the last sandwich to Annabel to hold at the cash register when they had finished. The boy handed Danny his change. When Danny handed him a five-dollar tip, the young man stared at Annabel. "Thank you," he said. "Please come back."

"You going to eat that later?" Annabel handed the paper wrapped sandwich to Danny.

"No, it's for Dakota. Restaurant handouts started serendipitously. They're just treats, he still gets dog food."

"Wow, Dad, that's like so cool of you," Nancy said. "Can I feed it to him?"

Danny unlocked the car. Nancy giggled as the pork on a bun disappeared, her hand dangling off the back seat, licked by a sawdust tongue until her finger grooves were dog sterililized.

Dakota pounced from the car as the girls scrambled out. The dog led the way vigorously in the chilly air. He tugged at the loose end of the leash.

Danny wrapped his fingers around his keys as they hovered at the front door. He dangled the leash to the girls to hold, and inserted the key. He stepped backwards perplexed. It was the right apartment number, eight. He tried the key again, but it wouldn't budge into the keyhole.

"Brrr," Nancy said locking her arm into Annabel's.

Danny mumbled under his breath as he tried to force the key. He jimmied the doorknob, then pulled and pushed the door.

"Here, try this." Nancy blew into the keyhole. "Maybe dirt got in it while you were gone."

"Stupid," Annabel said. "Fat chance."

Danny left the girls to their petty comments and walked around to the office. The door was open, but office hours were over, and no one was inside. Danny checked the clubhouse for the old man, who must have returned from vacation, but that door was locked. Danny peered in the bay window. There were no functions taking place and it was also empty.

"Come on girls," Danny said, resuming his spot in the breezeway. "I can't show you the inside tonight. I'll bring you both home and figure this out when I come back."

On the way to Sara's, the girls' attempts at explanations became almost plausible. Danny defended himself humorously, camouflaging his concern. No, Danny did have the right key. No, he didn't have Alzheimer's causing him to stumble to the wrong building. No, Dakota hadn't eaten the correct key. He had not dead bolted the inside and sneaked out a window. No, he didn't know how this could have been somebody's prank.

Silently, though, it was getting late to be solving a mystery and he wasn't in the mood.

Chapter 23

Before plodding with Dakota towards the office on his return, Danny tried one more time to open his apartment door. This time he found the office also locked. He pressed his forehead against the window and squinted to read the emergency maintenance number on the counter, but he couldn't decipher it.

Semi-plastered on the door and window were photocopied flyers. Twist your attacker into a pretzel in just three months read a martial arts studio ad. Another below it proclaimed Dispose of your bread handles with our diet dinners delivered to you door. Eventually he spotted a shiny laminated sign at the bottom of the bay window, which displayed office hours and the telephone number, including one for after-hour emergencies. He pulled his cell phone from his pocket and called.

"Hello," said a sleepy voice. "Maintenance."

"This is Dr. Tilson. Apartment number eight. I've got a problem."

"Mister, which apartment building? We service three complexes. I ain't a mind reader."

"I'm sorry. It's just that I am locked out of my apartment. Actually, my key doesn't seem to be working."

"You say you're number eight?"

"Yes, that's correct," Danny said.

"Let me check." There was a thud as the man put down the phone. "Yup, I guess it's you that's supposed to be locked out. That was our locksmith that changed the lock this evening."

Danny's blood boiled. "I live there. What are you talking about?"

"The office told us, we've got a service slip. They don't do anything unless it's warranted, so you talk to them tomorrow."

"But my personal things are in there. What am I supposed to do?"

The man hung up.

Dakota gleefully jumped again into the back of Danny's hatchback. Except for the recent addition of meaty sandwiches, two car rides in one night was doggie heaven. Danny put his hands on the wheel. Even his pager was in there. He pushed the consequences of not getting in out of his mind, started the engine, and headed to Mary's. He could spend the night there before blowing up at that manager and handling the wretched affair the next day.

After the hasty drive, Danny parked, let Dakota out, and rang Mary's bell. After pressing the bell for some time, he finally knocked. A dim light shone from the back of the house, but still no answer. Hadn't Casey mentioned something about going away? He had a key to the house, but it sat in an apartment drawer. "Shit," he said aloud.

Dakota sat, and then laid down on the doormat. "Let's go boy," Danny said. But the dog balked. Danny tugged the leash. Dakota stood, but refused to go forward or backward.

"I'm tired of this and want to lie down, too. But we need somewhere to sleep and it's almost midnight," Danny said.

Finally, they walked to the car, the bitter damp cold making him thankful for the layers he wore.

Danny wished he knew about area hotels. He drove toward the interstate where hotels were likely, stopped at the first one off an exit. A logo-vested employee sat in a room behind the counter, watching television. Danny pushed the little buzzer bell at the front desk and the woman poked her head out. Slowly she came forward. "Can I help you?" She put her glasses on from a dangling lanyard and moistened her chapped lips.

"Any rooms available?"

"Sure," she said. "Smoking or non?"

"Non, but enough room for a big dog."

"Sorry sir. We have a no pet policy."

Danny's patience waned. "You're kidding."

"No sir. We're no different than most hotels."

"Do you know any hotel that takes them?"

"Not really. Hotels around here do pretty well. No one really has to. Plus, dogs create disturbances for most guests."

Danny longed even more for a bed with white, crisp sheets with high cotton thread numbers. Even a cot would do. He was plum out of ideas. No bright notions of what to do or where to go. He got in the car, gripped the wheel and aimlessly drove. After awhile, he veered onto I-40 by sheer intuition. In a half hour, he stopped at an overnight drive-through and bought a coffee, then kept going.

At 2 a.m., he slowed the car down a hill and parked in the grass. He let Dakota out without his leash; they both relieved themselves in the brush, and walked to the water's edge. The outline of a three-quarter moon was sharp and defined. Individual stars of Orion's Belt brightened then dimmed as if a light dimmer controlled them. Light bounced off the Caney Fork as Danny breathed in the cold air, marveling at the celestial heaven. The stillness, the water, the expansiveness of the sky was even more peaceful than during the daytime. Dakota stood along side Danny's leg, the dog also seemingly composed by the magnificent night. The memories of this place. He remembered what his father had said, something about letting your life get so bad, you would have to fish here for your dinner, not for the fun or sport of it. He almost qualified. He missed Greg and realized his father wouldn't be proud of him right now. Danny turned, the dog at his heels, and went to the car.

Danny slid the front seats forward and collapsed the back seats. He wadded a rain jacket from a door pocket into a pillow and laid down. Dakota lengthened, his back providing warmth and comfort, and he soon twitched from his deep sleep dreams.

Within an hour, Danny's desire for fine comforts kept depreciating: a freshly made bed, to a cot, to a sleeping bag and tent, to the wholesome shelter of his vehicle. At one point, Dakota's dreaming intensified and he let out a muffled woof. Danny lightly laughed. Homeless at the Caney Fork in the dead of winter, sleeping with a dog. He thought back to Melissa's first ER visit for asthma and the subsequent weekend he'd brought his family fishing. The trip surfaced to the forefront of his mind like it had happened only yesterday …

It blanketed the Caney Fork. Fog like wispy cotton teased into miniature waterspouts. Greg and Annabel squatted in the gray gravel, poking at rocks in pools of water. Melissa pulled her white sunhat further back from her forehead and joined them as Danny and Sara unfolded three chairs. Annabel wore the new Alaska baseball cap her aunt had mailed her, with a long brim, like her grandfather's.

"That's a green mussel," Greg said, picking it up, putting it in the palm of his hand for display.

"Slimy green thing," Annabel said, taking it with amusement.

Melissa rolled over a mollusk in the water. "What's this one, Pop-Pop?"

"An olive nerite."

"How can I learn what you know?" Melissa asked. "About animals and things?"

"Well, sweetheart, I studied these things in college, besides business. If you want to work with animals and nature, then you study biology, like your mom."

She tilted her head to view a great blue heron sweep over the circular area of deep water in front of the Dam. "Then that's what I'll do when I grow up." Greg saw her nod to herself, resolute in her conviction.

"Poles are here," Sara said. "Chairs are ready."

Danny and Greg cast while Sara sat on the cooler, showing her small lure to Annabel. Nancy's hazel eyes grew wider when she saw her sister poke at the tiny sharp hook. She took a step back, throwing her arms in the air, chasing two turkey vultures that had landed on rocks behind them. The beasts raised their great black wings and flew heavily across the imitative cloud cover on the narrow part of the river.

"Any more news from the pediatrician?" Greg asked his son.

"No. Just confirmation. The blood work came back supporting the diagnosis of asthma," Danny said as Melissa fished around in the plastic container, selecting salmon eggs.

"Pop-Pop, it's okay. I have a special little puffy thing in case I can't breathe."

"An aerosol," Danny said. "Did you bring it?"

"It's in my bag, Daddy."

"Good girl."

Nancy ignored the chairs and sat on the coarse ground, causing her pants and underwear to be soggy within minutes.

She fingered the rocks and crushed seashells, not knowing the peeking pictures in them were fossils from ancient times.

Danny and Greg watched her, nodding approval. “Some things children do don’t change,” Greg said.

Both men cast again, the fine lines swallowed into the water after breaking its dark surface.

“Dad, I did some good cases this week. All my craniotomies went home except for the emergency I did yesterday. Maybe one of these years Bruce will make Harold and me partners.”

“He’s probably not ready to go out on a limb for you guys,” Greg said.

Danny watched Sara cast, her right arm fluid with motion. She stepped forward to the water’s edge while Annabel copied her movements.

“Come on, Melissa,” Danny said. “Unless your hip wader has leaks, we’re not fishing in this spot for the next hour. It’s going to be in the eighties before we know it.” He glanced at Greg, who already had underarm sweat stains on his swimming tilapia tee shirt.

“Let’s have breakfast at Cracker Barrel on the way home,” Sara said, raising her voice just enough for the family to hear. “I’m working up an appetite for scrambled eggs and blueberry muffins.” She reeled in her line. “False alarm,” she said, inverting her left palm, offended.

Danny thought she was a riot. She had a good appetite and yet kept a trim figure, even maintaining competitive running times for a thirty-three year old. Sara had dropped the teaching but had continued pounding the country roads around the subdivision, two or three times a week, especially the nights Danny cleared the dinner table. He eyed her trim white-skinned legs, solar kissed from outdoor activities and from rocking on the deck.

Danny and Melissa carefully took steps, aware of the moss, which clung like slippery snails to the river rocks below. They separated almost fifteen feet as an elderly couple perched themselves at the foot of the steep embankment across the way. Two teenaged boys waded further down, aware of the code for quiescent fishing.

After awhile, Sara and Greg saw the man across the way diverting his spouse's attention by pointing towards Danny and Melissa. Sara held her pole still, seeing the ripples and flopping in the dark water beyond Melissa. Danny waded towards his daughter, giving her a thumbs up.

In a few minutes, Danny and Melissa approached the bank. Melissa extended a rainbow trout. "Mommy, Pop-Pop, look what I caught!" she said, almost dropping the fish. She stood flushed from the blood that zipped through her arteries and she breathed faster. Danny thought she'd burst out of her waders.

"I bet it's almost a record," Greg said.

"At least five pounds," Danny said. The morning sun caught the trout's silvery underside while Annabel pointed to the pink stripe running lengthwise along its side.

Danny and Sara beamed at each other over the huddle, delighted with the trout that had been slicing through the river a few minutes ago.

"Time to let it go," Sara sighed.

"Let it swim off," Danny said to Melissa. "This is where it belongs. With its family."

At the most, Danny slept three hours. He drove out of the gravel, got back on the road, and headed west. He felt so tired, his thoughts fluttered like clothes airing to dry. As he neared Nashville, he could think of no other alternative than to call Annabel or Nancy. Indirectly, Sara.

"Dad, it's kind of early. You at work?" Annabel asked in a tired teenage droll.

"Not yet. I have a favor to ask you." Danny held his breath because it was Sara's cooperation he really needed. He heard a kitchen appliance in the background.

"Can you take Dakota today? Keep him at the house?"

"Sure," she said. "But I'll have to ask Mom."

Danny heard Annabel ask Sara, but couldn't hear Sara's response. "Mom said she doesn't do dogs."

Annabel lowered her voice again to Sara. "Okay, Dad. I told her you wouldn't have asked if it weren't important. And that Nancy and I really want to see Dakota."

Danny sighed with relief. Now he could get to work after all. "Thank you, sweetheart. I'll be by in a little while."

When Danny arrived, Annabel and Nancy were upstairs dressing for school. Sara opened the front door. "Hope I'm not disturbing you," Danny said. "I really do appreciate this."

Dakota stood, his tail waving furiously, his body swaying side-to-side. He nudged at Sara. Sara crouched to acknowledge him and Dakota pushed against her blue jeans before he plastered her with a single tongue swipe to her cheek.

"You look terrible, Danny," Sara said not looking up. She fixed a scowl. "I'm doing this for the girls and the dog, not you. We'll take good care of him. But I'm not saying 'any time.'"

Danny handed her the leash. "I know, but thank you. I'll call later." He turned to leave. "Sara, I don't have his food with me. If the girls can't get any, he'll eat a quarter-pounder or barbecue. And please, tell the girls I love them."

He left, but not without thinking that Sara looked amazing.

Danny contemplated his soiled tennis sneakers and rumpled blue jeans before entering the office. He gave his sweater and jacket a pass, but not the cotton-blended shirt which should have been ditched before the Tennezzee sleepover at the water's edge. His stubbly beard growth and smelly mouth with tartar-glossed teeth didn't help his attire either. He wasn't prone to rattling prayers off in his head; now was a good time to start. He had to sneak into a pair of scrubs before being spotted. Even then, wearing them in the office would elicit questions.

Taking a big breath and dropping his head, he entered. He slunk through the waiting room, and opened the inner door. The girls at the desk hadn't recognized him yet.

"Dr. Tilson, is that you?"

The voice came from the farthest distance inside the hallway, a bad thing since the volume reached Bruce, who had been busy around the corner of the viewing room. Bruce stuck his head out. Danny's office was past there, as well as the bathroom, as well as the kitchen. Danny was trapped.

"I didn't have time to clean up," Danny said. He slowed passing Bruce. "A fish gave me a decent fight. It took longer than expected. I'm going to use the washroom."

"Don't waste your time. See me in my office in ten minutes." Bruce steamed away while Danny slinked into the bathroom anyway and splashed water on his face.

On the ten-minute mark, Danny entered Bruce's office. It smelled like polished wood. Degrees and certificates from college through neurosurgery training, even continuing medical education, hung on every space of available wall. Unlike Danny's office, there were two windows. Besides a desk, two patient chairs and a couch, there was enough room for a round table, chairs and a bookcase to the left. Harold stood near a window and glanced down after a bewildered look in Danny's direction.

"This unprofessional behavior," Bruce began, "is the last such incident that the majority of The Neurosurgery Group of

Middle Tennessee is going to tolerate." He stood behind his desk, sank into his chair and signaled Danny to sit. Danny bit the tuft of skin inside the corner of his mouth and fell into the upholstery like a marionette on strings.

"In recent consultation with our group's attorney, it's a business decision to not disengage you as one of our partners. We won't fire you, as of yet, but put you on leave of absence for several months. Ample time to straighten yourself out."

Danny froze.

"Sorry, Danny," Harold tentatively added. "It's just that your behavior has serious repercussions for all of us. It's not just the malpractice tarnish. There are reports of being short tempered in the OR and not having your pager on. You disrupt office schedules and patients are unhappy with you. Your behavior substantiates run-away rumors of an affair and case foul-ups."

Bruce put his open palm forward to stop Harold. "And have you taken a look at yourself lately? You're a mess. When was the last time you had a haircut?"

Harold tinkled change in his pocket and sat in the adjacent chair next to Danny. "Jeez, Danny. It's not just your clothes that stink."

"When?" Danny asked.

"Starting now," Bruce said.

"How? My scheduled patients …"

"That's our problem," Bruce said as he rose. "We will deal with it."

"While you are suspended, no pay. That will be indicated on your statements."

The doctor's lounge provided Danny with the immediate tools he needed. His medical privileges were intact at the hospital; he was still a staff physician. He toasted a bagel, peeled an orange and drank coffee while waiting for nine o'clock to call the apartment office.

"Valley View," someone said at the other end. Danny recognized the elderly man's voice, just who he wanted to talk to.

"Hello. This is Doctor Tilson. Sir, my apartment number eight was re-keyed yesterday. What's this all about? I pay rent; I believe I have justification for legal action."

A perfusionist taking a break from the bypass machine glanced over so Danny leaned forward into the dictating machine cubicle. "Doctor Tilson, we would never do anything this drastic were it not for our legal counsel. You should know that already, since you received letters from Valley View and the attorney's office, after we warned your girlfriend."

"Do we speak the same language? I said I don't know what you are talking about."

"Well, it's in your rental agreement."

Danny thought he would explode. "What is?" he yelled. Most of the people in the doctor's lounge shot him a glance. His attire didn't help. Two doctors grinned at each other, as if Danny had lost it.

"No dogs allowed."

Danny couldn't believe it. One more thing. Was this defensible?

"Sir, I had no idea." Danny scooted the chair in another inch and practically whispered into the phone. "I desperately need to get my personal things out of there."

"The apartment is no longer yours to rent. And, you won't be getting a refund for the rest of the month on your paid-up rent, nor will you be getting your security deposit back. If you don't believe me, read your contract."

"Can I please move my personal possessions out this morning?"

"I'll be here. Whenever you want."

Besides getting Mary's house key from the drawer, so that he wouldn't be sleeping in his car again with Dakota, Danny's main concern was to get his leather case. His clothes and books were important, too, but paled in comparison. When he entered the business office, the man adjusted some paperwork, found the new apartment key, and signaled for Danny to follow. The trek to number eight reminded Danny of once being led to the principal's office in grade school.

The man abruptly stopped. "See those dead branches there?" he asked. "That's what happens to landscaping when apartments have dogs." Danny shook his head since the middle of January wasn't a month for non-evergreens to qualify as green. Why, Dakota had never paid any interest in that short-changed, scraggly excuse of a bush.

They got to Danny's recent living quarters. The man's key slipped straight away into the keyhole and he opened the door. He lingered at the edge of the kitchen counter, making it clear he wasn't leaving. "I'm locking up after you leave. It'll be the model apartment again with all this rental furniture, which we're going to assume the bill for."

Danny headed to the bedroom, everything looking exactly as he had left it. He swiped at the bedspread, picked up the end of the mattress and took his burgundy case. He went to the closet; all his personal items would go back into the suitcase and boxes he had stored there. He rolled the packed luggage in front of the kitchen counter, grasping his case with his free hand. After he placed it on the counter, he found Mary's key and his pager, put them separately with his most important item, and continued throwing drawer and kitchen pantry items into a box.

Danny had worked up a sweat, so unzipped his jacket, draped it near the phone. Piled mail lay there so he leafed through envelopes before dropping them into the box. He opened the Valley View and law firm letters, the man making a face as if he had better things to do. He should have opened them days ago. He now had more attorneys after him than the number of French style green beans in a sixteen ounce can.

Danny stood straight. Something triggered a curious thought, like when someone looks directly at something, but it doesn't register what he or she really sees, until later. His leather burgundy case, it didn't seem right. What was it?

He darted a glance to the keeper of his endeared items, a sinking feeling welling up from his gut. He inched his hand over, put his palm on top and pressed.

Danny's words came hesitantly, "Has anyone been in here before or after the apartment was re-keyed?"

"Just me. To evaluate for dog mischief, or owner damage like we usually do. The place looked like you left me with no trouble. But still don't expect that security deposit."

Danny discontinued listening to him. He was worried about someone else, not him. But first … He picked up Albert Einstein's book and Melissa's bracelet holder and opened the flap. It was as empty as a strewn red neck beer can.

Chapter 24

As much as Danny wanted to, he couldn't go get Dakota, yet. He had to unload his car at Mary's. Danny let himself into her house when no one answered the door, carried bags and boxes upstairs and stacked a neat pile in the original guest room, the only bedroom truly available. He called Sara and left a message that he'd pick up the dog later. Growing sleepier, he succumbed to the bed. His eyelids closed right away and the difference between consciousness and fading into a dream blurred. A cat's paw ruffled the river's surface as he stood watching, Dakota nearby, the moon a bright white ball overhead. Circular ripples grew, the water percolated, like humpback whales bubble feeding. Melissa appeared from the center and approached him, her arms outstretched. She wore a long, ethereal dress, but before she reached him, she disappeared back into the water, crying "Daddy, Daddy." The Caney Fork became quiet again.

Sara scanned the newspaper's TV guide and Nancy opened a new peanut butter jar and spread some on a slice of bread.

Dakota suddenly bolted up, sniffing the air. He sat, reeled backward, and pranced his two front legs into the air.

"What?" Nancy asked. "That's a pretty cool high-five."

"I think dogs like peanut butter," Annabel said as she peeled apple skin from her braces.

"That would explain it," Sara said, glancing over the top of the counter.

Nancy spread a pat of peanut butter on her index finger and extended it to Dakota. "But, like, be polite and don't eat my finger." Dakota gobbled the small mound and continued licking until he scoured the tile floor for any fallen residue.

"Would one of you call your father about Dakota?" Sara asked.

"I'll do it," Annabel said. "I want to talk to his office anyway."

Nancy asked for her father. "I'll put you through to Dr. Tilson's nurse," the receptionist said.

"Cheryl," Annabel said, "I need to talk to my Dad, but first I need your help. Dad told me to call about dates because I want to shadow him for a few days after school. I'm thinking about a medical career, but I don't know if I would like it."

"Your dad isn't here this afternoon, Nancy. We'll have to wait to schedule you, though. He won't be in the office for some time in the immediate future. Bye now."

Annabel grimaced at the receiver before putting it on the cradle. "Like, that was weird."

"What?" Nancy asked.

"Cheryl said Dad's not there, and he won't be there … 'in the immediate future.'"

Sara, Nancy and Annabel exchanged glances. Annabel waved her apple core at Dakota who politely took it in his mouth and trotted to the other side of the kitchen.

Annabel picked up the phone again and called Danny's apartment, her face showing disbelief as she listened to a telephone company recording. "Mom, maybe we get to keep Dakota tonight."

"I doubt it," Sara said. "Your father left a message here saying he'd pick him up. Don't call his cell, though, in case he's in surgery."

As Danny rolled over, he opened his eyes, readjusting them to old familiar surroundings. Recollection of Melissa's dream sent chills along his neck. His entire career hung in jeopardy. Actually, his whole life. He sat up and buried his head in his hands. He shut his eyelids tight, concentrating into the darkness.

Danny quickly showered and rummaged for clean pants, a tee shirt and sweatshirt from his duffel bag. He pulled his trousers up, zipped his fly and struggled with the button. Pants must have shrunk.

Downstairs Danny hesitated to scan the refrigerator for something to eat, because leaving Dakota at Sara's longer than necessary could be a problem, especially if the dog became mischievous. Since his morning bagel, Danny hadn't eaten, so he went through the drive-in on the way and bought two-quarter pounders with cheese, fries and coffee.

When Danny rang the bell at Sara's, Nancy opened the door while Dakota stopped barking and greeted him. Danny's heart warmed; nobody ever got that excited to see him.

"Dad, like what is going on with you?" Nancy said as Danny acknowledged Dakota. He planted a strong kiss on Nancy's forehead." She stood back and eyed him. "Like I said, Dad, what's going on with you?"

"Can't I kiss my daughter?"

"I guess that's okay. I mean, like everything else. The office said you weren't there and aren't going to be there. And your telephone's been disconnected."

Annabel came into the hallway and stood behind her sister. "Yeah, Dad, we are kind-of worried about you."

"Girls, it's not the time or place to talk about it. Actually, you have no idea how nice it is to see you both." Now he gave Annabel a hug and kiss as well.

The girls started to lead Danny to the back of the house. "I better just take Dakota and leave," he said.

"It's okay, Dad. You have to wait for Mom anyway. She went to get Dakota a bag of dog food."

"Does that mean I shouldn't feed him the cheeseburger I have?" Danny laughed. He ran to the car and brought his fast food. He sat with the girls at his old kitchen table, where he used to eat Sara's healthy meals. Which explained his tight trousers. He'd been eating fewer meals, but the quality had gone to the dogs.

"Dad, we are never going to see the inside of your apartment, are we?" Annabel asked, and then sampled a French fry.

"No." Danny said, embarrassed. He washed down a bite of burger with his coffee. "Do either of you know when Mary and Casey will be home?"

"They drove to the gulf coast for a few days," Annabel said. "They should be home tomorrow afternoon."

Danny promised the girls he'd see them more the next month as Sara came through the garage door hugging a dog food bag. She grumbled something as he got up to take it. "I almost left this beside your car," she said. "But I think Dakota needs some now."

"Sara, thanks," Danny said. "You didn't have to do that."

"It's what's best for the dog," she replied. She took a cereal bowl from a shelf while Danny split the top of the bag. Sara read the feeding directions. "What do you think he weighs?"

"Sixty pounds." Annabel said.

"Probably seventy-five, eighty." Danny said. Danny swiped at Annabel. "It's like a girl to underestimate weight."

"Okay, about two cups then," Sara said.

"Here, watch this," Danny said. Dakota followed him. "Dead dog, Dakota."

Sara smiled and placed the dish on the floor.

Danny and Dakota finished eating and Danny headed to the door.

"Dad," Annabel called after him, "where should we reach you?"

Danny shouted backward past Sara, who trailed him. "At Mary's."

"I thought you were living with your girlfriend," Sara said quietly.

"I haven't seen her in a while."

"Hmm. Well, did you burden the girls with all your problems?"

Danny looked down. "Despite everything falling apart, I spared them."

Sara contemplated, hooked her thumb into a belt loop on her jeans. "I guess, Danny, unless you're a politician, you end up being responsible for your actions."

"I suppose so," he said, clasping the Purina bag in his left arm. "Can I ask you something?"

"Sure."

"The legal maneuvers between us have been ... well ... surprising. Jim Dorsey's letter about my first child support being late, though, really hurt. You could have just reminded me."

Sara raised her voice. "What were you thinking, to give up what we had?" She held her tongue for a long moment. "I received a copy of that," she said in a lowered tone. "Jim asked me if I'd gotten the payment. When I said no, he said he'd take care of it. I had no idea he'd write such a malevolent letter."

Danny smelled subtle orange-ginger. He inhaled slowly through his nose, soaking up its familiarity. "Listen, thanks for taking Dakota and thanks for getting the dog food."

"Yeah, yeah," she said, waving.

Danny lightly held the middle of Dakota's leash. Dakota nipped at the free end as Danny tasted Sara's lingering scent on his way to the car.

The next day, Danny waited before unpacking his personal belongings. Crashing at Mary's for a day or two was one thing, but he couldn't presume staying for weeks on end. He'd have to divulge his whole mess to his sister and closest friend and hope for the best. He gritted his teeth thinking about his financial status. At the moment, he was cashless, and without an upcoming income stream. He would have to cash in his annuity to make payments to Sara. By the manner in which the Judge had decided his motion in court, trying to legally recalculate payments to her wasn't worth it. The Judge would ignore Danny's sob story and only see a useless nonworking professional filling his time with fishing and throwing sticks for a dog. A doctor should be a gold mine, despite his lousy circumstances.

Danny browsed through Mary's art room. Every completed picture was vastly different from the next; each one had a fresh quality about it, as if she were multiple artists in one. A work-in-progress stood on the easel, it smelled like oils; the palette nearby with thick colors piled at the edges, while a short painting knife and stubby brush laid horizontal on a can. The paraphernalia and woody texture of the bedroom itself made it more artistic than any gallery viewing room. He wanted to linger there longer. However, since Mary and Casey were arriving that afternoon after a long drive, he would contribute to groceries.

After going to the store, Danny stashed milk, cold cuts, orange juice, and frozen vegetables in the refrigerator. He stocked the bare fruit bowl and stacked dog food cans in the pantry, thinking of adding moist food to Dakota's dry meals. In case Casey and Mary wanted to eat when they got home, he had bought a deli chicken. As he petted Dakota, he felt pangs for the past and yearned for a normal dinner with some family.

Danny heard doors slamming at five o'clock after Casey's Jeep pulled into the garage next to Mary's Ford. "We've got a visitor!" Mary exclaimed, toddling into the kitchen and dropping a shopping bag to hug her brother. "And four-legged Dakota, too," she yelled back to Casey.

"Hey, Danny," Casey said. "What a nice surprise."

"How was your trip?" Danny asked.

"Gathered some sunshine from Florida," Casey said. "Even went fishing."

"We had a great time," Mary said. "A few days were all we needed." Mary acknowledged Dakota as Casey and Danny continued unloading the car and shaking sand from the floor mats.

"There's been an imposter here," Mary said, when Danny and Casey stopped going back and forth. She pointed to the lemon-peppered chicken and the fruit bowl.

"A take-in dinner," Danny said. "But do I have bucket loads to tell you. And a favor to ask as well."

For hours, mostly Danny talked. They retired to the family room, after cleaning up, walking Dakota, and popping a cork on a sweet Muscadine, like a dessert to linger over. Mary changed into loose fitting sweats and slipper socks and Casey took off his leather shoes. Danny discarded his sweatshirt - how many days had he worn it? The memory of which clothes he had worn the last few days were a blur. He extended his legs on the leather ottoman, and after awhile Dakota laid down, elongated on his side. Occasionally the roof creaked and the back door whispered from a breeze, causing Dakota to tilt his head in that direction, but he resumed his hunting and retrieving under his eyelids.

First, Danny explained his preoccupation with Rachel had something to do with him missing an obvious diagnosis on a CT scan and the resulting lawsuit filed against him. Casey grimaced at some of the details - Danny's round robin of depositions, meetings with attorneys and Bruce's disgust. "And the outcome is yet to be determined," Danny said. "The Parity attorneys and the plaintiff's lawyers are discussing an out of court settlement."

In a non-accusatory manner, Danny told them details of the divorce, the attorneys, the financial settlement, his day in court and the unfairness of it all. "It wasn't like the legal system judges what someone did," Danny said. "All they care about is the money. Who's got it, who doesn't, and who they can get to pay whom." Danny twirled the glass of wine. "I'm not mad at Sara about all that. The whole thing is ludicrous. They didn't take into account everything handed to her and the girls from Dad. Which I will never see."

"You could have come to us before," Mary said.

"I'm not finished," Danny said. "Now comes the part about my apartment eviction."

Casey widened his eyes and leaned forward as Danny put the pieces together. "They accused me of being told several times that the dog was not allowed. In essence, they told Rachel. I've been thrown out."

"Danny, Danny, Danny," Mary said. She split the remainder of the wine bottle contents into their three glasses and breathed deeply.

"I'm still not finished. I am an unemployed neurosurgeon, the result of Bruce getting disgusted by the things I've told you."

"Omigod," Casey said.

"Before you continue, and believe me, we've heard enough," Mary asked, "you obviously need a place to stay. I take it that's why we found you here?"

Danny's head bobbed up and down. "After sleeping overnight in my car with Dakota at the Caney Fork? Yes, that's why you found me here."

Mary's mouth fell open.

"I need a place only …"

Mary put her hand up, stopping him. "Danny, look, this is your house as much as it is mine. You stay as long as you want. I have so much to thank you for."

"I may be imposing on both of you though."

"No," Casey said. "Maybe I should leave for awhile, Danny. Until all of this gets sorted and you get back on your feet."

Mary raised her voice. "Nobody's going anywhere. And I mean it! Not even Dakota."

"Come to think of it, what is the story with Dakota?" Casey asked. Dakota raised his head, but lowered it drowsily back on the rug.

"He belongs to Rachel or used to belong to her, but I haven't heard a word from her. She high tailed out of town." Danny sighed. "And I'm heartsick over something else." Danny put his stemware to the side.

"Mary, do you remember the book Mom gave me by Albert Einstein?" Mary nodded, and then Danny proceeded to tell Casey about his mother's purchase of the 1920 book *Relativity: The Special and the General Theory*, the verification of Albert Einstein's signature, and her bequeathing it to him. Danny told Casey he kept it in the leather case he purchased at Christmas years ago, and how the book had traveled place to place with him. "And Casey, you must remember the opal bracelet you gave Melissa?"

"Like it was yesterday."

"Well, both the book and the bracelet are missing."

Chapter 25

Danny, Casey and Mary had no reason to get up early in the morning so they remained glued together several more hours as Danny told them every detail.

"You're positive the Valley View office manager didn't take them?" Casey asked.

"Extremely unlikely. He seemed clueless when I packed my belongings. Rachel frequented the apartment, with and without Dakota, and had been there the day she vanished. That's when she left Dakota and a small note."

The wine danced around in their heads, mellowing their thoughts. Casey slid over to Mary, put his arm on the back of the couch, and rubbed her left shoulder with his fingers. "Well, my friend," Casey said to Danny, "we need to make some plans. First off, you and I are going to hit every pawnshop around here."

"You think you're going to find a high end piece of history in a place like that?" Mary asked.

"If Rachel stole it, she has to know it's valuable. She wouldn't want it traced to her. I think she'd pawn it to get the cash."

"But Casey, if she's as devious as she sounds, she could always say Danny gave it to her. She was practically living with him and Danny can't prove anything. She could sell it to some kind of treasury collector."

"That's true," Casey said. "But we have to start somewhere and give it a shot. On the other hand, she may be planning on keeping the book until she's an old lady."

"But I've got the time to poke around pawn shops," Danny said. "Even merchandise for sale columns in newspapers."

"You know how you're always complaining about not having the time to attend CME neurosurgery conferences?" Casey asked.

"Yeah, now's my opportunity," Danny said. "But, I have to get my spot back with my group."

"Why don't you consider looking elsewhere?" Mary took her foot, toasty warm in her blue sock, and rubbed it on Casey's ankle. They had slithered further into the couch cushions, their legs extended on the cocktail table.

"I don't want to move out of town. I'm in a dilemma anyway. Even the two other neurosurgery groups in the region are not going to accept me under the present circumstances once they get wind of the reasons I was put on leave. No, I have to straighten this out."

"We need to know the outcome of the Parity case, too," Casey said. "I'll be your eyes and ears in the hospital. Sometimes I see your partners coming and going in the ER."

"Lord knows how Bruce and Harold are going to cover the call," Danny said. Dakota exposed his belly and Danny leaned to lightly stroke it. "Listen, thanks for letting me stay here. It's going to help not paying rent, but I'll chip in for bills and groceries."

"Casey has the utilities and extras covered," Mary said. "And don't worry about eating with us. But, what are you going to tell Annabel and Nancy?"

"I won't tell them everything. But I'll tell them the truth. I messed up in my practice and have to suffer the consequences. My job now is to right my wrongs."

They went to bed, Casey and Mary to the master bedroom, exhausted from the long drive and late night, and Danny to the guest bedroom. Dakota sniffed around the room, amazed he was spending another night in the same place.

In the morning, Danny and Casey listed all the pawnshops around Nashville then split them into regions, to thumb through their contents, even if it took months. They wore blue jeans and sneakers and filled a slender thermos with coffee, and reluctantly left Mary to her painting and Dakota at home.

For their first trip, they headed west fifty miles through an area bridging suburban Nashville and districts of farmland. They veered fifteen miles south off I-40 and found themselves driving in a cluster of gas stations, grocery marts and sleepy strip malls. They pulled into a gravel lot facing *Ritchie's Pawn* and *Lucky's Locksmith*, both gray wood buildings out of a cowboy movie. A woman with a long ponytail and a fake fur jacket hurriedly swept the front porch.

"You looking for a thrifty deal or key replicas for your girlfriends' apartments?" she asked, halting her broom. "I say that 'cus your girls probably aren't the trailer type."

"We're going into the pawnshop," Danny said.

"You visit us when you're finished. If you buy a gun in there, we got lock boxes for them, too. We don't just make keys."

Casey thanked her for the information as they opened the door to a neatly organized shop, a bell announcing their entrance. A clerk polishing a tarnished candleholder stood behind the counter, a large horizontal sign hanging above. We loan, we trade, we sell.

"Can I help you?" the man asked, peering over reading glasses.

Danny and Casey walked towards the glass case filled with rings, watches, gold jewelry and gemstones. Other shelves stored digital cameras, antiques, tools and knickknacks. Casey tapped Danny's arm, pointing to the far wall where the bulk of the items were old musical instruments. A scotch-taped sign hung on a large guitar: *Could've been used by The King himself.*

"Perhaps," Danny said. "We're searching for a very old book. Do you happen to have a book on relativity by Albert Einstein, or have you dealt with it recently?"

The man put down the polishing cloth, wiped his hands on a white towel. "That doesn't sound familiar," he said, adjusting the pen behind his ear. "I'd remember something like that. I have a fine motorcycle out back, though, be happy to give it away for just a few thousand dollars."

"We would be interested if we were in the market for one," Casey said.

"You two naïve to the pawn business?" the man asked.

"You can tell?" Casey laughed.

"Sure can," the man answered nicely. He smiled at them both and sat down on an oak stool behind the counter. "If this piece of history has been stolen, have you reported it to the police?"

"We can't prove it has," Danny lamented.

"I'll be straight with you. As a pawnshop clerk, I must keep a list of tickets on items. A detective or policeman is in charge of pawnshop detail. They compare the list of tickets with their list of stolen property. They make regular, unannounced visits to pawnshops."

"Interesting," Danny said. "Now we know."

"I've owned my shop a long time. Eat donuts with those guys. Best chance of finding your property is reporting it."

"You haven't recently gotten in a girl's opal bracelet, either, have you?" Danny asked.

"No. I'm sorry. Give me your contact info. If they come in, I'll call you since I can sell them back to you."

"Thanks. Appreciate that." Danny and Casey left, crossed off Ritchie's Pawn, which left seventeen remaining addresses on their list.

For over a month, Casey kept a lookout for Harold or Bruce in the ER. He knew Danny's partners in passing, but he hoped they would recognize him as the ER paramedic who was Danny's friend. One Sunday afternoon, as he stood talking at the curb with Mark, with a lull in an afternoon shift, Casey spotted Harold walking through the ER double doors. Casey tailed him inside but slowed when Harold ducked into the kitchen.

Harold hit the ice machine with a Styrofoam cup then dispensed a soda. "Hey, you're Danny Tilson's friend, aren't you?" Harold said when Casey stepped in behind him. Harold drank for several seconds. Danny recognized the dead dog tired look on Harold. Even his shoulders sagged, heavy for sleep.

"Danny and I do go back," Casey said.

"I sure do miss him," Harold said. "My partner and I are splitting call between us and I'm worn down. Feels like residency again. Maybe worse."

"Sounds tuff," Casey commented.

"Yeah, I grow sleepy drinking a cup of coffee. But it should change soon."

"Why, you changing practices?" Casey asked, pouring coffee.

Harold swigged more soda; hit the dispenser again to top off his cup. "Hell, no," Harold said. "We've hired a new doc."

Casey grimaced at the bad news. It had been a struggle for Mary and Casey to help Danny maintain a positive attitude; every day they encouraged him to believe his situation would improve.

"Hey, listen, if you see Danny, tell him I said hello and that Bruce plans on calling him real soon." Harold trudged away before Casey decided to pitch what he thought was moldy brew.

Mary and Casey lay in bed late at night, softly talking after making love. "I just don't know if I should tell him," Casey said, curled along Mary's back, his right arm running lengthwise down her forearm to squeeze her hand.

"Let's not meddle with any of Danny's professional business. Let him hear it from his partner." Mary rolled over and clutched the cream sheet to cover their moist bodies. "Our family Einstein book is another matter. Have you both visited every pawn shop on your list?"

"Only two more left with no leads from any of them. And every day Danny and I still skim through The Thrifty Nickel and other papers for merchandise for sale. Nothing." Casey tenderly nibbled at her shoulder. "I've overlooked something I didn't think of before."

Mary giggled from his nips. "What?"

"EBay. People dispose of stuff on-line all the time. I better start logging on to their site at least twice a week."

"You," she said gleaming, "are a smart frog turned prince."

"And you, princess, have mystical eyes."

"You liar," she said, tossing a handful of cotton sheet at him.

"Am not. Your dark blue eyes are pools from the deepest ocean abyss. Where mermaids thrive."

Every day at dawn, Dakota laid his muzzle on the bed, at Danny's face. He sniffed, making Danny believe the dog evaluated him for the presence or absence of breathing. Dakota followed that by placing his front end up next to Danny, keeping his rear legs on the floor. He dawdled there, nuzzling Danny or resting his head with patience or gurgling impetuous sounds as if it were time to rise.

"Oh, all right." Danny swiveled his legs to the side, pushing Dakota off the bed, and got up. He heard Casey in the hallway, leaving for a seven-to-three shift, as he stepped into brown corduroys and slid into a dark sweat shirt. He went downstairs and walked out the back door with Dakota. He tested the air without a jacket since spring had arrived, and made his way toward trees. Dakota sprang over several hills, marking trees and dispensing his morning duties. Danny surveyed; making mental notes for him and Casey. They wanted to rent equipment to aerate the lawn; they wanted to cull dead brush at the property line, prune some trees, and with the girls, cultivate a small patch to plant blueberry and strawberry bushes.

Danny turned, walked the decline briskly, and called Dakota, who ran up with a stout, foot long stick, obviously delighted with his prey. "Drop it," Danny said. Dakota let go, backed up with glued eyes on Danny. His tail sailed erect, not a muscle flinched, he readied in anticipation for the retrieve. Danny threw it as far as possible and Dakota full throttled forward to fetch it. He ran back, pleased. More of the same, his body pleaded.

"You would retrieve until you dropped," Danny said, shaking his head. He continued Dakota's instinctive game until he yearned to quench the rumbling in his stomach so they went back inside. When Mary came downstairs and joined him, they lazily made toast, and slowly read the newspaper, reading headline stories to each other. At 9 a.m, Danny answered the phone, surprised but fearful when he heard Bruce on the other end.

"If you get a chance, drop by so we can talk."

A chance? He had room on his plate for plenty of chances. "I can drop in later," he said, "if that's not too soon."

"Five o'clock at the office," Bruce said, and hung up.

Later in the day, Casey arrived home to ditch his uniform and change into workout clothes. He wanted to leave Mary undisturbed until he left for the gym. When he spied on her from the doorway, she looked sumptuous in a pale blue sleeveless sweater, her shiny hair pulled loosely behind her. She thumbed through a stack of wooden frame pieces.

Casey grabbed his duffel bag, stuffed in a towel, gym gloves and headset and left the bedroom. He hadn't checked eBay in a few days, so he ducked into the other bedroom to Mary's desktop. Casey searched using two methods. He had gotten familiar with the predictable items he'd stumble on, so he zipped through the forty-two pages of entries under *historical books*. The usual dozens of historical romances also popped up. They even categorized them as *American, French,* or *Italian*. Did that mean they were written in particular countries or the lovers involved lived in those countries? He came to the pages devoted to historical fiction, then major historical atlases and on and on, but didn't find his target. He finished that scroll and went back into eBay's search, typing *Albert Einstein*.

Here, Casey had developed a fondness for a poster of the most important mind of the twentieth century riding a bicycle, but a close second was the genius in full protuberance of his tongue. He looked at the page numbers at the bottom, and it hadn't changed: six total pages. On page four, he accessed books, but they were all new books about Albert Einstein, written by others. An old photograph of Einstein caught his attention, sitting in a chair, the seller claiming the signature at the bottom to be an Einstein original. There was only twenty-four hours remaining to bid on it.

Casey clicked next to page five. The very first item at the top made him catch his breath. Bingo. *Relativity: The Special and the General Theory*. Casey viewed the larger image. "Mary," he shouted. "I've found something."

Mary came around the corner. "You trying to scare me to death? I had no ..." She stopped, focusing on the monitor.

"Read it," she said, unwrapping a new paintbrush. She kneeled on the floor next to Casey's chair.

Own a genuine piece of museum quality history.
A 1920 book by Albert Einstein. Einstein's full authenticated signature resides on the front page!!!

"That has to be it," Mary said, tapping Casey's elbow with excitement.

"Minimum bid fourteen grand," Casey said.

"This has to be the mother of all pearls for people searching for Einstein collectibles."

Casey continued along the ad. "Hmm. Says here the seller is a well respected, trust-worthy dealer using eBay and to contact him if you are dead serious about purchasing it. If I receive the minimum bid or higher from you, I will answer questions about the book's authenticity, the ad says." Casey looked at Mary, perplexed. "Well, it doesn't appear to be Danny's golden girl who is the seller."

"Let's put in a bid, the minimum, and maybe he'll email us back with his name and number," Mary said. "It seems kind of fishy. I bet it's Danny's book."

At ten to five, the women at the front desk greeted Danny warmly and told him to wait in Bruce's office. Cheryl took a patient's blood pressure as the woman sat next to her counter. Cheryl gave Danny a sincere smile and gestured with her hand for Danny to stop. "Mrs. Andrews, please wait for Dr. Jacob in room three," she said.

The patient stepped away as Cheryl gave Danny a small hug. Danny reciprocated, puzzled by the strange doctor's name. "Who's Dr. Jacob?"

"Our new doctor," she said softly. "He doesn't do as many craniotomies as you did, and he's still getting his feet wet, but we like him. Anyway, how are you doing and how are your girls?"

"The girls are fine, and I'm taking a day at a time."

Cheryl nodded. "It's good to see you Danny. Please help yourself to the coffee pot and the newspaper." She pointed to the kitchen. "Bruce should be finished with a patient in a minute."

Danny poured a half cup and went into Bruce's office.

"Danny, Danny, how are you?" Bruce extended his hand when he walked in, gave Danny a healthy handshake and motioned to sit. Bruce settled behind the desk and took his lopsided stethoscope off his neck and put it on the desk. "Well, I bet you're wondering what happened with your lawsuit?"

"Yes, I'm anxious to hear and am cautiously optimistic."

"The Parity dynamic duo pulled it off. The plaintiff settled after her attorney played games, making a stink, and strutting his feathers."

Danny let out a sigh and nodded several times. “For how much?”

“A hundred and sixty thou. Stewart and Richard tried to split it between one and two hundred thousand, but it’s like the stiff attorney had something to prove. We threw in the towel to the extra ten grand. For legal roulette to go any further wouldn’t have been worth it.”

Danny thought it over. “Bruce, thanks. I appreciate your part in this.”

The horizontal lines from the corner of Bruce’s eyes seemed to smile. Danny reached over to drop his cup into an aluminum wastebasket alongside the mahogany desk.

“I’ve hired another doctor.”

Danny hesitated. “So I just found out.”

“He’s a fine addition. Obviously, Harold and I needed the help. So now we can get back to your situation.”

Danny braced himself. He couldn’t bear to think he would have to start over in another office, another town, hell, maybe even another country. He saw himself commuting to work on the Alaskan White Pass Railroad in the Yukon after applying for a Canadian license to practice.

“We would like for you to start accumulating CME paperwork, a copy of your state license renewal, drug enforcement agency renewal and anything else that’s changed and bring them in.” Bruce pushed back in his chair and crossed his legs. “I should have asked you before, but there is one more thing I’d like you to do. Before we ask you to come back to join us, that is. Lord knows, we can use the expansion and nobody does heads like you.”

Danny let go of clutching the left armrest and felt a tsunami of relief surge over him.

"Don't get me wrong, I'm not asking you to see a shrink. And even if I did, that's not a bad thing." Bruce scrambled through a set of papers. "Here, this is Linda Atkins number. You might know her, she's a psychologist in the building."

Anything to get his job back, Danny thought. There's a first time for everything, even being analyzed on a couch.

"She'll see you for awhile, help determine if you are straight enough for the demands of medicine without distraction. Use the sessions to your advantage, Danny. Parity also recommended we do this. You and I will be comfortable for the record that you have no mental illness or strange personality disorder and there are no major problems."

Danny bit his tongue. Bruce had a point, and Danny made the decision right then to not take it personally. "I'll schedule an appointment and make use of any and all sessions."

"Let's try this for two months. We'll look forward to her giving you a clean mental bill of health and on working with you then."

Danny left, thanking the stars for second chances.

Chapter 26

Danny arrived home and gushed forth the details of his meeting with Bruce. Casey and Mary listened enthusiastically, hoping that within a few months Danny would be a practicing neurosurgeon again. They had agreed to keep their eBay find a secret because it could just lead to a dead end.

The next day, Casey opened new email. Their minimum book bid had snagged a reply. Casey received a name and a number, in case he had pertinent questions. He saw Danny and Dakota from the window so quickly called the number. Within a few minutes, Casey slinked behind Mary in the kitchen and kissed the nape of her neck. She stopped squeezing a lemon wedge into an iced tea and spun around.

"How would you like to go to Knoxville with me for the weekend? We'll leave Danny and Dakota here."

"Sounds suspicious."

"It is."

Saturday morning Casey and Mary threw a few things into the Jeep. "Have a good time together," Mary said, scurrying out of the kitchen. She kissed Annabel and Nancy, rubbed Dakota's hind end and hugged Danny good-bye. Casey popped his head in. "You coming?" he asked.

"Where are you staying?" Danny asked.

"The Crowne Plaza, downtown Knoxville," Mary said out the door. She put their MapQuest directions between seats, powered on Casey's cell phone and also placed it between them while Casey backed out. They had a four hour drive so Mary took off her tennis shoes, ankle white peds and brought up her legs Indian style. She untied the drawstrings at the bottom of her pinstriped cotton pants, more like pajamas, and got very comfortable. "I'll admire the scenery for painting ideas," she said.

"It may get more interesting in the mountains," Casey said. "Especially with everything in bloom."

"By the way, what's his name, the man we're going to see? And what did you tell him?"

"His name is Ray. I told him he may have someone's book that he shouldn't be selling. We weren't going to make any trouble, but needed to talk to him."

"What do you think he'll do?" Mary asked.

"If my hunch is correct, I think he's okay. He said he'd take it off eBay until we paid him a visit."

Mary nodded off for twenty minutes at the very end as Casey followed the man's directions. "We're here," Casey said, prodding her elbow. She awoke to slip on her socks and shoes while craning her neck to look all around.

"I'll try and stay out of it," Mary said, "so he doesn't think we're ganging up on him." Casey pumped the pedal up the hill, pulled alongside the side of the house and stopped. They glanced around at the pristine remoteness. Young, leafy trees and underbrush grew on the forest floor, the first few lines of thicket so gnarled and entangled, that they imagined hundreds of acres of wildlife and organic thickening beyond it.

"Not another soul around," Casey said.

"Except for birds, it's so quiet."

Casey walked slightly off course from the front door to spy on a red pickup. Several pieces of lumber as well as an open box of drug store chocolates, a bucket and a personal pan pizza box lay strewn in the truck bed. A car battery and tire were set on the gravel near the front end.

Not far off, a dog barked, as a man came around the other shrub free corner of the ranch house. "Howdy, been expecting yah," he said, extending his hand to Casey. "I'm Ray."

"I'm Casey. This is Mary. I called you about the eBay book you're selling."

The man was wiry, half Casey's size. He had an outdoorsy, healthy appearance and settled a friendly smile on both of them.

"I guess you all got something tah tell me about that."

"If it's the same book," Danny said, "we think it was stolen. I don't know how you got it, but if that's the one, I'm sure we can work something out."

Ray fingered his mustache and looked down at his boots. "See that windshield on my truck? Got a hole from a interstate rock, spreading like cracked ice. Gonna replace it myself."

Casey pulled up the windshield wiper. "You need some help?"

"Maybe," said Ray, scrutinizing Casey's face.

Mary listened carefully to their conversation. A stout boxer with a dangling tongue trotted up the road and sat several feet away. Mary strove to understand the detail of what she saw. The dog was collarless but a fat, olive-looking thing hung from its neck then dropped to the ground. The dog moved in another foot, sat back down, as Mary looked closer. Something bulged between its front toes.

"Brown dog ticks," Ray said, following Mary's gaze.

Mary gasped. Another blood-engorged swollen female fell to the ground and waddled. It looked like a miniature armored military tank. "That is so disgusting. But it doesn't look brown."

"That's their color when they swell bigger'n a raisin." A drop of blood from the dog's chest followed the tick to the gravel. Mary shivered.

"It's a stray trying not to be," Ray said as he studied Mary. "Been hanging here the last few days."

"Poor thing," she said.

"Them city people come out here, open their vehicle doors and dispose of the best friends they got just like they's garbage."

Ray nodded his head to himself while he flipped the wiper back down onto the window. "You two have a seat there on the cement front step and I'll go get that book."

When he returned, they took turns passing the book and the New Orleans verification of Einstein's signature. "This is it," Mary said.

"Awesome," Casey said. "Ray, we're sure this is Mary's family book. It belongs to her brother, and my best friend. We believe a woman he knew stole it from his apartment."

"Was she pregnant?" he asked.

There was an uncomfortable pause; Casey and Mary felt as if they'd been shot by a stun gun. "Was her name Rachel?" Casey asked.

"That was it," Ray said. "I remember it because I remember thinking it a pretty name. But I can check to be sure."

"You keep records?"

"Like the internet says, I got a reputation, don't do nothing nobody wants that's shady. Everything comes and goes I got a track on. I'll get 'er name and number."

Casey and Mary couldn't hold back a smile. "I'd be indebted to you," Casey said to him.

"You don't have to debt me anything," he said. He turned around to walk into the house. "Just kidding with yah," he said. "Sit down again, if you'd like."

He came back out, leaving the door open, making it difficult for Mary to peel her eyes away from the inside. "This is her name and cell phone number. Now it was a couple months ago she sold me this. See, I wait awhile to put it back on the web. Market it under different categories than before, too, if I bought it through eBay. Turn a decent profit, for me, anyways."

Casey rolled this around. "But mostly," Ray said, "I sell and buy car parts. That's another story. We need to straighten what we're gonna do about the physical genius' book."

"You're right, Ray. How much did you pay her for this?"

"Twelve thousand dollars."

Casey got up from the step, placing his hand on Mary's shoulder to stay put. He walked in a circle, furrowing his eyebrows as Ray and Mary looked at each other. Casey faced them. "I have an idea which may work for all of us."

Casey carried the slip of paper with him to his Jeep and opened the driver's side. He sat sideways on the leather seat, picked up his cell and dialed. The boxer hoisted himself up with his dangling parasites and moved to monitor Casey.

On the second ring, a female voice answered. "Hello."

"Hello," Casey said. "Is this Rachel?"

"Yes," she said.

"Rachel, my name is Robert." He said the first name that popped into his head. He knew they had been introduced briefly in the doctor's lounge a long time ago by Danny. She might recall his true name and link him immediately to his friend. "I collect Albert Einstein memorabilia. I made a note months ago that you were selling a book of his, on relativity. I couldn't afford anything a few months ago, but I've come into some cash and was wondering if the book is still available."

"Hmm. Well, actually …" she began.

"I'm a serious collector, will pay top dollar. According to my note you were asking around eleven thousand dollars."

"What do you mean by 'top dollar?'" she asked, as if she were making a 42nd street corner hustle.

"Twenty thousand dollars, cash. But I can't go any higher than that," he said with disappointment. "I take it you still have the merchandise."

It went quiet on the other end.

"Robert," she purred, "give me your telephone number. I need to think about it. I will call you back."

"When?" Casey asked.

"Hopefully, today. But you'll hear from me one way or the other."

Casey gave her his cell phone number. He walked over to Mary, who was petting a brown and white spotted dog lying in the doorway, and Ray, who had taken off his baseball cap, the green bill sticking out of his blue jeans.

"Rachel should call you. She'll offer to buy Einstein back, and I believe you'll make a hefty profit. Then, call me."

The two men shook hands. "Thank you for helping us out," Mary said. She patted the beagle again on its head. Ray walked them to their vehicle and tipped his hand good-bye as the boxer in the road watched longingly at their departure.

Casey and Mary stopped for lunch along the way to downtown Knoxville. They approached the area known as the Old City and looked for the twelve-story building where they had booked a room. Spotting the concrete and glass hotel, they veered into its narrow covered drop-off entrance, and proceeded into the parking garage. They carried their belongings in the back glass doors to a rich wood, reserved lobby where they checked in, dumped their things in the room, and left again. They brought pamphlets with area maps and a visitor's guide to walk around the revitalized historic district. After two hours, they went back to their room. To wait.

By 10 p.m., Casey and Mary were satiated with repeat news and videos of the same CNN coverage. Mary slithered under the comforter and channel surfed again to look for movies. Casey hedged to mention that his plan wasn't working when his cell phone blared from the desk. He flipped open the cover. "Hello," he said.

"Casey, it's Ray. She left here a little while ago."

Casey sat on the edge of the bed, gave Mary a thumbs up.

"Everything go okay?" Casey asked

"Like a clock. Re-sourceful lady to gimme cash on a Saturday. She must've kept it under a mattress."

"Common hiding place these days. What did she give you? Or, to be more accurate," Casey laughed, "how much did you ask for?"

"Fifteen thousand dollars. Made a twenty-five percent profit for a few months doing nothing. And now I don't have to advahtise it again."

"We're happy for you, Ray."

"Hope she calls you."

"Oh, she will," Casey said. "You take care now. If I'm ever in the market for car parts, I'll pay you a call."

Casey showered and got under the sheets with Mary. They fell asleep, the volume low on *The Blade Runner*, but the phone did not ring.

Early in the morning, Casey jumped up to unplug his charging cell phone as it rang. “She could’ve let us sleep in,” he said before answering.

“Hello,” he said.

“Robert, this is Rachel. I’ve decided to sell you my book.”

“All right. I mean, good. I’m on the road today. I’ll be going through Knoxville. Do you think it would be possible to meet there?”

“That would be fine.”

“Twelve noon on the bike and walking path at the Tennessee River, past the City County Building and Walnut Street.”

“Okay,” she said. “If you’re bringing twenty-thousand dollars, I’ll bring Albert Einstein’s book on relativity.”

“Excellent,” Casey said. “How will I know you?”

“Look for a pregnant lady who’s going to pop any minute.”

At eleven-thirty, Casey and Mary left the hotel, walked across the street, between two building towers, down winding stairs and through Market Square. It was mostly sunny; couples strolled, a young man played a guitar and an elderly man with a long ponytail sat on a bench with a Yellow Lab and an inverted hat for handouts. Some change had missed the straw hat and lay on the ground in front of him. Customers from a few eclectic restaurants ate outside.

Mary was glad she had worn a corduroy skirt and button-down blouse; most tourists were dressed nicely. They continued walking down Market Street, between federal and county buildings with perfect lawns and a wide assortment of pansies, from deep royal blues to yellow, red and violets. Rounding the last official building, they came to the landing with a view of the Tennessee River.

“Mary, why don’t we separate and you sit on the bench down there?” Casey asked. Although he rarely wore a hat, he had brought one, so stuck on the logo baseball cap. Anything to change his appearance so Rachel wouldn't recall Danny's introduction.

"Okay, I'll see what happens," she said, and went ahead. She walked down the long descent to sit on a park bench where runners and walkers passed by between her and the brown current below. Casey walked slowly, looking in all directions. When he reached the walkway, he held the handrail along the path, watching for a pregnant pedestrian, occasionally glancing to the businesses and factory across the River.

After five minutes, he saw her approaching from his peripheral vision. She wore a pale purple knee length dress and a thin cardigan. He directly turned to her, but couldn't make out her hair color or style due to a wide lavender scarf worn as a headband, tied behind her neck.

She eyed him as she approached and he nodded. "You must be Rachel," he said, when she was close enough to have a conversation.

"And you're Robert?" She smiled.

"I am." Her flawless skin etched over high cheekbones. He remembered her now more clearly because her eyes were so dramatic; he wondered if their aqua color came from special contact lenses. He had never seen a woman so pregnant look so beautiful.

"I was fortunate to track you down," Casey said. "And I hope your walk was not too much trouble or far." He gestured to the front of her dress.

"I'm pregnant, not ill," she said. She followed that with an alluring smile.

"I'm looking forward to rounding out my collection. May I see the book?"

"Certainly." She picked a small gift bag from a vinyl pocket book she carried and handed it to him. Casey felt a rush of disgust. She had glanced at his left ring finger.

Beyond Rachel, Mary sat attentively watching the encounter. Casey tucked the gift bag under his arm and carefully examined the book he had held the day before. "Marvelous," he said. "This signature, verification and book are just what I've been looking for."

"Perhaps you can place the money in there with that sheet of tissue wrap paper," she said, pointing to the bag.

Casey placed the book back into the light gray bag with two little handles and stuck it back under his armpit.

"That won't be necessary," he said.

She pursed her lips and stopped leaning her hip on the railing. "Robert, either give me the money or hand me back my book." She took a step backwards. "Think how fast I'm going to have a cop here. A pregnant lady screaming?"

"Go ahead. A cop would be very interested in this stolen book. An officer would want me to return it to Danny Tilson, the real owner." Casey took off his cap.

She took a deep breath, caught, but not defeated. "Okay. Yes, bring it on. Danny gave it to me. After all, I was living with him and he gave it to me in a heat of passion."

"The only half credible thing you've mentioned is the two of you living together. We can drag Danny into this, if need be."

"So it's his, or yours, or whoever's word against mine."

"The middle man may make you look bad, too."

"What middle man?"

"Ray, from eBay."

"Why, you," she said, giving him a piercing glare.

"There is also the matter of an opal bracelet."

"I don't know what you're talking about," she smirked.

Casey took four steps, stopped, and walked back two. “You know if you weren’t pregnant, and if you weren’t a woman, I’d sock you.”

Chapter 27

Mary linked her arm into Casey's and listened closely to his account of the river walk talk with Rachel as they right angled into a vegetarian soup and sandwich place. Excited, they thumbed through the book one more time and gradually ate, but Casey still didn't mention the topic they both feared.

Mary pushed her lunch basket to the side. "Did you ask her?"

Casey rubbed his eyebrows, covering his face. "Danny doesn't need this, but a new life is always a blessing. Mary, we just don't know. So, like the book, let's not say anything. He'll find out if it's meant to be."

Annabel and Nancy had gone home to Sara's by the time Casey and Mary returned. Danny was in good spirits after spending the weekend with the girls. They had talked about school, safety on the internet and a part-time job for Annabel over the summer since she had turned sixteen. They had played Bananagrams and taken multiple long walks with Dakota. One walk had turned into hurling sticks, but after twenty minutes Danny's arm had tired before Dakota quit retrieving.

Dakota barked at the door, but quieted and pranced excitedly in the kitchen when he heard Casey's car stop in the garage.

"You two have a good time?" Danny asked when they walked in.

"Better than good," Casey said. "Except for one thing."

Mary bent over and gave Dakota the attention he begged for. "We have a surprise for you. Casey and I had continued to ask around about your book and you still had two pawnshops left on your search list. Anyway, we did further investigating."

"And we're not divulging the particulars," Casey said sternly.

Danny stared at their bemused smiles wondering. Dakota's thin pink lips relaxed into a good-natured grin. Casey handed Danny the small gift bag. Danny peered in, opened his hand to pull something out from the tissue wrapping paper.

"Wow! Holy smoke." He held onto his mom's book, embraced Casey, and then hugged Mary. "You don't know how much this means to me." His smile faded and he got teary eyed. "It's supposed to be with me, it's part of my past. This is like receiving some of what I've lost. I can't thank you enough." He held the book tight against his chest. "How much do I owe you?"

"Danny, you're welcome," Mary said. Casey sat on a stool and jostled Dakota's back end. "You don't owe us anything. We simply recovered it."

Danny gave his sister a hug again. "If you don't mind, it's going into its case." He peeled away from them, up the stairs.

"I apologize," Casey said to Mary. "There was something else on my agenda this weekend, but it's not too late." He stood and slipped his arms around Mary's back, into her hair. Dakota sat with attention. "Can you change your mind about marriage? I would love to marry you, Mary Tilson."

Mary gasped, a little sound popping up from her vocal cords, but it really came from her heart. An extra beat. "Casey, let's not have a long engagement," she said.

They kissed while Casey spun her in the air. "I come with a ring," he beamed, placing her on the floor. He dug into the bag Danny had left on the counter, opened a white box and slipped a diamond solitaire onto her finger.

Weeks later, Nancy waited outside school with a gaggle of girls, her eyes peeled for her father. The girls pointed out boys they expected would turn dicey over the summer, like betting at a horserace, as parents' cars grumbled to a stop. Nancy clutched books in one arm and jockeyed a knapsack on her back, which held all her locker contents of the last year. Danny inched up and saw her as she reluctantly waved to a friend not returning to the same school next fall.

"Congratulations. Another finish to a school year," Danny said, when she slid into the front seat. He noticed the addition of lipstick, a brownish rose, an "in color" for spring in the girl's magazine pictures. His daughter was in full bloom, and getting prettier by the day. Nancy glanced at her chest as she leaned over carefully stacking her books on the floor while Dakota tried to greet her, nudging forward from the back seat.

"Like all right already," she said to Dakota. "You'd think you haven't seen me in a month." Dakota licked her hand.

Danny was only driving her to Sara's. Nancy wanted to unpack her school things and spend time with her father in a day or two. Nancy was explaining to him when she would receive her final grades, when Danny's cell phone rang.

"Danny, it's Bruce. I'm at the office. Are you available?

"I'm driving and I have my daughter with me."

"You're being served with some kind of papers." With that, Bruce hung up.

Danny's heartbeat bounded so hard and fast, he could feel his fingertips pulsate on the steering wheel.

"Dad, Dad, slow down, it's a red light," Nancy said. "What's the matter anyway?"

He braked. "I'm sorry Nancy. That was Bruce. He'd like me to stop by."

"All right, no big deal." She turned on the radio to music he despised.

Danny went back to his thoughts. He was still within the statute of limitations for malpractice lawsuits. He racked his brain, imagining every scenario with patients he could think of. He couldn't remember anyone voicing comments to him that would make him suspicious, that they harbored resentment towards him or were truly dissatisfied with surgical or non-surgical results. Yet, that's how lawsuits were. They pop up when you least expect them. He had hoped that Susan Dexter's lawsuit would be the first and last brush with malpractice he would ever see in his career.

Bruce was behind the front desk when Danny and Nancy walked in. Nancy beamed when the staff warmly greeted her, telling her that her hair outdid spectacular salon cuts and she had grown into a young lady.

"Danny, have you had appointments yet with the psychologist?" Bruce asked.

"Once every two weeks. I think they're going well so I don't mind if you talk to her."

"I didn't want a uniformed man sitting out here," Bruce said. Patients in the waiting room read or thumbed through magazines and books. On TV, a shock-show talk host dramatically pranced before a couple's physical argument, but no one paid serious attention. Bruce motioned to Danny to come in. "I sent him to your unoccupied office."

Nancy sat on a teal cushioned chair and picked up a People magazine while Danny walked back through the hallway. Inside his office, the server jumped up from the couch upon seeing him. "If you're Doctor Danny Tilson, John Hancock here," he said. Danny signed and the bald man handed him a thick envelope. "Have a nice day," the man mumbled as he left.

Danny sat under his Rockwell fishing print. Beckett and Livingston must be a law firm, he thought, surmising the return address from Knoxville. He flinched while sliding his finger under the flap. A cream-colored cover letter sat inside on stapled legal sized papers. He was so accustomed to legal paperwork by now, he recognized a court's style and font, and his stomach knotted.

Rachel Hendersen vs. Daniel Tilson, it started at the upper left side. What the hell was this all about? He skimmed for the buzzwords quickly to explain what she claimed he had done to her.

Then he found it. *This Paternity Suit will seek to …* He read and reread the two major words as a tidal wave of disbelief and anger swept over him. She had taken birth control. Or he thought she had taken birth control pills because that's what she had told him. Just like she had told him about being an RN, just like she had told him about going to Wellington's Life Care.

He read on. *This suit seeks to reimburse the biological mother, Rachel Hendersen, for prenatal and post-natal expenses and establish child support from said biological father, Daniel Tilson, a physician neurosurgeon with The Neurosurgery Group for Middle Tennessee, who makes in excess of $200,000 per year. Said biologic mother is an unemployed parent ...*

Of course, details of all Rachel's maternity costs were attached, including all medical bills for a Caesarian section. Her attorney requested Danny to pay all costs since the biologic mother incurred the burden of providing for medical insurance (a minor medical insurance policy), and requested four thousand dollars a month for child support, to be slightly modified after Danny sends copies of his last three monthly pay stubs. If there were any questions as to the validity of the suit, then Danny could incur the costs for DNA testing.

He couldn't read any further.

They could test his DNA, he thought, he knew the results, so it wasn't worth it. Danny stuffed the cover letter from Phil, the first name of Beckett in Beckett and Livingston and the official suit into the envelope. He waved good-bye at the front desk, and then motioned to Nancy.

Nancy scrambled to catch him through the door. "Dad, you look terrible. What's the matter?"

"I'll tell you in the car," but he wasn't sure about that. Dakota greeted them, sticking his face out the half-rolled down window. Danny started the car and headed to Sara's. He flipped the sun visor down, after squinting from the bright sun, while Nancy studied his ghostly face.

"Well?" she asked. "Your white color hasn't changed."

"I just found out I'm a father."

"Well, duh," she said.

"No, I mean a father again. You have a half-brother or sister."

Initially Nancy tried to make sense out of that; she kept silent thinking about it. For months, there had been no mention of her father's affair; the woman her father had fooled around with seemed to have disappeared from the picture. That's it, she thought, that woman. That woman was now linked to her family.

Now Nancy steamed. She clammed shut, although Danny paid no attention because he was lost in his own world. They pulled into the driveway. Nancy tore out of the car, through the front door and up into her bedroom. Danny got out, dumbfounded, going after her. Sara came to the open door.

"What was that all about?" Sara asked. Sara wore no shoes and lightly stepped onto the front porch. She had just changed into fresh clothes after showering. She looked radiant and smelled great from her shampoo.

"Can I sit?"

Sara nodded. "Danny, you look terrible. But, you've looked terrible ever since you left me." Danny winced, his shoulders dropped in the glider. "I'm sorry," she said. "I didn't mean it to be nasty. It came out because it's true."

"And you are truthful," he said.

"Sit here a minute. Do you mind if I let Dakota out of the car?"

"No."

Sara walked gingerly across the grass, and opened the door for Dakota's escape. Dakota used the closest bush, then darted around the front lawn looking for sticks.

Sara leaned against the railing but decided to pull an Adirondack rocker close to avoid sitting in the glider with Danny.

"Sara, I have a favor to ask," Danny said. "Can you cut me some slack? I haven't had a paycheck come in for months. I'm using annuity money for your alimony and child support but in addition, something else just came up. I have to retain Mark Cunningham again, besides our mess."

"It's not a mess, Danny, at least not to me."

"I know, I know. I'm the mess."

Sara crossed her legs, pushed the rocker with the sole of her left foot. Dakota dropped a branch in front of the railing, egging them to play.

"Okay, just let me know when you would like to cut the next checks. They can be late.
Now, why is Nancy upset with you?"

"I just discovered … I was just served with … I've got a new baby."

"Oh, Danny." Sara stopped moving, furrowed her face with concern.

"I don't even know where she went, or if it's a boy or a girl."

Sara shook her head, tucked her knees to her chest and gained momentum to rock. "Nancy must feel like she's been replaced."

Danny twisted his hands. He ignored Dakota, who dropped more sticks in front of the bushes, hoping Danny would pitch one for him. "How, Sara?"

"She's your youngest," Sara said softly. "Now she's not the baby any more. She'll get over it, just give her time."

Danny rubbed his chin. "That's one thing I possess…time for waiting." At the car door, he glanced back to his ex-wife and waved good-bye.

Danny called his attorney and for the remainder of the afternoon trimmed bushes flanking the back patio. At dinnertime, he prepared salads while Mary heated leftovers. He waited for Casey to spill the news about Rachel and the legal papers.

"I heard indirectly from Rachel today," Danny said when Casey arrived.

Casey held from shooting a glance to Mary. "What does she want?" he asked.

Danny tapped his knife on the placemat. "Plenty. Brace yourself. I'm apparently a father. She was pregnant, hasn't worked and wants me to pay her child support and her pre-and post-natal medical expenses."

Mary caught Casey's glance. She sighed heavily for her brother.

"Congratulations, I think, for the first part. But, child support to support her?"

"Danny, this is a shock," Mary said. "What are you going to do?"

"I'm seeing Mark Cunningham in two days. His schedule is jammed, but he'll see me."

"Is the baby healthy?" Mary asked. "Is it a girl or boy?"

"I have no idea."

"She's going to make a hell of a mother, and a hell of a role model," Mary said. Danny and Casey stared at her, allowing those thoughts to seep in.

"My sister and my best friend, now engaged to each other, suggested this eatery," Danny said to Mark. "The green curry is the way to go."

"We'll make it two, then," Mark said.

Danny glanced at a tourist industry's poster of Thailand and the deep green walls with white trim. A college student came to the table and they placed their order with extra rice.

"So you're in more deep water, Doctor Tilson?" Mark asked, his bushy hair thicker than the last time Danny had seen him.

"Unfortunately." Danny opened the Barrett and Livingston envelope and handed him the contents. He kept silent, letting Mark read it all, as the waiter returned and poured hot tea.

"Have you had any contact with her lately?" Mark asked. "I take it from this she doesn't know you aren't working."

"I don't even know where she is, there's been no communication," Danny said. "They sent the papers to my group's address. It appears she has no knowledge of my job situation."

"At least you've done something right." Danny looked puzzled. "She can't get much out of you under the circumstances, Danny."

"Really?"

"I'll take care of this. I'll fire off correspondence to her attorney. You bring your pay stubs?"

Danny handed him copies for the last few months.

"You've been suspended; she can't get money out of a rock. If my hunch is correct, she's the reason for your present pitiful set of circumstances, anyway." Mark shook his head and took a sip of Thai tea. "A man's downfall comes from his crotch."

Danny felt like ducking under the table; Mark was so direct. "But, for now, you'll probably have to pay her something extremely minimal. Since she won't know when or if you resume working, she'll have to take the chance of paying her own legal fees later if she wants to find out, so she can up the ante."

"I get it," Danny said. "But it says in there, she also wants reimbursement for Mr. Barrett's services."

"No kidding. You're not working right now. You're in the same boat as her. You will both pay your own legal fees. I'll see to that," Mark said, emphatically.

"But won't they say I'm capable of making a ton of money?"

"The occurrence of your circumstances happened independent of hers. You never planned on being jobless so you wouldn't have to pay her bills. So eat your curry and relax." Mark placed the papers on the chair next to him. "When you see your baby, why don't you hand deliver your pay stubs to the mother?"

Chapter 28

Mary closed her wooden paint box and got comfortable. She'd been working outside on the patio for several hours and considered the finger lake acrylic painting finished. Casey had worked a seven-to-three and came outside longing to relax. He wiggled behind Mary, in the same lounge chair, as the Chessie whiffed the air and hummingbirds zoomed between two red feeders.

"I'm going to find Rachel," Danny said, putting his novel aside. "Before Mark gets her address from the attorney in Knoxville."

Casey pinched Mary on her side. "What are you contemplating?" Casey asked.

"I want to see my new baby. And give Rachel copies of my zero gross pay stubs."

Danny squinted at the draining feeders while Casey gave Mary a peck on the cheek and whispered something in her ear.

"We can arrange a meeting if you'd like," Casey said.

"You can?" Clueless, Danny stared at the two lovebirds. "Then let's go for it."

"This weekend when I have off?" Casey asked.

"We know a hotel that takes dogs, Danny," Mary said. "Let's bring Dakota."

"That's fine with me," Danny said, "and I'm sure that would be fine with Dakota." He hoisted himself out of the chair to play fetch with Dakota. "You two haven't divulged the big day. When is it?"

Casey caressed Mary from behind. "In the fall," Casey said. "You're going to be my best man, right?"

"Now that I've been formally asked, absolutely."

"Sara, Annabel and Nancy will be the maid of honor and bridesmaids," Mary said. "We're going to do it right here, Danny. Set chairs and trellises of flowers on the lawn. We'll have a string quartet over there." She signaled to the oak tree and the excitement in her voice mounted.

"Mom and Dad would be so proud of you and thrilled with the ceremony at the house. And the groom." Danny laughed and pointed at Casey.

They drove in Casey's Jeep on Saturday morning. Dakota sat alert, peering out the back window at I-40 traffic as they wound through the Cumberland Plateau passing undeveloped countryside and expansive forests. The valleys between ridges looked fertile and deep green from a wet spring. The lakes and rivers streamed full, replenished from the drought of 2007. The steep mountain curves and windy trip made Mary queasy every time she attempted to read the paper, so she folded it and passed it to Danny sitting in the back seat. She slipped off her leather sandals and turned on Middle Tennessee's talk radio, which faded as they approached Knoxville. They took a downtown exit, parked in the Crowne Plaza's garage and walked Dakota. At the lobby's front desk, clerks complimented Danny on his good-looking, well-mannered Chesapeake, and then the three of them checked into two rooms.

They rode the elevator alone for four floors, Dakota puzzled at the sudden upward start off the ground. "How does it stand right now with Bruce?" Casey asked Danny. "Is there any indication that he's hoping you resign so he doesn't have to fire you?" They reached their floor and jockeyed their overnight bags, dog supplies and Dakota into the hallway.

"Bruce may be the dictatorial grandfather of the group, but I totally trust his business sense and his word. If he's satisfied with the psychologist's report, he'll take me. Talking with her has gone smoothly. Having input from Linda Atkins was probably to cover the group's butt that I'm rational, or whatever."

"I've never known you to be rational," Mary said. "Anybody that goes through neurosurgery training has some screws loose."

They unlocked their side-by-side doors. "No canine pillow clutching or curling on the bed in here," Danny said sternly to Dakota, who made headway first into the room.

Danny unpacked his overnight bag, rechecked the papers he had brought and freshened up in the bathroom. He finished the paper while propped against pillows on the headboard, and at four o'clock, rapped next door.

Mary slipped her shoes on and fastened her hair in a bunch while Casey opened the door. "We'll be early, so we can order something to eat," Casey said. "Mary and I looked at maps before calling Rachel, so we suggested a good landmark to meet." He patted Dakota on the head as the dog waited politely.

"You both seem to have this well arranged. I can't thank you enough. I probably would have lost my temper if I had found her and called." Danny tugged on Dakota's leash and they left the front entrance of the hotel. The temperature hovered at seventy, but without a breeze and no clouds, it felt warmer. Dakota lightly panted after they walked down all the steps before Market Square.

Danny, Casey and Mary leisurely strolled the Market district. They had time before Rachel appeared, but scanned the faces of local pedestrians and tourists just in case. A gray haired man wearing a white undershirt fed squirrels from a park bench and a little girl with lighted sneakers tossed a balloon. A man wearing a felt fedora and a woman strum guitars and sang. They were better than karaoke singers, but not ready for the Music City.

"Doesn't this sound delicious?" Mary asked. A chalkboard sign placed on the pavement read *Mulligatawny Soup and half sandwich – special of the day*. "Let's order and sit outside. We can tether Dakota to this pole."

Danny looped Dakota's leash, refastened the snap to his collar and followed Mary into the gated outside area. They took the empty table and chairs in the corner next to Dakota on the other side. "I'll go in and order," Casey said. "Three specials?"

"Sure," Mary said, while Danny nodded his head.

"Half roast beef and cheese on sourdough?" Casey asked.

"Sounds scrumptious," Mary said.

"Here," Danny said, and handed him two twenties.

"Yeah, yeah. Okay, and I'll get three iced teas."

They nibbled at their sandwiches and finished the turmeric yellow soup. Mary gazed upward to feel the sun's warmth on her winter complexion as onlookers passed asking about Dakota. Two little girls, sisters, with their mother in attendance, asked if they could pet him, but stroked him all over before waiting for a response. Dakota's delight fueled their giggles.

"My turn to go inside," Danny said. "I'll buy something to take home tomorrow."

Casey could spot her anywhere. This time she pushed a blue baby stroller, and her figure had miraculously transformed into the slim, curvy female he had met in the doctor's lounge, now shapelier than ever. He motioned to Mary, subtly pointing her out. "Wait here," Casey said, "I want a few words with her alone." He slid out of the iron chair.

Casey walked briskly, surprising her when he landed dead in front of the carriage. "Rachel," he said. "Beautiful day, isn't it?"

"Very beautiful," she said.

A blue canvas top shielded the baby from the sun. A rattle hung from the handrail and a diaper bag fit into the basket underneath. A stuffed koala bear clasped its arms around the front handle, hanging on by Velcro paws. Rachel looked the picture of motherhood.

"May I?" Casey asked, wanting to peer at the baby swaddled into too big a seat, with the smallest white sunhat Casey had ever seen.

Rachel nodded as Casey dropped into a squatting position.

"Robert, thank you for arranging this meeting. Danny is coming with his pay stubs, right?"

Casey looked under the hat and guessed it was a girl by the splashes of pink in the carriage more than by the infant's facial features. This miniature person encapsulated the essence of innocence and beauty, for that he was sure.

"You're welcome. It's the least I could do after you graciously returned Danny's book. Now he can return the favor and personally deliver those copies. Plus, he's dying to see his new baby." Casey took his right hand and smoothed his fingers on the baby's cheek, as smooth as butter. Her eyes opened and her lips sought for his fingers. "She's beautiful. Is she hungry?"

"Most of the time." Rachel laughed.

"What's her name?"

"Julia."

Casey hunted for her tiny hand. "But why Danny, Rachel? Why did you pick him?" Casey stayed crouched on purpose, minimizing his intimidating size. He wanted questions and answers to flow between them in a non-confrontational manner.

Rachel liked him giving attention to her infant and stepped to the side to display Julia's miniature fingers. She kneeled down. "Just like you, Robert, I'm single. I want to stay that way and not deal with a full-time man. I didn't pick just anybody to be the father of my child, you know."

"I don't blame you," Casey said. "I would want the guy to be handsome, smart and rich."

"You said it. Danny makes tons. Neurosurgeons with thriving practices are like a tri-state lottery win. But Bruce is getting up there in age, so I wasn't interested in hitting on him."

"But you broke up a family, Rachel."

"Hell," she said abruptly, "I didn't expect him to leave his wife. Why did he go and do that?"

"I guess he wanted a future with you," Casey said. Julia squirmed and clasped at his fingers.

"Well, that's his problem."

"I still don't understand why you didn't just use a sperm bank. Can't you fire off a check list about the donor, like eye color, and race, list your specifications?"

"Robert," she said, exasperated, "I want to be a single mom but not a working single mom. I should do just fine with Danny's child support, and a few other interests I pursue."

"Like stealing valuable books?"

She glared at him, raised her hand to block the sun as her cotton blouse sleeve fell away from her wrist.

"Sorry," he said. "I didn't mean to criminalize you. You had a window of opportunity, I can see that." She lightened back into a smile. "Why Knoxville?"

"I had to get far away enough from the father," she said softly, almost to herself. "I want to raise my kid on my own."

Danny strutted outside with a brown bag and set it on the table. "Where's Casey?"

"You're about to meet your baby," Mary said. "Casey's over there."

Danny gave Mary the bag, picked up his envelope and stepped around the railing to get Dakota. Danny and Mary walked over together

Rachel stayed planted at the side of the stroller. "Danny, it's nice to see you," she said.

"This is my sister, Mary," Danny said. The two women smiled at each other. "And I take it you just met Casey."

"I did," she said, quickly.

Dakota sniffed at Rachel, wagging his tail. She petted the top of his head. "Hey Dakota."

Danny and Mary crouched down. "It's been a long time since I had a newborn," Danny said to Mary. "I forgot what it's like. She's beautiful."

The baby gurgled at him. Danny took her sunhat off for a moment to study her eyes and her thin light hair. "What's her name?"

"Julia."

Casey tapped Mary lightly on her shoulder. "Why don't we give Danny some time with his daughter? Rachel, too."

"Good idea." Casey and Mary walked to a nearby bench and sat next to a young man texting on his cell phone.

"That's a beautiful name," Danny said. "You certainly didn't need my input."

"Yes, I should do just fine. You won't have to bother about us, after we get all this legal stuff taken care of."

Julia had Danny mesmerized. He tried to stifle the tears of joy that were pooling in his eyes. Another daughter, as pretty as Annabel and Nancy, as pretty as Melissa was, with her whole life ahead of her. Even though the mother wasn't Sara, he loved this little girl as much as he loved the others.

Dakota stretched his neck into the carriage to see what all the fuss was about. He pushed his snout around Danny's hand, planting a cold nose on baby Julia, who reflexively squinted. Danny got up and stamped his foot. "Dakota, sit please," he said. Dakota obeyed and Rachel jealously noticed their rapport.

"Here, I have your papers," Danny said. He slipped her the envelope. She opened the steel clasp and dug inside, brought the papers out. She stood with her name brand sunglasses and manicured fingers, reading carefully.

"This doesn't make sense. This is crazy, it does say The Neurosurgery Group for Middle Tennessee and this is your name. But gross pay can't be zero, not even one month." She tapped her foot.

Danny listened, the tables turning on her. He shifted his eyes back towards his lovely daughter and remained silent.

"This is your sick attempt at a joke, right?"

"I was so love struck by you, I couldn't work any more."

Like the Times Square New Year's Eve ball, Rachel's world tumbled down within a minute. With a thud. For once, she couldn't think of anything to say.

"A great lady once told me, you have to be responsible for your actions," Danny said. "You are also going to be financially responsible for Julia."

Casey pinched at Mary's denim capris. "I think they're finished," he said. "Let's go."

Danny played with Julia as Casey and Mary stood next to him again. "Danny," Casey said. "Rachel is wearing Melissa's bracelet. She's keeping it in safekeeping until it fits Julia. You don't mind, do you?"

Rachel shot Casey a piercing look. Danny stood up. "How?"

He didn't know how. But one thing was for sure. "Rachel, you don't think this is it, do you? I intend to make Julia a part of my life. I'm going to fight you for custody."

"Bye-bye, Julia," Casey and Mary said and tugged at Danny. Danny leaned into the stroller and kissed his daughter. Dakota wagged his tail and they headed away.

"Danny, wait," Rachel said. "I want my dog back."

"Over my dead body," Danny yelled over his shoulder. Dakota reached for the tail end of the leash and pranced proudly along Danny's side.

The next morning Danny walked Dakota, the two men paid their bills, and they loaded the Jeep. "Hurry up Dakota, get in there," Danny said holding open the hatchback. Danny also raced around and jumped into a back passenger seat.

"Let's stop for breakfast," Mary said, while sliding on her seat belt. Casey started the engine.

"Let's not stop," Danny said. He opened the bag of muffins he had bought the day before and shoved it to the front seat. "Have one of these."

"Jeez, Danny," Mary said. "What's your hurry?"

"I have to get back to Nashville."

Casey grabbed a cranberry muffin from the bag before putting the car in reverse. "What's so important right now in Nashville?"

"I want to ask Sara something…"

Mary unbuckled her belt and turned all the way to face her brother.

"To go fishing at the Caney Fork with me."

Mary smiled.

Danny shrugged. “Maybe I can romance her to fall in love with me again.”

Casey looked in the rearview mirror. “And you need to start working again.”

“Absolutely. In my one and only career passion. Neurosurgery.”

“God knows, you lack instinct about how people think, so you better tinker inside their heads instead.”

“Shut up, Casey, you’re just an ambulance driver.”

“I am not. I’m a highly trained EMT. A paramedic.”

The two men broadly smiled as Mary slipped off her shoes. They headed west and didn’t stop.

Acknowledgments

To my encouraging, behind-the-scenes editor, and to the astute readers who trudged through my early manuscripts … thank you.

About the Author

Barbara Ebel lives with her husband and pets in a Tennessee protected wildlife corridor. She no longer actively practices medicine and is the author and illustrator of Chester the Chesapeake, a children's book about her therapy dog.

http://www.Chesterthechesapeake.com

Made in the USA